PENGUIN CRIME FICTION

THE CHEYNE MYSTERY

Freeman Wills Crofts was born in Dublin, Ireland, in 1879. He was educated privately and at the Methodist and Campbell Colleges, Belfast. In 1897 he joined the civil-engineering staff of the Belfast Counties Railway as a pupil, and after holding various positions in railway engineering, he became chief assistant engineer to the same railway—then the L.M.S. Northern Counties Committee. In 1929 he retired from railway work in order to give his whole time to writing. He wrote over thirty-nine books, including *The Cask, Death of a Train, The 12:30 from Croydon, The Loss of the Jane Vosper, The Groote Park Murder, Inspector French and the Starvel Tragedy, Fatal Venture, Golden Ashes, The Sea Mystery, Crime at Guildford, Mystery in the English Channel, Inspector French's Greatest Case, The Pit-Prop Syndicate* (the latter two titles are available from Penguin Books), and one religious book, *The Four Gospels in One Story*; several short stories; a play, *Sudden Death*; and a number of short plays for the British Broadcasting Corporation. In 1939 he was elected a fellow of the Royal Society of Arts. He died in 1957.

FREEMAN WILLS CROFTS

—

THE
CHEYNE MYSTERY

PENGUIN BOOKS

Penguin Books Ltd, Harmondsworth,
Middlesex, England
Penguin Books, 625 Madison Avenue,
New York, New York 10022, U.S.A.
Penguin Books Australia Ltd, Ringwood,
Victoria, Australia
Penguin Books Canada Limited, 2801 John Street,
Markham, Ontario, Canada L3R 1B4
Penguin Books (N.Z.) Ltd, 182–190 Wairau Road,
Auckland 10, New Zealand

First published 1926
Published in Penguin Books 1965
Reprinted 1978

Copyright 1926 by Freeman Wills Crofts
All rights reserved

Printed in the United States of America by
Offset Paperback Mfrs., Inc., Dallas, Pennsylvania
Set in Linotype Baskerville

This edition published by arrangement with
The Society of Authors

CONTENTS

1 The Episode in the Plymouth Hotel   7
2 Burglary!   20
3 The Launch "Enid"   31
4 Concerning a Peerage   44
5 An Amateur Sleuth   55
6 The House in Hopefield Avenue   68
7 Miss Joan Merrill   77
8 A Council of War   90
9 Mr. Speedwell Plays His Hand   102
10 The New Firm Gets Busy   115
11 Otto Schulz's Secret   127
12 In the Enemy's Lair   140
13 Inspector French Takes Charge   153
14 The Clue of the Clay-marked Shoe   165
15 The Torn Hotel Bill   178
16 A Tale of Two Cities   191
17 On the Flood Tide   203
18 A Visitor from India   216
19 The Message of the Tracing   229
20 The Goal of the "L'Escaut"   242

CHAPTER I

The Episode in the Plymouth Hotel

WHEN the White Rabbit in *Alice* asked where he should begin to read the verses at the Knave's trial the King replied: "Begin at the beginning; go on till you come to the end; then stop."

This would seem to be the last word on the subject of narration in general. For the novelist no dictum more entirely complete and satisfactory can be imagined—in theory. But in practice it is hard to live up to.

Where is the beginning of a story? Where is the beginning of anything? No one knows.

When I set myself to consider the actual beginning of Maxwell Cheyne's adventure, I saw at once I should have to go back to Noah. Indeed I was not at all sure whether the thing could be adequately explained unless I carried back the narrative to Adam, or even further. For Cheyne's adventure hinged not only on his own character and environment, brought about by goodness knows how many thousands of generations of ancestors, but also upon the contemporaneous history of the world, crystallized in the happening of the Great War and all that appertained thereto.

So then, in default of the true beginning, let us commence with the character and environment of Maxwell Cheyne, following on with the strange episode which took place in the Edgecombe Hotel in Plymouth, and from which started that extraordinary series of events which I have called The Cheyne Mystery.

Maxwell Cheyne was born in 1891, so that when his adventure began in the month of March, 1920, he was just twenty-nine. His father was a navy man, commander of one of His Majesty's smaller cruisers, and from him the

boy presumably inherited his intense love of the sea and
of adventure. Captain Cheyne had Irish blood in his veins
and exhibited some of the characteristics of that irritating
though lovable race. He was a man of brilliant attain-
ments, resourceful, dashing, spirited and, moreover, a fine
seaman, but a certain impetuosity, amounting at times to
recklessness, just prevented his attaining the highest rank
in his profession. In character he was as straight as a die,
and kindly, generous, and openhanded to a fault, but he
was improvident and inclined to live too much in the
present. And these characteristics were destined to affect
his son's life, not only directly through heredity, but indi-
rectly through environment also.

When Maxwell was nine his father died suddenly, and
then it was found that the commander had been living up
to his income and had made but scant provision for his
widow and son and daughter. Dreams of Harrow and
Cambridge had to be abandoned and, instead, the boy was
educated at the local grammar school, and then entered
the office of a Fenchurch Street shipping firm as junior
clerk.

In his twentieth year the family fortunes were again
reversed. His mother came in for a legacy from an uncle,
a sheep farmer in Australia. It was not a fortune, but it
meant a fairly substantial competence. Mrs. Cheyne bought
back Warren Lodge, their old home, a small Georgian
house standing in pleasant grounds on the estuary of the
Dart. Maxwell thereupon threw up his job at the shipping
office, followed his mother to Devonshire, and settled down
to the leisurely life of a country gentleman. Among other
hobbies he dabbled spasmodically in literature, producing
a couple of novels, one of which was published and sold
with fair success.

But the sea was in his blood. He bought a yacht, and
with the help of the gardener's son, Dan, sailed her in
fair weather and foul, thereby gaining skill and judgment
in things nautical, as well as a first-hand knowledge of the

8

shores and tides and currents of the western portion of the English Channel.

Thus it came to pass that when, three years after the return to Devon, the war broke out, he volunteered for the navy and was at once accepted. There he served with enthusiasm if not with distinction, gaining very much the reputation which his father had held before him. During the intensive submarine campaign he was wounded in an action with a U-boat, which resulted in his being invalided out of the service. On demobilization he returned home and took up his former pursuits of yachting, literature, and generally having as slack and easy a time as his energetic nature would allow. Some eighteen months passed, and then occurred the incident which might be said definitely to begin his Adventure.

One damp and bleak March day Cheyne set out for Plymouth from Warren Lodge, his home on the estuary of the Dart. He wished to make a number of small purchases, and his mother and sister had entrusted him with commissions. Also he desired to consult his banker as to some question of investments. With a full program before him he pulled on his oilskins, and having assured his mother he would be back in time for dinner, he mounted his motor bicycle and rode off.

In due course he reached Plymouth, left his machine at a garage, and set about his business. About one o'clock he gravitated towards the Edgecombe Hotel, where after a cocktail he sat down in the lounge to rest for a few minutes before lunch.

He was looking idly over *The Times* when the voice of a page broke in on his thoughts.

"Gentleman to see you, sir."

The card which the boy held out bore in fine script the legend: "Mr. Hubert Parkes, Oakleigh, Cleeve Hill, Cheltenham." Cheyne pondered, but he could not recall anyone of the name, and it passed through his mind that the page had probably made a mistake.

"Where is he?" he asked.

"Here sir," the boy answered, and a short, stoutly built man of middle age with fair hair and a toothbrush mustache stepped forward. A glance assured Cheyne that he was a stranger.

"Mr. Maxwell Cheyne?" the newcomer inquired politely.

"My name, sir. Won't you sit down?" Cheyne pulled an easy chair over towards his own.

"I've not had the pleasure of meeting you before, Mr. Cheyne," the other went on as he seated himself, "though I knew your father fairly intimately. I lived for many years at Valetta, running the Maltese end of a produce company with which I was then connected, and I met him when his ship was stationed there. A great favorite, Captain Cheyne was! The dull old club used to brighten up when he came in, and it seemed a national loss when his ship was withdrawn to another station."

"I remember his being in Malta," Cheyne returned, "though I was quite a small boy at the time. My mother has a photograph of Valetta, showing his ship lying in the Grand Harbor."

They chatted about Malta and produce company work therein for some minutes, and then Mr. Parkes said:

"Now, Mr. Cheyne, though it is a pleasure to make the acquaintance of the son of my old friend, it was not merely with that object that I introduced myself. I have, as a matter of fact, a definite piece of business which I should like to discuss with you. It takes the form of a certain proposition of which I would invite your acceptance, I hope, to our mutual advantage."

Cheyne, somewhat surprised, murmured polite expressions of anxiety to hear details and the other went on:

"I think before I explain the thing fully another small matter wants to be attended to. What about a little lunch? I'm just going to have mine and I shall take it as a favor if you will join me. After that we could talk business."

Cheyne readily agreed and the other called over a waiter

and gave him an order. "Let us have a cocktail," he went on, "and by that time lunch will be ready."

They strolled to the bar and there partook of a wonderful American concoction recommended by the young lady in charge. Presently the waiter reappeared and led the way, somewhat to Cheyne's surprise, to a private room. There an excellent repast was served, to which both men did full justice. Parkes proved an agreeable and well informed companion and Cheyne enjoyed his conversation. The newcomer had, it appeared, seen a good deal of war service, having held the rank of major in the department of supply, serving first at Gallipoli and then at Salonica. Cheyne knew the latter port, his ship having called there on three or four occasions, and the two men found they had various experiences in common. Time passed pleasantly until at last Parkes drew a couple of arm chairs up to the fire, ordered coffee, and held out his cigar case.

"With your permission I'll put my little proposition now. It is in connection with your literary work and I'm afraid it's bound to sound a trifle impertinent. But I can assure you it's not meant to be so."

Cheyne smiled.

"You needn't be afraid of hurting my feelings," he declared. "I have a notion of the real value of my work. Get along anyway and let's hear."

Parkes resumed with some hesitation.

"I have to say first that I have read everything that you have published and I am immensely impressed by your style. I think you do your descriptions extraordinarily well. Your scenes are vivid and one feels that one is living through them. There's money in that, Mr. Cheyne, in that gift of vivid and interest-compelling presentation. You should make a good thing out of short stories. I've worked at them for years and I know."

"Huh. I haven't found much money in it."

Parkes nodded.

"I know you haven't, or rather I guessed so. And if you don't mind, I'll tell you why." He sat up and a keener interest crept into his manner. "There's a fault in those stories of yours, a bad fault, and it's in the construction. But let's leave that for the moment and you'll see where all this is leading."

He broke off as a waiter arrived with the coffee, resuming:

"Now I have a strong dramatic sense and a good working knowledge of literary construction. As I said I've also tried short stories, and though they've not been an absolute failure, I couldn't say they've been really successful. On the whole, I should think, yours have done better. And I know why. It's my style. I try to produce a tale, say, of a shipwreck. It is intended to be full of human feeling, to grip the reader's emotion. But it doesn't. It reads like a Board of Trade report. Dry, you understand; not interesting. Now, Mr. Cheyne," he sat up in his chair once more, this time almost in excitement, "you see what I'm coming to. Why should we not collaborate? Let me do the plots and you clothe them. Between us we have all the essentials for success."

He sat back and then saw the coffee.

"I say," he exclaimed, "I'm sorry, but I didn't notice this had come. I hope it's not cold." He felt the coffee pot. "What about a liquor? I'll ring for one. Or rather," he paused suddenly. "I think I've got something perhaps even better here." He put his hand in his pocket and drew out a small flask. "Old Cognac," he said. "You'll try a little?"

He poured some of the golden brown liquid into Cheyne's cup and was about to do the same into his own when he was seized with a sudden fit of choking coughing. He had to put down the flask while he quivered and shook with the paroxysm. Presently he recovered, breathless.

"Since I was wounded," he gasped apologetically, "I've been taken like that. The doctors say it's purely nervous— that my throat and lungs and so on are perfectly sound. Strange the different ways this war leaves its mark!"

He picked up the flask, poured a liberal measure of its

contents into his own cup, drank off the contents with evident relish and continued:

"What I had in my mind, if you'll consider it, was a series of short stories—say a dozen—on the merchant marine in the war. This is the spring of 1920. Soon no one will read anything connected with the war, but I think that time has scarcely come yet. I have fair knowledge of the subject and yours of course is first hand. What do you say? I will supply twelve plots or incidents and you will clothe them with, say, five thousand words each. We shall sell them to *The Strand* or some of those monthlies, and afterwards publish them as a collection in book form."

"By Jove!" Cheyne said as he slowly sipped his coffee. "The idea's rather tempting. But I wish I could feel as sure as you seem to do about my own style. I'm afraid I don't believe that it is as good as you pretend."

"Mr. Cheyne," Parkes answered deliberately, "you may take my word for it that I know what I am talking about. I shouldn't have come to you if I weren't sure. Very few people are satisfied with their own work. No matter how good it is it falls short of the standard they have set in their minds. It is another case in which the outsider sees most of the game."

Cheyne felt attracted by the proposal. He had written in all seventeen short stories, and of these only three had been accepted, and those by inferior magazines. If it would lead to success he would be only too delighted to collaborate with this pleasant stranger. It wasn't so much the money—though he was not such a fool as to make light of that part of it. It was success he wanted, acceptance of his stuff by good periodicals, a name and a standing among his fellow craftsmen.

"Let's see what it would mean," he heard Parkes's voice, and it seemed strangely faint and distant. "I suppose, given the synopses, you could finish a couple of tales per week—say, six weeks for the lot. And with luck we should sell for £50 to £100 each—say £500 for your six week's work, or nearly £100 per week. And there might be any amount more for the book rights, filming and so on. Does the idea appeal to you, Mr. Cheyne?"

Cheyne did not reply. He was feeling sleepy. Did the idea appeal to him? Yes. No. Did it? Did the idea . . . the idea . . . Drat this sleepiness! What was he thinking of? Did the idea . . . What idea? . . . He gave up the struggle and, leaning back in his chair, sank into a profound and dreamless slumber.

Ages of time passed and Cheyne slowly struggled back into consciousness. As soon as he was sufficiently awake to analyze his sensations he realized that his brain was dull and clouded and his limbs heavy as lead. He was, however, physically comfortable, and he was content to allow his body to remain relaxed and motionless and his mind to dream idly on without conscious thought. But his energy gradually returned and at last he opened his eyes.

He was lying, dressed, on a bed in a strange room. Apparently it was night, for the room was dark save for the light on the window blind which seemed to come from a street lamp without. Vaguely interested, he closed his eyes again, and when he reopened them the room was lighted up and a man was standing beside the bed.

"Ah," the man said, "you're awake. Better, I hope?"

"I don't know," Cheyne answered, and it seemed to him as if some one else was speaking. "Have I been ill?"

"No," the man returned, "Not that I know of. But you've slept like a log for nearly six hours."

This was confusing. Cheyne paused to take in the idea, but it eluded him, then giving up the effort, he asked another question.

"Where am I?"

"In the Edgecombe: the Edgecombe Hotel, you know, in Plymouth. I am the manager."

Ah, yes! It was coming back to him. He had gone there for lunch—was it today or a century ago?—and he had met that literary man—what was his name? He couldn't remember. And they had had lunch and the man had made some suggestion about his writing. Yes, of course! It was all coming back now. The man had wanted to collaborate with him. And during the conversation he had suddenly felt sleepy. He supposed he must have fallen asleep then, for he remembered nothing more. But why had he felt sleepy like that? Suddenly his brain cleared and he sat up sharply.

"What's happened, Mr. Jesse? I never did anything like this before!"

"No?" the manager answered. "I dare say not. I'll tell you what has happened to you, Mr. Cheyne, though I'm sorry to have to admit it could have taken place in my hotel. You've been drugged. That's what has happened."

Cheyne stared incredulously.

"Good Lord!" he ejaculated. "Drugged! By—not by that literary man, surely?" He paused in amazed consternation and then his hand flew to his pocket. "My money," he gasped. "I had over £100 in my pocket. Just got it at the bank." He drew out a pocket-book and examined it hurriedly. "No," he went on more quietly. "It's all right." He took from it a bundle of notes and with care counted them. "A hundred and eight pounds. That's quite correct. My watch? No, it's here." He got up unsteadily, and rapidly went through his pockets. "Nothing missing anyway. Are you sure I was drugged? I don't understand the thing a little bit."

"I am afraid there is no doubt about it. You seemed so ill that I sent for a doctor. He said you were suffering from the effects of a drug, but were in no danger and would be all right in a few hours. He advised that you be left quietly to sleep it off."

Cheyne rubbed his hand over his eyes.

"I can't understand it," he repeated. "Tell me exactly what happened."

"About three o'clock or shortly before it, Mr. Parkes appeared at the office and asked for his bill. He paid it, complimented the clerk on the excellent lunch he had had, and left the hotel. He was perfectly calm and collected and quite unhurried. Shortly after the waiter went up to clear away the things and he found you lying back in your chair, apparently asleep, but breathing so heavily that he was uneasy and he came and told me. I went up at once and was also rather alarmed at your condition, so I sent at once for the doctor."

"But," Cheyne objected, "that's all right, only I *wasn't* drugged. I know exactly what I ate and drank, and Parkes had precisely the same. If I was drugged, he must have been also, and you say he wasn't."

"He certainly was not. But think again, Mr. Cheyne. Are you really quite certain that he had no opportunity of putting powder over your food or liquid into your drink? Did he divert your attention at any time from the table?"

Cheyne was silent. He had remembered the flask of old brandy.

"He put cognac in my coffee from his own flask," he admitted at length, "but it couldn't have been that."

"Ah," the manager answered in a satisfied tone, "it *was* that, I should swear. Why don't you think so?"

"I'll tell you why I don't think so; why, in fact, I know it wasn't. He put an even larger dose out of the same flask into his own cup and he drank his coffee before I drank mine. So that if there was anything in the flask he would have got knocked over first."

The manager looked puzzled.

"Don't think me discourteous, Mr. Cheyne, but I confess I have my doubts about that. That episode of the flask looks too suspicious. Are you sure it was the same flask in each case? Did he pour straight into one cup after the other or was there an interval in between? You realize of course that a clever conjurer could substitute a second flask for the first without attracting your notice?"

"I realize that right enough, but I am positive he didn't do so in this case. Though," he paused for a moment, "that reminds me that there was an interval between pouring into each cup. He got a fit of coughing after giving me mine and had to put down the flask. But when the paroxysm was over he lifted it again and helped himself."

"There you are," the manager declared. "During his fit of coughing he substituted a different flask."

"I'll swear he didn't. But can't we settle the thing beyond doubt? Have the cups been washed? If not, can't we get the dregs analyzed?"

"I have already asked the doctor to have it done. He said he would get Mr. Pringle to do it at once: that's the city analyst. They're close friends, and Mr. Pringle would do it to oblige him. We should have his report quite soon. I am also having him analyze the remains on the plates which were used. Fortunately, owing to lunch being served in a private room, these had been stacked together and none had been washed. So we should be able to settle the matter quite definitely."

Cheyne nodded as he glanced at his watch. "Good Lord!" he cried, "it's eight o'clock and I said I should be home by seven! I must ring up my mother or she'll think something is wrong."

The Cheynes had not themselves a telephone, but their nearest neighbors, people called Hazelton, were good-natured about receiving an occasional message through theirs and transmitting it to Warren Lodge. Cheyne went down to the lounge and put through his call, explaining to Mrs. Hazelton that unforeseen circumstances had necessitated his remaining overnight in Plymouth. The lady promised to have the message conveyed to Mrs. Cheyne and Maxwell rang off. Then as he turned to the dining room, a page told him that the manager would like to see him in his office.

"I've just got a report from the doctor about that coffee, Mr. Cheyne," the other greeted him, "and I must say it confirms what you say, though it by no means clears up the mystery. There was brandy in those cups, but no drug: no trace of a drug in either."

"I knew that," Cheyne rejoined. "Everything that I had

17

for lunch Parkes had also. I was there and I ought to know. But it's a bit unsettling, isn't it? Looks as if my heart or something had gone wrong."

The manager looked at him more seriously. "Oh, I don't think so," he dissented. "I don't think you can assume that. The doctor seemed quite satisfied. But if it would ease your mind, why not slip across now and see him? He lives just round the corner."

Cheyne reflected.

"I'll do so," he answered presently. "If there's nothing wrong it will prevent me fancying things, and if there is I should know of it. I'll have some dinner and then go across. By the way, have you said anything to the police?"

The manager hesitated.

"No, I have not. I don't know that we've evidence enough. But in any case, Mr. Cheyne, I trust you do not wish to call in the police." The manager seemed quite upset by the idea and spoke earnestly. "It would not do the hotel any good if it became known that a visitor had been drugged. I sincerely trust, sir, that you can see your way to keep the matter quiet."

Cheyne stared.

"But you surely don't suggest that I should take the thing lying down? If I have been drugged, as you say, I must know who has done it, and why. That would seem to me obvious."

"I agree," the manager admitted, "and I should feel precisely the same in your place. But it is not necessary to apply to the police. A private detective would get you the information quite as well. See here, Mr. Cheyne, I will make you an offer. If you will agree to the affair being hushed up, I will employ the detective on behalf of the hotel. He will work under your direction and keep you advised of every step he takes. Come now, sir, is it a bargain?"

Cheyne did not hesitate.

"Why, yes," he said promptly, "that will suit me all right. I don't specially want to advertise the fact that I have been made a fool of. But I'd like to know what has really happened."

"You shall, Mr. Cheyne. No stone shall be left unturned to get at the truth. I'll see about a detective at once. You'll have some dinner, sir?"

Cheyne was not hungry, but he was very thirsty, and he had a light meal with a number of long drinks. Then he went round to see the doctor, to whom the manager had telephoned, making an appointment.

After a thorough examination he received the verdict. It was a relief to his mind, but it did not tend to clear up the mystery. He was physically perfectly sound, and his sleep of the afternoon was not the result of disease or weakness. He had been drugged. That was the beginning and the end of the affair. The doctor was quite emphatic and ridiculed the idea of any other explanation.

Cheyne returned to the Edgecombe, and sitting down in a deserted corner of the lounge, tried to puzzle the thing out. But the more he thought of it, the more mysterious it became. His mind up till then had been concentrated on the actual administration of the drug, and this point alone still seemed to constitute an insoluble problem. But now he saw that it was but a small part of the mystery. *Why* had he been drugged? It was not robbery. Though he had over £100 in his pocket, the money was intact. He had no other valuables about him, and in any case nothing had been removed from his pockets. It was not to prevent his going to any place. He had not intended to do anything that afternoon that could possibly interest a stranger. No, he could form no conception of the motive.

But even more puzzling than this was the question: How did Parkes, if that was really his name, know that he, Cheyne, was coming to Plymouth that day? It was true that he had mentioned it to his mother and sister a couple of days previously, but he had told no one else and he felt sure that neither had they. But the man had almost certainly been expecting him. At least it was hard to believe that the whole episode had been merely the fruits of a chance encounter. On the other hand there was the difficulty that any other suggestion seemed even more unlikely. Parkes simply *couldn't* have known that he, Cheyne, was coming. It was just inconceivable.

He lay back in his deep armchair, the smoke of his pipe curling lazily up, as he racked his brains for some theory which would at least partially meet the facts. But without success. He could think of nothing which threw a gleam of light on the situation.

And then he made a discovery which still further befogged him and made him swear with exasperation. He had taken out his pocket-book and was once more going through its contents to make absolutely sure nothing was missing, when he came to a piece of folded paper bearing memoranda about the money matters which he had discussed with his banker. He had not opened this when he had looked through the book after regaining consciousness, but now half absent-mindedly he unfolded it. As he did so he stared. Near the crease was a slight tear, unquestionably made by some one unfolding it hurriedly or carelessly. But that tear had not been there when he had folded it up. He could swear to it. Someone therefore had been through his pockets while he was asleep.

CHAPTER II

Burglary!

The discovery that his pockets had been gone through while he was under the influence of the drug reduced Cheyne to a state of even more complete mystification than ever. What *had* the unknown been looking for? He, Cheyne, had nothing with him that, so far as he could imagine, could possibly have interested any other person. Indeed, money being ruled out, he did not know that he possessed anywhere any paper or small object which it would be worth a stranger's while to steal.

Novels he had read recurred to him in which desparate enterprises were undertaken to obtain some document of importance. Plans of naval or military inventions which would give world supremacy to the power possessing them were perhaps the favorite instruments in these romances, but treaties which would mean war if disclosed to the wrong power, maps of desert islands on which treasure was buried, wills of which the existence was generally unknown and letters compromising the good name of wealthy personages had all been used time and again. But Cheyne had no plans or treaties or compromising letters from which an astute thief might make capital. Think as he would, he could frame no theory to account for Parkes's proceedings.

He yawned and, getting up, began to pace the deserted lounge. The effects of the drug had not entirely worn off, for though he had slept all the afternoon he still felt slack and drowsy. In spite of its being scarcely ten o'clock, he thought he would have a whisky and go up to bed, in the hope that a good night's rest would drive the poison out of his system and restore his usual feeling of mental and physical well-being.

But Fate, once more in the guise of an approaching page, decreed otherwise. As he turned lazily towards the bar a voice sounded in his ear.

"Wanted on the telephone, sir."

Cheyne crossed the hall and entered the booth.

"Well?" he said shortly. "Cheyne speaking."

A woman's voice replied, a voice he recognized. It belonged to Ethel Hazelton, the grown-up daughter of that Mrs. Hazelton whom he had asked to inform Mrs. Cheyne of his change of plans. She spoke hurriedly and he could sense perturbation in her tones.

"Oh, Mr. Cheyne, I'm afraid I have rather disturbing news for you. When you rang up we sent James over to Warren Lodge. He found Mrs. Cheyne and Agatha on the doorstep trying to get in. They had been ringing for some time, but could not attract attention. He rang also, and then eventually found a ladder and got in through one of the upper windows. He opened the door for Mrs. Cheyne and Agatha. Can you hear me all right?"

"Yes, clearly. Go on, please, Miss Hazelton."

"They searched the house and they discovered cook and Susan in their bedrooms, both tied up and gagged, but otherwise none the worse. They released them, of course, and then found that the house had been burgled."

"Burgled!" Cheyne ejaculated sharply. "Great Scott!" He was considerably startled and paused in some consternation, asking then if much stuff was missing.

"They don't know," the distant voice answered. "Your safe had been opened, but they hadn't had time to make an examination when James left. The silver seems to be all there, so that's something. James came back here with a message from Mrs. Cheyne asking us to let you know, and I have been ringing up hotels in Plymouth for the last half hour. You know, you only said you were staying the night in your message; you didn't say where. Mrs. Cheyne would like you to come back if you can manage it."

There was no hesitation about Cheyne's reply.

"Of course I shall," he said quickly. "I'll start at once on my bicycle. What about telling the police?"

"I rang them up immediately. They said they would go out at once. James has gone back also. He will stay and lend a hand until you arrive."

"Splendid! It's more than good of you both, Miss Hazelton. I can't thank you enough. I'll be there in less than an hour."

He delayed only to tell the news to the manager.

"There's the explanation of this afternoon's affair at all events," he declared. "I was evidently fixed up so that I couldn't butt in and spoil sport. But it's good-bye to your keeping it quiet. The police have been called in already and the whole thing is bound to come out."

The manager made a gesture of concern.

"I'm sorry to hear your news," he said gravely. "Are you properly insured?"

"Partially. I don't know if it will cover the loss because I don't know what's gone. But I must be getting away."

He was moving off, but the manager laid a detaining hand on his arm.

"Well, I'm extremely sorry about it. But see here, Mr. Cheyne, it may not prove to be necessary to bring in about the drugging. It would injure the hotel. I sincerely trust you'll do what you can in the matter, and if you find the private detective sufficient, you'll let our arrangement stand."

"I'll decide when I hear just what has happened. You'll let me have a copy of the analyst's report?"

"Of course. Directly I get it I shall send it on."

Fifteen minutes later Cheyne was passing through the outskirts of Plymouth on his way east. The night was fine, the mists of the day having cleared away, and a three-quarter moon shone brilliantly out of a blue-black sky. Keenly anxious to reach home and learn the details of the burglary and the extent of his loss, Cheyne crammed on every ounce of power, and his machine snored along the deserted road at well over forty miles an hour. In spite of slacks for villages and curves he made a record run, turning into the gate of Warren Lodge at just ten minutes before eleven.

As he approached the house everything looked normal. But when he let himself in this impression was dispelled, for a constable stood in the hall, who, saluting, informed him that Sergeant Kirby was within and in charge.

But Cheyne's first concern was with his mother and sister. An inquiry produced the information that the two ladies were waiting for him in the drawing room, and thither he at once betook himself.

Mrs. Cheyne was a frail little woman who looked ten years older than her age of something under sixty. She welcomed her son with a little cry of pleasure.

"Oh, I am relieved to see you, Maxwell," she cried.

"I'm so glad you were able to come. Isn't this a terrible business?"

"I don't know, mother," Cheyne answered cheerily, "that depends. I hear no one is any the worse. Has much stuff been stolen?"

"Nothing!" Mrs. Cheyne's tone conveyed the wonder she evidently felt. "Nothing whatever! Or at least we can't find that anything is missing."

"Unless something may have been taken from your safe," Agatha interposed. "Was there much in it?"

"No, only a few pounds and some papers, none valuable to an outsider." He glanced at his sister. She was a pretty girl, tall and dark and in features not unlike himself. Both the young people had favored the late commander's side of the house. He turned towards the door, continuing: "I'll go and have a look, and then you can tell me what has happened."

The safe was built into the wall in his own sanctum, "the study," as his mother persisted in calling it. It had been taken over with the house when Mrs. Cheyne bought the little estate. As Cheyne now entered he saw that its doors were standing open. A tall man in the uniform of a sergeant of police was stooping over it. He turned as he heard the newcomer's step.

"Good-evening sir," he said in an impressive tone. "This is a bad business."

"Oh, well, I don't know, sergeant," Cheyne answered easily. "If no one has been hurt and nothing has been stolen it might have been worse."

The sergeant stared at him with some disfavor.

"There's not much but what might have been worse," he observed oracularly. "But we're not sure yet that nothing's been stolen. Nobody knows what was in this here safe, except maybe yourself. I'd be glad if you'd have a look and see if anything is gone."

There was very little in the safe and it did not take Cheyne many seconds to go through it. The papers were tossed about—he could swear someone had turned them over—but none seemed to have been removed. The small packet of Treasury notes was intact and a number of gold and silver medals, won in athletic contests, were all in evidence.

"Nothing missing there, sergeant," he declared when he had finished.

His eye wandered round the room. There was not much of value in it; one or two silver bowls—athletic trophies also, a small gold clock of Indian workmanship, a pair of high-power prism binoculars and a few ornaments were about all that could be turned into money. But all these were there, undisturbed. It was true that the glass door of a locked bookcase had been broken to enable the bolt to be unfastened and the doors opened, but none of the books seemed to have been touched.

"What do you think they were after, sir?" the sergeant queried. "Was there any jewelry in the house that they might have heard of?"

"My mother has a few trinkets, but I scarcely think you could dignify them by the name of jewelry. I suppose these precious burglars have left no kind of clue?"

"No, sir, nothing. Except maybe the girls' description. I've telephoned that into headquarters and the men will be on the lookout."

"Good. Well, if you can wait here a few minutes I'll go and send my mother to bed and then I'll come back and we can settle what's to be done."

Cheyne returned to the drawing room and told his news. "Nothing's been taken," he declared. "I've been through the safe and everything's there. And nothing seems to be missing from the room either. The sergeant was asking about your jewels, mother. Have you looked to see if they're all right?"

"It was the first thing I thought of, but they are all in their places. The cabinet I keep them in was certainly examined, for everything was left topsy-turvy, but nothing is missing."

"Very extraordinary," Cheyne commented. It seemed to

him more than ever clear that these mysterious thieves were after some document which they believed he had, though why they should have supposed he held a valuable document he could not imagine. But the searching first of his pockets and then of his safe and house unmistakably suggested such a conclusion. He wondered it he should advance this theory, then decided he would first hear what the others had to say.

"Now, mother," he went on, "it's past your bedtime, but before you go I wish you would tell me what happened to you. Remember I have heard no details other than what Miss Hazelton mentioned on the telephone."

Mrs. Cheyne answered with some eagerness, evidently anxious to relieve her mind by relating her experiences.

"The first thing was the telegram," she began. "Agatha and I were sitting here this afternoon. I was sewing and Agatha was reading the paper—or was it the *Spectator*, Agatha?"

"The paper, mother, though that does not really matter."

"No, of course it doesn't matter," Mrs. Cheyne repeated. It was evident the old lady had had a shock and found it difficult to concentrate her attention. "Well, at all events we were sitting here as I have said, sewing and reading, when your telegram was brought in."

"*My* telegram?" Cheyne queried sharply. "What telegram do you mean?"

"Why, your telegram about Mr. Ackfield, of course," his mother answered with some petulance. "What other telegram could it be? It did not give us much time, but—"

"But, mother dear, I don't know what you are talking about. I sent no telegram."

Agatha made a sudden gesture.

"There!" she exclaimed eagerly. "What did I say? When we came home and learned what had happened and thought of your not turning up," she glanced at her brother, "I said it was only a blind. It was sent to get us away from the house!"

Cheyne shrugged his shoulders good-humoredly. What he had half expected had evidently taken place.

"Dear people," he protested, "this is worse than getting blood from a stone. Do tell me what has happened. You were sitting here this afternoon when you received a telegram. Very well now, what time was that?"

"What time? Oh, about—what time did the telegram come, Agatha?"

"Just as the clock was striking four. I heard it strike immediately after the ring."

"Good," said Cheyne in what he imagined was the manner of a cross-examining K.C. "And what was in the telegram?"

The girl was evidently too much upset by her experience to resent his superior tone. She crossed the room, and taking a flimsy pink form from a table, handed it over to him.

The telegram had been sent out from the General Post Office in Plymouth at 3:17 that afternoon, and read:

You and Agatha please come without fail to Newton Abbot by 5:15 train to meet self and Ackfield about unexpected financial development. Urgent that you sign papers today. Ackfield will return Plymouth after meeting. You and I will catch 7:10 home from Newton Abbot — MAXWELL.

Three-seventeen; and Parkes left the Edgecombe about three! It seemed pretty certain that he had sent the telegram. But if so, what an amazing amount the man knew about them all! Not only had he known of Cheyne's war experiences and literary efforts and of his visit that day to the Edgecombe, but now it seemed that he had also known his address, of his mother and sister, and, most amazing thing of all, of the fact that Mr. Ackfield of Plymouth was their lawyer and confidential adviser! Moreover, he had evidently known that the ladies were at home as well as that they alone comprised the family. Surely, Cheyne thought, comparatively few people possessed all this knowledge, and the finding of Parkes should therefore be a correspondingly easy task.

"Extraordinary!" he said aloud. "And what did you do?"

"We got a taxi," Mrs. Cheyne answered. "Agatha arranged it by telephone from Mrs. Hazelton's. You tell him, Agatha. I'm rather tired."

The old lady indeed looked worn out and Cheyne interposed a suggestion that she should go at once to bed, leaving Agatha to finish the story. But she refused and her daughter took up the tale.

"We caught the 5:15 ferry and went on to Newton Abbot. But when the Plymouth train came in there was no sign of you or Mr. Ackfield, so we sat in the waiting-room until the 7:10. I telephoned for a taxi to meet the ferry. It brought us to the door about half-past eight, but unfortunately it went away before we found we couldn't get in."

"You rang?"

"We rang, and knocked, but could get no answer. The house was in darkness and we began to fear something was wrong. Then just as I was about to leave mother in the summer-house and run up to the Hazeltons' to see if James was there, he appeared to say that you were staying in Plymouth overnight. He rang and knocked again. But still no one came. Then he tried the windows on the ground floor, but they were all fastened, and at last he got the ladder from the yard and managed to get in through the window of your dressing room. He came down and opened the door and we got in."

"And what did you find?"

"Nothing at first. We wondered where the maids could possibly have got to, or what could have happened. I found your electric torch and we began to search the rooms. Then we saw that your safe had been broken open and we knew it was burglary. That terrified us on account of the maids and we wondered if they had been decoyed away also. I don't mind admitting now that I was just shaking with fear lest we should find that they had been injured or even murdered. But it wasn't so bad as that."

"They were tied up?"

"Yes, we found them in cook's bedroom, lying on the

floor with their hands and feet tied, and gagged. They were both very weak and could scarcely stand when we released them. They told us—but you'd better see them and hear what they have to say. They're not gone to bed yet."

"Yes, I'll see them directly. What did you do then?"

"As soon as we were satisfied the burglars had gone James went home to call up the police. Then he came back and we began a second search to see what had been stolen. But the more we looked, the more surprised we became. We couldn't find that anything had been taken."

"Extraordinary!" Cheyne commented again. "And then?"

"After a time the police came out, and then James went home again to see whether they had been able to get in touch with you. He came back and told us you would be here by eleven. He had only just gone when you arrived. I really can't say how kind and helpful he has been."

"Yes, James is a good fellow. Now you and mother get to bed and I'll fix things up with the police."

He turned his steps to the kitchen, where he found the two maids shivering over a roaring fire and drinking tea. They stood up as he entered, but he told them to sit down again, asked for a cup for himself, and seating himself on the table chatted pleasantly before obtaining their statements. They had evidently had a bad fright and cook still seemed hysterical. As he sat he looked at them curiously.

Cook was an elderly woman, small and plain and stout. She had been with them since they had bought the house, and though he had not seen much of her, she had always seemed good-tempered and obliging. He had heard his mother speak well of her and he was sorry she should have had so distressing an experience. But he didn't fancy she would be one to give burglars much trouble.

Susan, the parlormaid, was of a different quality. She was tall with rather heavy features, and good looking after a somewhat coarse type. If a trifle sullen in manner, she was competent and by no means a fool, and he felt that nefarious marauders would find her a force to be reckoned with.

By dint of patient questioning he presently knew all they had to tell. It appeared that shortly after the ladies had left a ring had come at the door. Susan had opened it to find two men standing outside. One was tall and powerfully built, with dark hair and clean shaven, the other small and pale—pale face, pale hair, and tiny pale mustache. They had inquired for Mr. Maxwell Cheyne, and when she had said he was out. the small man had asked if he could write a note. She had brought them into the hall and was turning to go for some paper when the big man had sprung on her and before she could cry out had pressed a handkerchief over her mouth. The small man had shut the door and begun to tie her wrists and ankles. Susan had struggled and in spite of them had succeeded in getting her mouth free and shouting a warning to cook, but she had been immediately overpowered and securely gagged. The men had laid her on the floor of the hall and had seemed about to go upstairs when cook, attracted by Susan's cry, had appeared at the door leading to the back premises. The two men had instantly rushed over, and in a few seconds cook also lay bound and gagged on the floor. They had then disappeared, apparently to search the house, for in a few minutes they had come back and carried first Susan and then cook to the latter's room at the far end of the back part of the house. The intruders had then withdrawn, closing the door, and the two women had neither heard nor seen anything further of them.

The whole episode had a curious effect on Cheyne. It seemed, as he considered it, to lose its character of an ordinary breach of the law, punishable by the authorized forces of the Crown, and to take on instead that of a personal struggle between himself and these unknown men. The more he thought of it the more inclined he became to accept the challenge and to pit his own brain and powers against theirs. The mysterious nature of the affair appealed to his sporting instincts, and by the time he rejoined the sergeant in the study, he had made up his mind to keep his own counsel as to the Plymouth incident. He would call up the manager of the Edgecombe, tell him to carry on with his private detective, and have the latter down to Warren Lodge to go into the matter of the burglary.

He found the sergeant attempting ineffectively to discover finger-prints on the smooth walls of the safe, sympathized with him in the difficulty of his task, and asked a number of deliberately futile questions. On the ground that nothing had been stolen he minimized the gravity of the affair, questioned his power to prosecute should the offenders be forthcoming, and instilled doubts into the other's mind as to the need for special efforts to run them to earth. Finally, the man explaining that he had finished for the time being, he bade him good night, locked up the house and went to bed. There he lay for several hours tossing and turning as he puzzled over the affair, before sleep descended to blot out his worries and soothe his eager desire to be on the track of his enemies.

CHAPTER III
The Launch "Enid"

FOR several days after the attempted burglary events in the Cheyne household pursued the even tenor of their way. Cheyne went back to Plymouth on the following morning and interviewed the manager of the Edgecombe, and the day after a quiet, despondent-looking man with the air of a small shopkeeper arrived at Warren Lodge and was closeted with Cheyne for a couple of hours. Mr. Speedwell, of Horton and Lavender's Private Detective Agency, listened with attention to the tales of the drugging and the

31

burglary, thenceforward appearing at intervals and making mysterious inquiries on his own account.

On one of these visits he brought with him the report of the analyst relative to the dishes of which Cheyne had partaken at lunch, but this document only increased the mystification the affair had caused. No trace of drugs was discernible in any of the food or drink in question, and as the soiled plates or glasses or cups of *all* the courses were available for examination, the question of how the drug had been administered—or alternatively whether it really had been administered—began to seem almost insoluble. The cocktail taken with Parkes before lunch was the only item of which a portion could not be analyzed, but the evidence of the barmaid proved conclusively that Parkes could not have tampered with it.

But in spite of the analysis, the coffee still seemed the doubtful item. Cheyne's sleepy feeling had come on very rapidly immediately after drinking the coffee, before which he had not felt the slightest abnormal symptoms. Mr. Speedwell laid stress on this point, though he was pessimistic about the whole affair.

"They know what they're about, does this gang," he admitted ruefully as he and Cheyne were discussing matters. "That man in the hotel that called himself Parkes—if we found him tomorrow we should have precious little against him. However he managed it, we can't prove he drugged you. In fact it's the other way round. He can prove on our evidence that he didn't."

"It looks like it. You haven't been able to find out anything about him?"

"Not a thing, sir; that is, not what would be any use. I can prove that he sent your telegram all right; the girl in the Post Office recognized his description. But I couldn't get on to his trail after that. I've tried the stations and the docks and the posting establishments and the hotels and I can't get a trace. But of course I'll maybe get it yet."

"What about the address given on his card?"

"Tried that first thing No good. No one of the name known in the district."

"When did the man arrive at the hotel?"

"Just after you did, Mr. Cheyne. He probably picked you up somewhere else and was following you to see where you'd get lunch."

"Oh, well, that explains something. I was wondering how he knew I was going to the Edgecombe."

"It doesn't explain so very much, sir. Question still is, how did he get all that other information about you; the name of your lawyer and so on?"

Cheyne had to admit that the prospects of clearing up the affair were not rosy. "But what about the burglary?" he went on more hopefully. "That should be an easier nut to crack."

Speedwell was still pessimistic.

"I don't know about that, sir," he answered gloomily. "There's not much to go on there either. The only chance is to trace the men's arrival or departure. Now individually the private detective is every bit as good as the police; better, in fact, because he's not so tied up with red tape. But he hasn't their organization. In a case like this, when the police with their enormous organization have failed, the private detective hasn't a big chance. However, of course I've not given up."

He paused, and then drawing a little closer to Cheyne and lowering his voice, he went on impressively: "You know, sir, I hope you'll not consider me out of place in saying it, but I had hoped to get my best clue from yourself. There can be no doubt that these men are after some paper that you have, or that they think you have. If you could tell me what it was, it might make all the difference."

Cheyne made a gesture of impatience.

"Don't I know that," he cried. "Haven't I been racking my brains over that question ever since the thing happened! I can't think of anything. In fact, I can tell you there *was* nothing—nothing that I know of anyway," he added helplessly.

Speedwell nodded and a sly look came into his eyes.

"Well, sir, if you can't tell, you can't, and that's all there is to it." He paused as if to refer to some other matter, then apparently thinking better of it, concluded: "You have my address, and if anything should occur to you I hope you'll let me know without delay."

When Speedwell had taken his departure Cheyne sat on in the study, thinking over the problem the other had presented, but as he did so he had no idea that before that very day was out he should himself have received information which would clear up the point at issue, as well as a good many of the other puzzling features of the strange events in which he had become involved.

Shortly after lunch, then, on this day, the eighth after the burglary and drugging, Cheyne, on re-entering the house after a stroll round the garden, was handed a card and told that the owner was waiting to see him in his study. Mr. Arthur Lamson, of 17 Acacia Terrace, Bland Road, Devonport, proved to be a youngish man of middle height and build, with the ruggedly chiselled features usually termed hard-bitten, a thick black toothbrush mustache, and glasses. Cheyne was not particularly prepossessed by his appearance, but he spoke in an educated way and had the easy polish of a man of the world.

"I have to apologize for this intrusion, Mr. Cheyne," he began in a pleasant tone, "but the fact is I wondered whether I could interest you in a small invention of mine. I got your name from Messrs. Holt & Stavenage, the Plymouth ship chandlers. They told me you dealt with them and how keen you were on yachting, and as my invention relates to the navigation of coasting craft, I hoped you might allow me to show it to you."

Cheyne, who had had some experience of inventors during six weeks' special naval war service after his convalescence, made a noncommittal reply.

"I may tell you at once, sir," Mr. Lamson went on,

"that I am looking for a keen amateur who would be willing to allow me to fit the device to his boat, and who would be sufficiently interested to test it under all kinds of varying conditions. You see, though the thing works all right on a motor launch I have borrowed, I have exhausted my leave from my business, and am therefore unable to give it a sufficiently lengthy and varying test to find out whether it will work continuously under ordinary everyday sea-going conditions. If it proves satisfactory I believe it would sell, and if so I should of course be willing to take into partnership to a certain extent anyone who had helped me to develop it."

In spite of himself Cheyne was impressed. This man was different from those with whom he had hitherto come in contact. He was not asking for money, or at least he hadn't so far.

"Have you patented the device?" he asked, reckoning willingness to spend money on patent fees a test of good faith.

"No, not yet," the visitor answered. "I have taken out provisional protection, which will cover the thing for four months more. If it promises well after a couple of months' test it will be time enough to apply for the full patent."

Cheyne nodded. This was a reasonable and proper course.

"What is the nature of the device?" he asked.

The young man's manner grew more alert. He leaned forward in his chair and spoke eagerly. Cheyne frowned involuntarily as he recognized the symptoms.

"It's a position indicator. It would, I think, be useful at all times, but during fog it would be simply invaluable: that is, for coasting work, you know. It would be no good for protection against collision with another ship. But for clearing a headland or making a harbor in a fog it would be worth its weight in gold. The principle is, I believe, old, but I have been lucky enough to hit on improvements in detail which get over the defects of previous instruments. Speaking broadly, a fixed pointer, which may if

35

desired carry a pen, rests on a moving chart. The chart is connected to a compass and to rollers operated by devices for recording the various components of motion: one is driven off the propeller, others are set, automatically mostly, for such things as wind, run of tide, wave motion and so on. The pointer always indicates the position of the ship, and as the ship moves, the chart moves to correspond. Steering then resolves itself into keeping the pointer on the correct line on the chart, and this can be done by night without guide lamps, or in a fog, as well as in day-time. The apparatus would also assist navigation through unbuoyed channels over covered mud flats, or in time of war through charted mine fields. I don't want to be a nuisance to you, Mr. Cheyne, but I do wish you would at least let me show you the device. You could then decide whether you would allow me to fix it to your yacht for experimental purposes."

"I should like to see it," Cheyne admitted. "If you can do all you claim, I certainly think you have a good thing. Where is it to be seen?"

"On my launch, or rather, the launch I have borrowed." The young man's eagerness now almost approached excitement. His eyes sparkled and he fidgeted in his chair. "She is lying off Johnson's boat slip at Dartmouth. I left the dinghy there."

"And you want me to go now?"

"If you really will be so kind. I should propose a short run down the estuary and along the coast towards Exmouth, say for two or three hours. Could you spare so much time?"

"Why, yes, I should enjoy it. I shall be back, say, between six and seven."

"I'll have you back at Johnson's slip at six o'clock. I have a taxi waiting now, and I'll arrange with Johnson to call another for you as soon as he sees us coming up the estuary."

"I'll go," said Cheyne. "Just a moment until I tell my people and get a coat."

The day was ideal for the run. Spring was in the air. The brilliant April sun poured down from an almost cloudless sky, against which the sea horizon showed a hard, sharp line of intensest blue. Within the estuary it was calm, but multitudinous white flecks in the distance showed a stiff breeze was blowing out at sea. Cheyne's spirits rose. It was a glorious sport, this of battling with the foaming, tumbling waves in the open. How he loved their blue-black depth with its suggestion of utter and absolute cleanness, the creamy purity of their seething crests, their steady, irresistible onward movement, the restless dancing and swirling of the wavelets on their flanks! To him it was life to feel the buoyant spring of the craft beneath him, to hear the crash of the bows into the troughs and the smack of the spindrift striking aft. He was glad this Lamson had called. Even if the matter of the invention was a washout, as he more than half expected, he felt he was going to enjoy his afternoon.

Three or four minutes brought them to Johnson's boat slip on the outskirts of Dartmouth. There Lamson drew the proprietor aside.

"See here," he directed, "we're going out for a run. I want you to keep a lookout for us coming back. We shall be in about six. As soon as you see us send for a taxi and have it here when we get ashore. Now, Mr. Cheyne, if you're ready."

They climbed down into a small dinghy and Lamson, taking the oars, pulled out towards a fair-sized motor launch which lay at anchor some couple of hundred yards from the shore. She was not a graceful boat, but looked strongly built, showing a high bluff bow, a square stern and lines suggestive of speed.

"A sea boat," said Cheyne approvingly. "You surely don't run her by yourself?"

"No, a motoring friend has been giving me a hand. I am skipper and he engineer. We hug the coast, you know, and don't go out if it is blowing."

As he spoke he pulled round the stern of the launch

upon which Cheyne observed the words "Enid, Devonport." At the same time a tall, well-built figure appeared and waved his hand. Lamson brought the dinghy up to the tiny steps and a moment later they were on deck.

"Mr. Cheyne has come out to see the great invention, Tom. I almost hope that he is interested. My friend, Tom Lewisham, Mr. Cheyne."

The two men shook hands.

"Lamson thinks he is going to make his fortune with this thing, Mr. Cheyne," the big man remarked, smiling. "We must see that there is no mistake about our percentages."

"If you want a percentage you must work for it, my son," Lamson declared. "Mr. Cheyne must be back by six, so get your old rattletrap going and we'll run down to the sea. If you don't mind, Mr. Cheyne, we'll get under way before I show you the machine, as it takes both of us to get started."

"Right-o," said Cheyne. "I'll bear a hand if there's anything I can do."

"Well, that's good of you. It would be a help if you would take the tiller while I'm making all snug. There's a bit of a tumble on outside."

The boat was certainly a flier. The charmingly situated old town dropped rapidly astern while Lamson "made snug." Then he came aft, shouted down through the engine room skylight for his friend, and when the latter appeared told him to take the tiller.

"Now, Mr. Cheyne," he went on, "now comes the great moment! I have not fixed the apparatus up here in front of the tiller, partly to keep it secret and partly to save the trouble of making it weatherproof. It's down in the cabin. But you understand it should be up here. Will you come down?"

He led the way down a companion to a diminutive saloon. "It's in the sleeping part, still forward," he pointed, and the two men squeezed through a door in the bulkhead into a tiny cabin, lit by electric light and with a table in

the center and two berths on either side. On the table was
a frame on the top of which was stretched a chart, and a
light rod ran out from one side to a pointer fixed over the
middle of the chart.

"You can see that it's very roughly made," Lamson went
on, "but if you look closely I think you'll find that it works
all right."

Cheyne bent forward and examined the machine, and
as he did so mystification grew in his mind. The chart was
not of the estuary of the Dart, nor, stranger still, was it
connected to rollers. It was simply tacked on what he now
saw was merely the lid of a box. How it was moved he
couldn't see.

"I don't follow this," he said. "How do you get your
chart to move if it's nailed down?"

There was no answer, but as he swung round with a
sudden misgiving there was a sharp click. Lamson had
disappeared and the door was shut!

Cheyne seized the handle and turned it violently, only
to find that the bolt of the lock had been shot, but before
he could attempt further researches the light went off,
leaving him in almost pitch darkness. At the same moment
a significant lurch showed that they were passing from the
shelter of the estuary into the open sea.

He twisted and tugged at the handle. "Here you,
Lamson!" he shouted angrily. "What do you mean by this?
Open the door at once. Confound you! Will you open the
door!" He began to kick savagely at the woodwork.

A small panel in the partition between the cabins shot
aside and a beam of light flowed into Cheyne's. Lamson's
face appeared at the opening. He spoke in an old-
fashioned, stilted way, aping extreme politeness, but his
mocking smile gave the lie to his protestations.

"I'm sorry, Mr. Cheyne, for this incivility," he declared,
"and hope that when you have heard my explanation you
will pardon me. I must admit I have played a trick on you
for which I offer the fullest apologies. The story of my
invention was a fabrication. So far as I am aware no appa-

ratus such as I have described exists: certainly I have not made one. The truth is that you can do me a service, and I took the liberty of inveigling you here in the hope of securing your good offices in the matter."

"You've taken a bad way of getting my help," Cheyne shouted wrathfully. "Open the door at once, damn you, or I'll smash it to splinters!"

The other made a deprecatory gesture.

"Really I beg of you, Mr. Cheyne," he said in mock horror at the other's violence. "Not so fast, if you please, sir. I have an answer to both your observations. With regard to the door you will—"

Cheyne interrupted him with a savage oath and a fierce onslaught of kicks on the lower panels of the door. But he could make no impression on them, and when in a few moments he paused breathless, Lamson went on quietly.

"With regard to the door, as I was about to observe, it would be a waste of energy to attempt to smash it to splinters, because I have taken the precaution to have it covered with steel plates. They are bolted through and the nuts are on the outside. I mention this to save you—"

Cheyne was by this time almost beside himself with rage. He expressed his convictions and desires as to Lamson and his future in terms which from the point of view of force left little to be desired, and persistently reiterated his demand that the door be opened as a prelude to further negotiation. In reply Lamson shook his head, and remarking that as the present seemed an inopportune moment for discussing the situation, he could postpone the conversation, he closed the panel and left the inner cabin once more in darkness.

For an hour Cheyne stormed and fumed, and with pieces which he managed to knock off the table tried to break through the door, the bulkheads, and the dead-lighted porthole, all with such a complete absence of success that when at last Lamson appeared once more at the panel he was constrained to listen, though with suppressed fury, to what he had to say.

"You see, it's this way, Mr. Cheyne," the erstwhile inventor began. "You are completely in our power, and the sooner you realize it and let us come to business, the sooner you'll be at liberty again. We don't wish you any harm; please accept my assurances on that. All we want is a slight service at your hands, and when you perform it you will be free to return home; in fact we shall take you back as I said, with profuse apologies for your inconvenience and loss of time. But it is only fair to point out that we are determined to get what we want, and if you are not prepared to come to terms now we can wait until you are."

Cheyne, still at a white heat, cursed the other savagely. Lamson waited until he had finished, then went on in a smooth, almost coaxing tone:

"Now do be reasonable, Mr. Cheyne. You must see that your present attitude is only wasting time for us both. Not to put too fine a point on it, the situation is this: You are there, and you can't get out, and you can't attract attention to your predicament—that is why the deadlights are shipped. It grieves me to say it," Lamson smiled sardonically, "but I must tell you that you will stay there until you do what we want. In order to prevent Mrs. Cheyne becoming uneasy we shall wire her in your name that you have left for an extended trip and won't be back for some days. 'To Cheyne, Warren Lodge, Dartmouth. Gone for yachting cruise down French coast. Address Poste Restante, St. Nazaire. All well. Maxwell.' You see, we know exactly how to word it. All suspicion would be lulled for some days and then," he paused and something sinister and revolting came into his face, "then it wouldn't matter, for it would be too late. For you see there is neither food nor drink in the cabin and we don't propose to pass any in. You won't get any, Mr. Cheyne, no matter how many days you remain aboard: that is," his manner changed, "unless you are reasonable, which of course you will be. In that case no harm is done. Now won't you hear our little proposition?"

"I'll see you in hell first," Cheyne shouted, his rage once

again overwhelming him. "You'll pay for this, I can tell you. It'll be the dearest trip you ever had in your life," and he proceeded with threats and curses to demand the immediate opening of the door. Lamson, a whimsical smile curling his lips, shrugged his shoulders at the outburst, and replied by withdrawing his head from the opening and sliding the panel to.

Cheyne, left once more in almost complete darkness, sat silent, his mind full of wrath against his captors. But as time passed and they made no sign, his fury somewhat evaporated and he began to wonder what it was they wanted with him. His rage had made him thirsty, and the mere fact that Lamson had stated that nothing would be given him to drink, made his thirst more insistent. It was impossible, he said to himself, that the scoundrels could carry out so diabolical a threat, but in spite of his assurance, little misgivings began to creep into his mind. At all events the vision of his usual cup of afternoon tea grew increasingly alluring. When therefore after what seemed to him several hours, but what was in reality about forty minutes only, the panel suddenly opened, he admitted sullenly that he was prepared to listen to what Lamson had to say.

"That's good," the young man answered heartily. "If you could just see your way to humor us in this little matter there is no reason why we should not part friends."

"There's no question of friends about it," Cheyne declared sharply. "Cut your chatter and get on to business. What do you want?"

A smile suffused Mr. Lamson's roughhewn countenance.

"Now that's talking," he cried. "That's what I've been hoping to hear. I'll tell you the whole thing and you'll see it's only a mere trifle that we're asking. I can put it in five words: We want Arnold Price's letter."

Cheyne stared.

"Arnold Price's letter?" he repeated in amazement. "What on earth do you know about Arnold Price's letter?"

"We know all about it, Mr. Cheyne—a jolly sight more than you do. We know about his giving it to you and the conditions under which he asked you to keep it. But you don't know why he did so or what is in it. We do, and we can justify our request for it."

The demand was so unexpected that Cheyne sat for a moment in silence, thinking how the letter in question had come into his possession. Arnold Price was a junior officer in one of the ships belonging to the Fenchurch Street firm in whose office Cheyne had spent five years as clerk. Business had brought the two young men in contact during the visits of Price's ship, and they had become rather friendly. On Cheyne's leaving for Devonshire they had drifted apart, indeed they had only met on one occasion since. That was in 1917, shortly before Cheyne received the wound which invalided him out of the service. Then he found that his former companion had volunteered for the navy on the outbreak of hostilities. He had done well, and after a varied service he had been appointed third officer of the *Maurania,* an eight-thousand-ton liner carrying passengers, as well as stores from overseas to the troops in France. The two had spent an evening together in Dunkirk renewing their friendship and talking over old times. Then, two months later, had come the letter. In it Price asked his friend to do him a favor. Some private papers, of interest only to himself, had come into his possession and he wished these to be safely preserved until after the war. Knowing that Cheyne was permanently invalided out, he was venturing to send these papers, sealed in the enclosed envelope, with the request that Cheyne would keep them for him until he reclaimed them or until news of his death was received. In the latter case Cheyne was to open the envelope and act as he thought fit on the information therein contained.

The sealed envelope was of a size which would hold a foolscap sheet folded in four, and was fairly bulky. It was inscribed: "To Maxwell Cheyne, of Warren Lodge, Dartmouth, Devonshire, from Arnold Price, third officer, S.S.

Maurania," and on the top was written: "Please retain this envelope unopened until I claim it or until you have received authentic news of my death. Arnold Price." Cheyne had acknowledged it, promising to carry out the instructions, and had then sent the envelope to his bank, where it had since remained.

The insinuating voice of Lamson broke through his thoughts.

"I think, Mr. Cheyne, when you hear the reasons for our request, you will give it all due consideration. For one—"

What? Break faith with Price? Go back on his friend? Rage again choked Cheyne's utterance. Stutteringly he cursed the other, once again demanding under blood-curdling threats of future vengeance his immediate liberty. Through his passion he heard the voice of the other saying he was sorry but he really could not help it, the panel slid shut, and darkness and silence, save for the sounds of the sea, reigned in the *Enid's* cabin.

CHAPTER IV

Concerning a Peerage

WHEN MAXWELL Cheyne's paroxysm of fury diminished and he began once more to think collectedly about the unpleasant situation in which he found himself, a startling idea occurred to him. Here at last, surely, was the explanation of his previous adventures! The drugging in the hotel in Plymouth, the burglary at Warren Lodge, and now his kidnaping on the *Enid* were all part and parcel of the same scheme. It was for Price's letter that his pocketbook was investigated while he lay asleep in the private room at the Edgecombe; it was for Price's letter that his safe was broken open and his house searched by other members of the conspiracy, and it was for Price's letter that he now lay, a prisoner aboard this infernal launch.

A valuable document, this of Price's must surely be, if it was worth such pains to acquire! Cheyne wondered how it had never occurred to him that it might represent the motive of the earlier crimes, but he soon realized that he had never thought of it as being of interest to anyone other than Price. Indeed, Price himself referred to his enclosure as "some private papers, of interest to myself only." In that last phrase Price had evidently been wrong, and Cheyne wondered whether he had been genuinely mistaken, or whether he had from distrust of himself deliberately misstated the case in order to minimize the value of the document. Price had certainly not shown himself anxious to regain it at the earliest possible moment. On the conclusion of peace he had not accepted demobilization. He had applied for and obtained a transfer to the Middle East, where he had commanded one of the transports plying between Basrah and Bombay in connection with the Mesopotamian campaign. So far as Cheyne knew, he was still there. He hadn't heard of him for many months, not, indeed, since he went out.

While Cheyne had been turning over these matters in his mind the launch had evidently been approaching land, as its rather wild rolling and pitching had gradually ceased and it was now floating on an even keel. Cheyne had been conscious of the fact despite his preoccupation, but now his musings were interrupted by the stopping of the motor and a few seconds later by the plunge of the anchor and the rattle of the running chain. In the comparative silence he shouted himself hoarse, but no one paid him the least attention. He heard, however, the dinghy being drawn up to the side and presently the sound of oars retreating, but whether one or both of his captors had left he could not tell. In an hour or two the boat returned, but though he again shouted and beat the door of his cabin, no notice was taken of his calls.

Then began for Cheyne a period which he could never afterwards look back on without a shudder. Never could he have believed that a night could be so long, that time could drag so slowly. He made himself as comfortable as he could in one of the bunks, but as the clothes and the mattress had been removed, his efforts were not crowned with much success. In spite of his weariness and of the growing exhaustion due to hunger, he could not sleep. He wanted something to drink. He was surprised to find that thirst was not localized in a parched throat or dry mouth. His whole being cried out for water. He could not have described the sensation, but it was very intense, and with every hour that passed it grew stronger. He turned and tossed in the narrow bunk, his restlessness and discomfort continually increasing. At last he dozed, but only to fall into horrible dreams from which he awoke unrefreshed and thirstier than ever.

Cheyne had plenty of spirit and dash, but he lacked in staying power, and when the inevitable period of reaction to his excitement and rage came he became plunged in a deep depression. These fellows had him in their power. If this went on and they really carried out their threat he would have to give way sooner or later. He hated to think he might betray a trust; he hated still more to be coerced into doing anything against his own will, but when, as it seemed to him, weeks later, the panel shot back and Lamson's face appeared, his first decision was shaken and he waited sullenly to hear what the other had to say.

The man was polite and deprecating rather than blustering, and seemed anxious to make it as easy as possible for Cheyne to capitulate.

"I hope, Mr. Cheyne," he began, "you will allow me to explain this matter more fully, as I cannot but think you have at least to some extent misunderstood our proposal. I did not tell you the whole of the facts, but I should like to do so now if you will listen."

He paused expectantly. Cheyne glowered at him, but did not reply, and Lamson resumed:

"The matter is somewhat complicated, but I will do my best to explain it as briefly as I can. In a word, then, it relates to a claim for a peerage. I must admit to you that

Lamson is not my name—it is Price, and the Arnold Price whom you knew during the war is my second cousin. Arnold's uncle and my father's cousin, St. John Price, is, or rather was, in the diplomatic service, and it is through his discoveries that the present situation has arisen.

"It happened that this St. John Price had occasion to visit South Africa on diplomatic business during the war, and as luck would have it he took his return passage on the *Maurania,* the ship on which his nephew Arnold was third officer. But he never reached England. He met his death on the journey under circumstances which involved a coincidence too remarkable to have happened otherwise than in real life."

In spite of himself Cheyne was interested. Price glanced at him and went on:

"One night at the end of the voyage when they were running without lights up the Channel, a large steamer going in the same direction as themselves suddenly loomed up out of the darkness and struck them heavily on the starboard quarter. My cousin was on deck, though not in charge. He saw the outlines of the vessel as she was closing in, and he also saw that a passenger was standing at the rail just where the contact was about to take place. At the risk of his own life he sprang forward and dragged the man back. Unfortunately he was not in time to save him, for a falling spar broke his back and only just missed killing Arnold. Then, as you may have guessed from what I said, it turned out that the passenger was none other than St. John Price. My cousin had tried to save his own uncle."

Once more Price paused, but Cheyne still remaining silent, he continued:

"St. John lingered for some hours, during most of which time he was conscious, and it was then that he told Arnold about his belief, that he, Arnold, was heir to the barony of Hull. I don't know, Mr. Cheyne, if you are aware that the present Lord Hull is a man well on to eighty and is in failing health. He has no known heir, and unless some claimant comes forward speedily, the title will in the course of nature become extinct. As you probably know also, Lord Hull is a man of enormous wealth. St. John Price believed that he, Arnold, and myself were all descended from the eldest son of Francis, the fifth Baron Hull. This man had lived an evil, dissolute life, and England having become too hot to hold him, he had sailed for South Africa in the early part of the last century. On his father's death search was made for him, but without result, and the second son, Alwyn, inherited. St. John had after many years' labor traced what he believed was a lineal descent from the scapegrace, and he had utilized his visit to South Africa to make further inquiries. There he had unearthed the record of a marriage, which, he believed, completed the proofs he sought. As he knew he was dying, he handed over the attested copy of the marriage certificate to Arnold, at the same time making a new will leaving all the other documents in the case to Arnold also.

"When Arnold received his next leave he went fully into the matter with his solicitor, only to find that one document, the register of a birth, was missing. Without this he could scarcely hope to win his case. The evidence of the other papers tended to show that the birth had taken place in India, probably at Bombay, and Arnold therefore applied for a transfer into a service which brought him to that country, in the hope that he would have an opportunity to pursue his researches at first hand. It was there that I met him—I am junior partner in Swanson, Reid & Price's of that city—and he told me all that I have told you.

"Before going to the East he sealed up the papers referring to the matter and sent them to you. If you will pardon my saying so, I think that there he made a mistake. But he explained that he knew too much about lawyers to leave anything in their hands, that they would fight the case for their own fees whether there was any chance of winning it or not, and that he wanted the papers to be in the hands of an honest man in case of his death.

"I pointed out that I was interested in the matter also,

but he said No, that he was the heir and that during his life the affair concerned him alone. Needless to say, we parted on bad terms.

"Now, Mr. Cheyne, you can see why I want those papers. Though Arnold is my cousin I doubt his honesty. I want to see exactly how we both stand. I want nothing but what is fair—as a matter of fact I can get nothing but what is fair—the law wouldn't allow it. But I don't want to be done. If I had the papers I would show them to a first-rate lawyer. If Arnold is entitled to succeed he will do so, if I am the heir I shall, if neither of us no harm is done. We can only get what the law allows us. But in any case I give my word of honor that, if I succeed, Arnold shall never want for anything in reason."

Price was speaking earnestly and his manner carried conviction to Cheyne. Without waiting for a reply he proceeded.

"You, Mr. Cheyne, if you will excuse my saying it, are an outsider in the matter. Whether Arnold or I or neither of us succeeds is nothing to you. You want to do only what is fair to Arnold, and you have my most solemn promise that that is all I propose. If you enable me to test our respective positions by handing over the papers to me you will not be letting Arnold down."

When Price ceased speaking there was silence between the two men as Cheyne thought over what he had heard. Price's manner was convincing, and as far as Cheyne could form an opinion, the story might be true. It certainly explained the facts adequately, and Cheyne believed that the statements about Lord Hull were correct. All the same he did not believe this man was out for a square deal. If he could only get what the law allowed, would not the same apply whether he or Arnold conducted the affair? Cheyne, moreover, was still sore from his treatment, and he determined he would not discuss the matter until he had received satisfactory replies to one or two personal questions.

"Did you drug me in the Edgecombe Hotel in Plymouth

a week ago and then go through my pockets, and did you the same evening burgle my house, break open my safe, and mishandle my servants?"

It was not exactly a tactful question, but Price answered it cheerfully and without hesitation.

"Not in person, but I admit my agents did these things. For these also I am anxious to apologize."

"Your apologies won't prevent your having a lengthened acquaintance with the inside of a prison," Cheyne snarled, his rage flickering up at the recollection of his injuries. "How do your confederates come to be interested?"

"Bought," the other admitted sweetly. "I had no other way of getting help. I have paid them twenty pounds on account and they will get a thousand guineas each if my claim is upheld."

"A self-confessed thief and crook as well as a liar! And you expect me to believe in your good intentions towards Arnold Price!"

An unpleasant look passed across the other's face, but he spoke calmly.

"That may be all very well and very true if you like, but it doesn't advance the situation. The question now is: Are you prepared to hand over the letter? Nothing else seems to me to matter."

"Why did you not come to me like an ordinary honest man and tell me your story? What induced you to launch out into all this complicated network of crime?"

Price smiled whimsically.

"Well, you might surely guess that," he answered. "Suppose you had refused to give me the letter, how was I to know that you would not have put it beyond my reach? I couldn't take the risk."

"Suppose I refuse to give it to you now?"

"You won't, Mr. Cheyne. No one in your position could. Circumstances are too strong for you, and you can hand it over and retain your honor absolutely untarnished. I do not wish to urge you to a decision. If you would prefer to take today to think it over, by all means do so. I sent the wire to Mrs. Cheyne shortly before six last night, so she will not be uneasy about you."

Though the words were politely spoken, the threat behind them was unmistakable and fell with sinister intent on the listener's ears. Rapidly Cheyne considered the situation. This ruffian was right. No one in such a situation could resist indefinitely. It was true he could refuse his consent at the moment, but the question would come up again and again until at last he would have to give way. He knew it, and he felt that unless there was a strong chance of victory, he could not stand the hours of suffering which a further refusal would entail. No, bitter as the conclusion was, he felt he must for the moment admit defeat, trusting later to getting his own back. He turned back to Price.

"I haven't got the letter here. I can only get it for you if you put me ashore."

That this was a victory for Price was evident, but the young man showed no elation. He carefully avoided anything in the nature of a taunt, and spoke in a quiet, businesslike way.

"We might be able to arrange that. Where is the letter?"

"At my bank in Dartmouth."

"Then the matter is quite simple. All you have to do is to write to the manager to send the letter to an address I shall give you. Directly you do so you shall have the best food and drink on the launch, and directly the letter is in our hands you will be put ashore close to your home."

Cheyne still hesitated.

"I'll do it provided you can prove to me your statements. How am I to know that you will keep your word? How am I to know that you won't get the letter and then murder me?"

"I'm afraid you can't know that. I would gladly prove it to you, but you must see that it's just not possible. I give you my solemn word of honor and you'll have to accept it because there is nothing else you can do."

Cheyne demurred further, but as Price showed signs of

retreating and leaving him to think it over until the evening, he hastily agreed to write the letter. Immediately the electric light came on in his cabin and Price passed in a couple of sheets of notepaper and envelopes. Cheyne gazed at them in surprise. They were of a familiar silurian gray and the sheets bore in tiny blue embossed letters the words "Warren Lodge, Dartmouth, S. Devon."

"Why, it's my own paper," he exclaimed, and Price with a smile admitted that in view of some development like the present, his agents had taken the precaution to annex a few sheets when paying their call to Cheyne's home.

"If you will ask your manager to send the letter to Herbert Taverner, Esq., Royal Hotel, Weymouth, it will meet the case. Taverner is my agent, and as soon as it is in his hands I will set you ashore at Johnson's wharf."

Seeing there was no help for it, Cheyne wrote the letter. Price read it carefully, then sealed it in its envelope. Immediately after he handed through the panel a tumbler of whisky and water, then hurried off, saying he was going to dispatch the letter and bring Cheyne his breakfast.

Oh, the unspeakable delight of that drink! Cheyne thought he had never before experienced any sensation approaching it in satisfaction. He swallowed it in great gulps, and when in a few moments Price returned, he demanded more, and again more.

His thirst assuaged, hunger asserted itself, and for the next half-hour Cheyne had the time of his life as Price handed in through the panel a plate of smoking ham and eggs, fragrant coffee, toast, butter, marmalade and the like. At last with a sigh of relief Cheyne lit his pipe, while Price passed in blankets and rugs to make up a bed in one of the bunks. Some books and magazines followed and a handbell, which Price told him to ring if he wanted anything.

Comfortable in body and fairly easy in mind, Cheyne made up his bed and promptly fell asleep. It was afternoon when he awoke, and on ringing the bell, Price appeared with a well-cooked lunch. The evening passed comfortably if tediously and that night Cheyne slept well.

Next day and next night dragged slowly away. Cheyne was well looked after and supplied with everything he required, but the confinement grew more and more irksome. However, he could not help himself and he had to admit he might have fared worse, as he lay smoking in his bunk and brooding over schemes to get even with the men who had tricked him.

About half-past ten on the second morning he suddenly heard oars approaching, followed by the sounds of a boat coming alongside and some one climbing on board. A few moments later Price appeared at the panel.

"You will be pleased to hear, Mr. Cheyne, that we have received the letter safely. We are getting under way at once and you will be home in less than three hours."

Presently the motor started, and soon the slow, easy roll showed they were out in the open breasting the Channel ground swell. After a couple of hours, Price appeared with his customary tray.

"We are just coming into the estuary of the Dart," he said. "I thought perhaps you would have a bit of lunch before going ashore."

The meal, like its fellows, was surprisingly well cooked and served, and Cheyne did full justice to it. By the time he had finished the motion of the boat had subsided and it was evident they were in sheltered waters. Some minutes later the motor stopped, the anchor was dropped, and someone got into a boat and rowed off. A quarter of an hour passed and then the boat returned, and to Cheyne's misgivings and growing concern, the motor started again. But after a very few minutes it once more stopped and Price appeared at the panel.

"Now, Mr. Cheyne, the time has come for us to say good-bye. For obvious reasons I am afraid we shall have to ask you to row yourself ashore, but the tide is flowing and you will have no difficulty in that. But before parting I wish to warn you very earnestly for your own sake and your own safety not to attempt to follow us or to set the police on our track. Believe me, I am not speaking idly when I assure you that we cannot brook interference with our plans. We wish to avoid 'removals'," he lingered over the word and a sinister gleam came into his eyes, "but please understand we shall not hesitate if there is no other way. And if you try to give trouble there will be in your case no other way. Take my advice and be wise enough to forget this little episode." He took a small automatic pistol from his pocket and balanced it before the panel. "I warn you most earnestly that if you attempt to make trouble it will mean your death. And with regard to trying to follow us, please remember that this launch has the heels of any craft in the district and that we have a safe hiding-place not far away."

As Price finished speaking he unlocked and threw open the cabin door, motioning his prisoner to follow him on deck. There Cheyne saw that they were far down the estuary, in fact, nearly opposite Warren Lodge and a mile or more from the town.

"I thought you were going to take me to Johnson's jetty," he remarked.

"An obvious precaution," the other returned smoothly. "I trust you won't mind."

The freshness and the freedom of the deck were inexpressibly delightful to Cheyne after his long confinement in the stuffy cabin. He stood drawing deep draughts of the keen invigorating air into his lungs, as he gazed at the familiar shores of the estuary, lighted up in the brilliant April sunlight. Nature seemed in an optimistic mood and Cheyne, in spite of his experiences and Price's gruesome remarks, felt optimistic also. He still felt he would devote all his energies to getting even with the scoundrels who had robbed him, but he no longer regarded them with a sullen hatred. Rather the view of the affair as a game in which he was pitting his wits against theirs gained force in his mind, and he looked forward with zest to turning the tables upon them in the not too distant future.

In the launch's dinghy, which was made fast astern, was Lewisham, engaged in untying the painter of a second dinghy which bore on its stern board the words "S. Johnson, Dartmouth." The explanation of the starting and stopping of the motor now became clear. The conspirators had evidently gone in to pick up this boat and had towed it down the estuary so as to insure their escape before Cheyne could reach the shore to lodge any information against them.

The painter untied, Lewisham passed it aboard the launch and Price, drawing the boat up to the gunwale, motioned Cheyne into it.

"As I said, I'm sorry we shall have to ask you to row yourself ashore, but the run of the tide will help you. Good-bye, Mr. Cheyne. I deeply regret all the inconvenience you have suffered, and most earnestly I urge you to regard the warning which I have given you."

As he spoke he threw the end of the painter into the dinghy and, the launch's motor starting, she drew quickly ahead, leaving Cheyne seated in the small boat.

Full of an idea which had just flashed into his mind, the latter seized the oars and began pulling with all his might not for Johnson's jetty, but for the shore immediately opposite. But try as he would, he did not reach it before the launch *Enid* had become a mere dot on the seaward horizon.

CHAPTER V

An Amateur Sleuth

CHEYNE's great idea was that instead of proceeding directly to the police station and lodging an information against his captors, as he had at first intended, he should himself attempt to follow them to their lair. To enter upon a battle of wits with such men would be a sport more thrilling than big game hunting, more exciting than war, and if by his own unaided efforts he could bring about their undoing he would not only restore his self-respect, which had suffered a nasty jar, but might even recover for Arnold Price the documents which he required for his claim to the barony of Hull.

Whether he was wise in this decision was another matter, but with Maxwell Cheyne impulse ruled rather than colder reason, the desire of the moment rather than adherence to calculated plan. Therefore directly a way in which he could begin the struggle occurred to him, he was all eagerness to set about carrying it out.

The essence of his plan was haste, and he therefore bent lustily to his oars, sending the tiny craft bounding over the wavelets of the estuary and leaving a wake of bubbles from its foaming stem. In a few minutes he had reached the shore immediately beneath Warren Lodge, tied the painter round a convenient boulder, and racing over the rocky beach, had set off running towards the house.

It was a short though stiff climb, but he did not spare himself, and he reached the garden wall within three minutes of leaving the boat. As he turned in through the gate he looked back over the panorama of sea, the whole expanse of which was visible from this point, measuring with his eye the distance to Inner Froward Point, the headland at the opposite side of the bay, around which the *Enid* had just disappeared. She was going east, up channel, but he did not think she was traveling fast enough to defeat his plans.

Another minute brought him to the house, and there, in less time than it takes to tell, he had seen his sister, explained that he might not be back that night, obtained some money, donned his leggings and waterproof, and starting up his motor bike, had set off to ride into Dartmouth.

Pausing for a moment at the boat slip to tell Johnson of the whereabouts of his dinghy, he reached the ferry and got across the river to Kingswear with the minimum of delay possible. Then once more mounting his machine, he rode rapidly off towards the east.

The land lying eastward of Dartmouth forms a peninsula shaped roughly like an inverted cone, truncated, and connected to the mainland by a broad isthmus at the northwest corner. The west side is bounded by the river Dart, with Dartmouth and Kingswear to the southwest, while on the other three sides is the sea. Brixham is a small town at the northeast corner, while further north beyond the isthmus are the larger towns of Paignton and, across Tor Bay, Torquay.

Most of the ground on the peninsula is high, and the road from Kingswear in the southwest corner to Brixham in the northeast crosses a range of hills from which a good view of Tor Bay and the sea to the north and east is obtainable. Should the *Enid* have been bound for Torquay, Teignmouth, Exmouth, or any of the seaports close by, she would pass within view of this road, whereas if she was going right up Channel past Portland Bill she would go nearly due east from the Froward Points. Cheyne's hope was that he should reach this viewpoint before she would have had time to get out of sight had she been on the former course, so that her presence or absence would indicate the route she was pursuing.

But when, having reached the place, he found that no trace of the *Enid* was to be seen, he realized that he had made a mistake. From Inner Froward Point to Brixham was only about seven miles, to Paignton about ten, and to Torquay eleven or twelve. The longest of these distances the launch should do in about twenty-five minutes, and as in spite of all his haste no less than forty-seven minutes had elapsed since he stepped into the dinghy, the test was evidently useless.

But having come so far, he was not going to turn back without making some further effort. The afternoon was still young, the day was fine, he had had his lunch and cycling was pleasant. He would ride along the coast and make some inquiries.

He dropped down the hill into Brixham, and turning to the left, pulled up at the little harbor. A glance showed him that the *Enid* was not there. He therefore turned his machine, and starting once more, ran the five miles odd to Paignton at something well above the legal limit.

Inquiries at the pier produced no result, but as he turned away he had a stroke of unexpected luck. Meeting a coast-guard, he stopped and questioned him, and was overjoyed when the man told him that though no launch had come into Paignton that morning, he had about three-quarters of an hour earlier seen one crossing the bay from the south and evidently making for Torquay.

Quivering with eagerness, Cheyne once more started up his bicycle. He took the three miles to Torquay at a reck-less speed and there received his reward. Lying at moorings in the inner harbor was the *Enid*.

Leaving the bicycle in charge of a boy, Cheyne stepped up to a group of longshoremen and made his inquiries. Yes, the launch there had just come in, half an hour or more back. Two men had come off her and had handed her over to Hugh Leigh, the boatman. Leigh was a tall stout man with a black beard: in fact, there he was him-self behind that yellow and white boat.

Impetuous though he was, Cheyne's knowledge of human nature told him that in dealing with his fellows the more haste frequently meant the less speed. He there-fore curbed his impatience and took a leisurely tone with the boatman.

"Good-day to you," he began. "I see you have the *Enid* there. Is she long in?"

" 'Bout 'arf an hour, sir," the man returned.

"I was to have met her," Cheyne went on, "but I'm afraid I have missed my friends. You don't happen to know which direction they went in?"

"Took a keb, sir: taxi. Went towards the station."

The station! That was an idea at least worth investi-gating. He slipped the man a couple of shillings lest his good offices should be required in the future, and hurrying back to his bicycle was soon at the place in question. Here, though he could find no trace of his quarry, he

learned that a train had left for Newton Abbot at 3:33—
five minutes earlier. It looked very much as if his friends
had traveled by it.

For those who are not clear as to the geography of
South Devon, it may be explained that Newton Abbot lies
on the main line of the Great Western Railway between
Paddington and Cornwall, with Exeter twenty miles to the
northeast and Plymouth some thirty odd to the southwest.
At Newton Abbot the line throws off a spur, which, passing
through Torquay and Paignton, has its terminus at Kingswear, from which there is a ferry connection to Dartmouth
on the opposite side of the river. From Torquay to Newton
Abbot is only about six miles, and there is a good road
between the two. Cheyne, therefore, hearing that the train
had left only five minutes earlier and knowing that there
would be a delay at the junction waiting for the main line
train, at once saw that he had a good chance of overtaking
it.

He did not stop to ask questions, but leaping once more
on his machine, did the six miles at the highest speed he
dared. At precisely 4:00 P.M. he pushed the bicycle into
Newton Abbot station, and handing half a crown to a
porter, told him to look after it until his return.

Hasty inquiries informed him that the train with which
that from Torquay connected was a slow local from
Plymouth to Exeter. It had not yet arrived, but was due
directly. It stopped for seven minutes, being scheduled out
at 4:10 P.M. On chance Cheyne bought a third single to
Exeter, and putting up his collar, pulling down his hat
over his eyes and affecting a stoop, he passed on to the
platform. A few people were waiting, but a glance told
him that neither Price nor Lewisham was among them.

As, however, they might be watching from the shelter
of one of the waiting rooms, he strolled away towards the
Exeter end of the platform. As he did so the train came in
from Plymouth, the engine stopping just opposite where he
was standing. He began to move back, so as to keep a
sharp eye on those getting in. But at once a familiar figure

caught his eye and he stood for a moment motionless.

The coach next the engine was a third, and in the corner of its fourth compartment sat Lewisham!

Fortunately he was sitting with his back to the engine and he did not see Cheyne approaching from behind. Fortunately, also, the opposite corner was occupied by a lady, as, had Price been there, Cheyne would unquestionably have been discovered.

Retreating quickly, but with triumph in his heart, Cheyne got into the end compartment of the coach. It was already occupied by three other men, two sitting in the corner seats next the platform, the third with his back to the engine at the opposite end. Cheyne dropped into the remaining corner seat—facing the engine and next the corridor. He did not then realize the important issues that hung on his having taken up this position, but later he marveled at the lucky chance which had placed him there.

As the train proceeded he had an opportunity, for the first time since embarking on this wild chase, of calmly considering the position, and he at once saw that the fugitives' moves up to the present had been dictated by their circumstances and were almost obligatory.

First, he now understood that they *must* have landed at Brixham, Paignton, or Torquay, and of these Torquay was obviously most suitable to their purpose, being larger than the others and their arrival therefore attracting correspondingly less attention. But they must have landed at one of the three places, as they were the only ports which they could reach before he, Cheyne, would have had time to give the alarm. Suppose he had lodged information with the police immediately on getting ashore, it would have been simply impossible for the others to have entered any other port without fear of arrest. But at Paignton or Torquay they were safe. By no possible chance could the machinery of the law have been set in motion in time to apprehend them.

He saw also how the men came to be seated in the train

from Plymouth when it reached Newton Abbot, and here again he was lost in admiration at the way in which the pair had laid their plans. The first station on the Plymouth side of Newton Abbot was Totnes, and from Torquay to Totnes by road was a matter of only some ten miles. They would just have had time to do the distance, and there was no doubt that Totnes was the place to which their taxi had taken them. In the event, therefore, of an immediate chase, there was every chance of the scent being temporarily lost at Torquay.

These thoughts had scarcely passed through Cheyne's mind when the event happened which caused him to congratulate himself on the seat he was occupying. At the extreme end of the coach, immediately in advance of his compartment, was the lavatory, and at this moment, just as they were stopping at Teignmouth, a man carrying a small kitbag passed along the corridor and entered. Approaching from behind Cheyne, he did not see the latter's face, but Cheyne saw him. It was Price!

Cheyne took an engagement book from his pocket and bent low over it, lest the other should recognize him on his return. But Price remained in the lavatory until they reached Dawlish, and here another stroke of luck was in store for Cheyne. At Dawlish, at which they stopped a few moments later, his vis-à-vis alighted, and Cheyne immediately changed his seat. When, therefore, just before the train started, Price left the lavatory, he again approached Cheyne from behind and again failed to see his face.

As he passed down the corridor Cheyne stared at him. While in the lavatory he had effected a wondrous change in his appearance. Gone now was the small dark mustache and the glasses, his hat was of a different type and his overcoat of a different color. Cheyne watched him pause hesitatingly at the door of the next compartment and finally enter.

For some moments as the train rattled along towards Exeter, Cheyne failed to grasp the significance of this last move. Then he saw that it was, as usual, part of a well-thought-out scheme. Approaching Teignmouth, Price had evidently left his compartment—almost certainly the fourth, where Lewisham sat—as if he were about to alight at the station. Instead of doing so, he had entered the lavatory. Disguised, or, more probably, with a previous disguise removed, he had left it before the train started from Dawlish, and appearing at the door of the second compartment, had attempted to convey the idea, almost certainly with success, that he had just joined the train.

A further thought made Cheyne swing across again to the seat facing the engine. They were approaching Starcross. Would Lewisham adopt the same subterfuge at this station? But he did not, and they reached Exeter without further adventure.

The train going no further, all passengers had to alight. Cheyne was in no hurry to move, and by the time he left the carriage Price and Lewisham were already far down the platform. He wished that he in his turn could find a false mustache and glasses, but he realized that if he kept his face hidden, his clothes were already a satisfactory disguise. He watched the two men begin to pace the platform, and soon felt satisfied that they were proceeding by a later train.

They had reached Exeter at 5:02 P.M. Two expresses left the station shortly after, the 5:25 for Liverpool, Manchester and the north, and the 5:42 for London. Cheyne sat down on a deserted seat near the end of the platform and bent his head over his notebook while he watched the others.

The 5:25 for the north arrived and left, and still the two men continued pacing up and down. "For London," thought Cheyne, and slipping off to the booking hall he bought a first single for Paddington. If the men were traveling third, he would be better in a different class.

When the London express rolled majestically in, Price and Lewisham entered a third near the front of the train. Satisfied that he was still unobserved, Cheyne got into the first class diner farther back. He had not been very close to the men, but he noticed that Lewisham had also made some alteration in his appearance, which explained his not having changed in the lavatory on the local train.

The express was very fast, stopping only once—at Taunton. Here Cheyne, having satisfied himself that his quarry had not alighted, settled himself with an easy mind to await the arrival at Paddington. He dined luxuriously, and when at nine precisely they drew up in the terminus, he felt extremely fit and ready for any adventure that might offer itself.

From the pages of the many works of detective fiction which he had at one time or another digested, he knew exactly what to do. Jumping out as the train came to rest, he hurried along the platform until he had a view of the carriage in which the others had traveled. Then, keeping carefully in the background, he awaited developments.

Soon he saw the men alight, cross the platform and engage a taxi. This move also he was prepared for. Taking a taxi in his turn, he bent forward and said to the driver what the sleuths of his novels had so often said to their drivers in similar circumstances: "Follow that taxi. Ten bob extra if you keep it in sight."

The driver looked at him curiously, but all he said was: "Right y'are, guv'nor," and they slipped out at the heels of the other vehicle into the crowded streets.

Cheyne's driver was a skillful man and they kept steadily behind the quarry, not close enough to excite suspicion, but too near to run any risk of being shaken off. Cheyne was chuckling excitedly and hugging himself at the success of his efforts thus far when, with the extraordinary capriciousness that Fate so often shows, his luck turned.

They had passed down Praed Street and turned up Edgware Road, and it was just where the latter merges into Maida Vale that the blow fell. Here the street was up and the traffic was congested. Both vehicles slackened down, but whereas the leader got through without a stop, Cheyne's was held up to give the road to cross traffic. In vain Cheyne chafed and fretted; the raised arm of the law could not be disregarded, and when at last they were free to go forward, all trace of the other taxi had vanished.

In vain the driver put on a spurt. There were scores of vehicles ahead and a thousand and one turnings off the straight road. In a few minutes Cheyne had to recognize that the game was up and that he had lost his chance.

He stopped and took counsel with his driver, with the result that he decided to go back to Paddington in the hope that when the other taxi had completed its run it would return to the station rank. He had been near enough to take its number, and his man was able to give him the other driver's address, in case the latter went home instead of to the station.

Having reserved a room at the Station Hotel and written a brief note to his sister saying that his business had brought him to London and that he would let her know when he was returning, he lit his pipe, and turning up the collar of his coat, fell to pacing up and down the platform alongside the cab rank. He was relieved to find that vehicles were still turning up and taking their places at the end of the line, and he eagerly scanned the number plate of each arrival. For endless aeons of time he seemed to wait, and then at last, a few minutes before ten, his patience was rewarded. Taxi Z1729 suddenly appeared and drew into position.

In a moment Cheyne was beside its driver.

"Ten bob over the fare if you'll take me quickly to where you set down those two men you got off the Cornish express," he said in a low eager voice.

This man also looked at him curiously and answered, "Right y'are, guv'nor," then having paused to say something to the driver of the leading car on the rank, they turned out into Praed Street.

The man drove rapidly along Edgware Road, through Maida Vale and on into a part of the town unfamiliar to Cheyne. As they rattled through the endless streets Cheyne instructed him not to stop at the exact place, but slightly short of it, as he wished to complete the journey on foot. It seemed a very long distance, but still the man kept steadily on. The town was now taking on a suburban appearance and here and there vacant building lots were to be seen.

Presently they passed an ornate building which Cheyne recognized as the tube station at Hendon, and shortly afterwards the vehicle stopped. Cheyne got out and looked about him, while the driver explained the lie of the land.

They had turned at right angles off the main thoroughfare leading from town into a road which bore the imposing title of "Hopefield Avenue." This penetrated into what seemed to be an estate recently handed over to the jerry-builder, for all around were small detached and semi-detached houses in various stages of construction. Many were complete and occupied, but in scores of other cases the vacant lots still remained, untouched save for their "To let for building" signboards.

Leaving the taxi in a deserted crossroad, the driver signified to Cheyne that they should go forward on foot. A hundred yards farther on they reached another cross-road —the place was laid out in squares like an American city —and there the driver pointed to a house in the opposite angle, intimating that this was their goal.

It was a small detached villa surrounded by a privet hedge and a few small trees and shrubs, evidently not long planted. The two adjoining lots, both along Hopefield Avenue and down the crossroad—Alwyn Road, Cheyne saw its name was—were vacant. Facing it on both streets were finished and occupied houses, but in the angle diagonally opposite was a new building whose walls were only half up.

Thrilled with eager anticipation and excitement, Cheyne dismissed the driver with his ten-shilling tip and then turned to examine his surroundings more carefully, and to devise a plan of campaign for his attack on the enemy's stronghold.

He began by crossing Alwyn Road and walking along Hopefield Avenue past the house, while he examined it as well as he could by the light of the street lamps. It was a two-story building of rather pleasing design, apparently quite new, and conforming to the type of small suburban villas springing up by thousands all around London. As far as he could make out it had the usual rectangular plan, a red-tiled roof with deep overhanging eaves and a large porch with above it a balcony, roofed over but open in front. A narrow walk edged with flower beds led across the forty or fifty feet of lawn between the road and the hall door. On the green gate Cheyne could just make out the words "Laurel Lodge" in white letters. So far as he could see the house appeared to be deserted, the windows and fanlight being in darkness. After the two vacant lots was a half-finished house.

Returning presently, he passed the house again, this time rounding its corner and walking down Alwyn Road. Between the first vacant lot and Laurel Lodge ran a narrow lane, evidently intended to be the approach to the back premises of the future houses.

Glancing round and seeing that no one was in sight, Cheyne slipped into this lane, and crouching behind a shrub, examined the back of Laurel Lodge.

It was very dark in the lane. Presently it would be lighter, as a quadrant moon was rising, but for the moment everything outside the radius of the street lamps was hidden in a black pall. The outline of the house was just discernible against the sky, though Cheyne could not from here make out the details of its construction. But, standing out sharply against its black background, was one brightly illuminated rectangle—a window on the first floor.

The window was open at the top, and the light colored blind was pulled down, though even from where he stood Cheyne could see that it did not entirely reach the bottom of the opening. Even as he watched a shadow appeared on the blind. It was a man's head and shoulders and it remained steady for a moment, then moved slowly out of sight.

Stealthily Cheyne edged his way forward. The back premises of Laurel Lodge were separated from the lane by a gate, and this Cheyne opened silently, passing within. Gradually he worked his way round a tiny greenhouse and between a few flower beds until he reached the wall of the house. There he listened intently, but no sound came from above.

"If only I could get up to the window," he thought, "I could see in under the blind."

But there was no roof or tree upon which he might have climbed, and he stood motionless, undecided what to do next.

Suddenly an idea occurred to him, and full once more of eager excitement, he carefully retraced his steps until he reached the lane. It ran on between rough wire palings, past the two vacant lots and behind the adjoining half-finished house. Cheyne followed it until he reached the half-completed building, and then entering, he began to search for a short ladder.

Every moment the light of the rising moon was increasing, and after stumbling about and making noises which sent him into a cold sweat of apprehension, he succeeded, partly by sight and partly by feeling, in finding what he wanted. Then with great care he lifted it into the lane and bore it back to Laurel Lodge.

With infinite pains he carried it through the gate, round the greenhouse, and past the flower beds to the house. Then fixing the bottom on the grass plot which surrounded the building, he lowered it gently against the wall at the side of the window.

A moment later he reached the slot of clear glass showing beneath the blind and peered into the room. There he saw a sight so unexpected that in spite of his precarious position a cry of surprise all but escaped him.

CHAPTER VI

The House in Hopefield Avenue

THE room was of medium size and plainly though comfortably furnished as a man's study or smoking room. In one corner was a small roll-top desk, in another a table bearing books and papers and a tantalus. Two large leather-covered armchairs stood one at each side of the grate, in which burned a cheerful fire. In the corner opposite the window was a press or cupboard built into the wall, and in front of this all furniture had been cleared away, leaving a wide unoccupied space on the floor. Beside the wall near this space was a large camera, already set up, and on a table beside it lay a flashlight apparatus and two dark slides, apparently of full plate size.

In the room were four persons, and it was the identity of the last of these that had so amazed Cheyne. Standing beside the camera were Price and Lewisham, while no less a personage than Mr. Hubert Parkes of Edgecombe Hotel notoriety stood looking on with his back to the fire. But it was not on these that Cheyne's eyes were glued. Reclining in one of the armchairs with her feet on the fender was Susan, the house and parlormaid at Warren Lodge!

Cheyne gasped. Here was the explanation of one mystery at all events. He saw now where the gang's knowledge of himself and his surroundings had been obtained. He remembered that he had discussed his visit to Plymouth during dinner, a day or two before the event. Susan had been waiting at table, and Susan had been the channel through which the information had been passed on. And the burglary! He could see Susan's hand in this also. In all probability she had taken full advantage of her opportunities to make a thorough search of the house for Price's letter, and it was doubtless only when it became necessary to deal with the safe that her friends had been called in.

Probably also she had been waiting for them, and had admitted them and shown them over the house before submitting to be tied up as a blind to mislead the detectives who would presumably be called in. Cheyne suspected also that Price's visit was timed at a propitious moment, when he himself was available and with a free afternoon to be filled up. No doubt Susan's part in the affair had been vital to its success.

But her participation also showed the extraordinary importance which the conspirators attached to the letter. Susan's makeup for the part she was to play, the forging of her references, her installation in the Cheyne household and her undertaking nearly two months of domestic service in order to gain the document, showed a tenacity of purpose which could only have been evoked to attain some urgent end. Evidently the gang believed that Price's claim on the barony was good, and evidently the others intended to share the spoils.

Cheyne watched breathlessly what was going on in the room, and to his delight he presently found that through the open upper sash he could also hear a good deal of what was said.

The camera had been set up to face the cupboard, and Cheyne now saw that a document of some kind was fastened with drawing pins to its door. Price put his head under the cloth and moved the camera back and forwards, evidently focusing it on the document. Lewisham lifted and examined the flashlight apparatus, then stood waiting. Parkes stooped and said something in a low tone to Susan, at which she laughed sarcastically.

"Do you think two will be enough or should we take four?" said Price when he had arranged the camera to his satisfaction.

"Two, I should say," Parkes answered. "Even if we lost the tracing, two negatives should be an ample record."

"I should take four," Lewisham declared. "After all we've done what is the extra trouble of developing a couple of negatives? One or two might be failures."

"Sime is right," Price decided. "I shall cake four."

Sime? Cheyne thought perplexedly that the man who had run the motor on the *Enid* had been introduced to him as Lewisham. Sime, was it? Then it occurred to him that probably each one of the four had met him under an assumed name, and he listened even more intently in the hope of finding this out.

"I wonder if that ass Cheyne put the cops on to us," went on Sime to the company generally. "James talked to him like a father and he seemed to swallow it all down as sweet as milk. Lordy! But you should have heard old James spouting. He rattled off his patter like a good 'un. Fresh absurdities each time and all that. Didn't you, James?"

"He didn't give much trouble," Price replied. "I shouldn't have believed anyone would have given in as soft as he did. I pitched him a yarn about yours truly being heir to the barony of Hull that wouldn't have deceived an oyster, and he sucked it in like a sponge. But it wasn't that that worked. It was keeping him without water that did the trick. When I offered him another day to think it over he collapsed like a pricked bubble."

"So would you if you had been in his shoes," Susan declared. "I'd like to see you standing out for anything against your own comfort."

"You wouldn't have seen me get into his shoes," Price retorted, fitting a dark slide into the camera. "Now, Sime, if you're ready."

Price pressed the bulb uncovering the lens and at the same time Sime burned a length of magnesium wire before the document on the door, while Cheyne writhed with impotent rage at the discovery that he had been duped in still another particular.

"We've done uncommonly well," Parkes remarked when the photograph had been taken, "but we're not by any means out of the wood yet. In fact, the real work is only beginning. We don't even yet know the size of the problem we're up against. We've got to find that out and then we've got to make a plan and put it through, and all the time we've got to lie low in case that infernal ass has reported us to the police."

"We've got to get these photographs taken and then we've got to get our supper," retorted Price. "For goodness sake let's have one thing at a time, Blessington. If you'd lend a hand instead of standing there preaching, it would be more to the point."

Here was another alias. Parkes's real name was Blessington. Cheyne was beginning to wonder what Price and Susan were really called, when the next remark satisfied his curiosity.

Parkes—or Blessington—took Price's remark easily.

"Now that's where you make the mistake, Mr. James Dangle," he said with a twinkle in his eye. "Miss Dangle and I do the real work in this joint: don't we, Miss Dangle? We supply the brains, you and Sime only rise to the muscles. Eh, Miss Dangle?"

But Miss Dangle was not in a mood for pleasantries.

"We shall want all the brains that you can supply and more," she answered irritably, and then turning lazily to the others demanded if they weren't ever going to be done messing with the darned camera.

At last Cheyne thought he had got the four fixed in his mind. The man on the rug—the man who had drugged him in the Plymouth hotel—was Blessington. The man who had introduced himself as Lamson and afterwards said his name was Price bore neither of these appellations: his name was Dangle. Susan was "Miss Dangle" and almost certainly sister to James. Lewisham, the motorman of the *Enid,* was Sime.

Dangle, Sime, and Blessington! Why, there was something sinister in the very names, and as Cheyne peeped guardedly in beneath the blind, he felt there was something even more sinister in their owners. Dangle, with his hard-bitten features and without his veneer of polish, looked a crafty scoundrel. There was a nasty gleam in his foxy eyes. He looked a man who would sell his best friend for a shilling. Perhaps Cheyne's imagination had by this time run away with him, but Sime now struck him as a murderous-looking ruffian, and Blessington's smug features seemed but to cloak an evil and cruel nature. He was smiling, but there was nothing mirthful about his smile. Rather was it the expression that a wolf might be supposed to wear when he sees a sheep helpless before his attack. Cheyne did not know if Susan was dangerous, but he had always suspected she could be vindictive and bad-tempered. A nice crew, he thought, and he shivered in spite of himself as he pictured his fate were some accident to lead to his discovery.

And what inventive genius they had shown! They had now told him three yarns, all convincing, well-thought-out statements, and all entirely false. There was first of all Blessington's dissertation of his, Cheyne's, literary efforts, told to get him off his guard so that a drug might be administered to him and his pockets be searched. Then there was the account of the position indicator for ships, detailed and plausible, a bait to lure him voluntarily aboard the *Enid*. Lastly there was the story of the Hull succession, including the interesting episode of the attempted rescue of the uncle St. John Price, undoubtedly related with the object of reducing Cheyne's scruples in handing over the letter. These people were certainly past masters in the art of decorative lying, and once again he marveled at the trouble which had been taken in making each story watertight so as to assure its success. It was for no small reward that this had been done.

Cheyne was getting stiff with cold on the ladder. Though keenly interested in what he saw, he wished his enemies would make some move so that he might advance or, if necessary, retreat. But they appeared in no special hurry, proceeding with the photographs in the most careful and deliberate way.

A desultory conversation was kept up, only part of which he heard, but nothing further was said which threw any light on the identity of the conspirators or on the objects for which they were assembled. The work with the camera progressed, however, and presently three photographs had been taken.

"Once more," he heard Dangle remark, and having pulled out the shutter, the whilom skipper of the *Enid* pressed the bulb and another photograph was taken.

"That's four altogether," Dangle went on in satisfied tones. "I guess we're well provided for against accidents. What about that bit of supper, old lady?"

"Aren't we waiting for you?" Susan demanded as she slowly pulled herself up out of the chair. "Gosh!" she went on, lazily stretching herself and yawning, "but it's good to be done with Devonshire! I was fed up, I can tell you! Susan this and Susan that! 'Susan, we'll have tea now,' 'Susan, you might bring a tray and take up the mistress's breakfast,' 'Susan, you might light the fire in the study; Mr. Cheyne wants to work.' Yah! I guess I've about done my share."

The men exchanged glances, but only Dangle spoke.

"I guess you have, old girl," he conceded. "But finish out this job and you'll live like a lady for the rest of your life."

"It'll be a poor look out for you if I don't," she grumbled, and Sime having opened the door, she passed out, followed by the others. Cheyne, watching breathlessly, saw a light spring up in a ground floor window, fortunately not below him, but at the far end of the house.

His heart beat quickly. Was it possible that his great chance had come already and that the gang had delivered themselves into his hands? A little coolness, a little daring, a little nerve, and he believed he could carry off a *coup* that would entirely reverse the situation. The document on the wall must surely be that which these criminals had stolen from him. Could he not regain it while they were downstairs at their supper? He decided with fierce delight that he would try. It was an adventure after his own heart.

Carefully he grasped the lower sash and pressed gently

upwards. To his delight it moved. With infinite care he pushed it higher and higher until at last he was able to work his way into the room. Evidently he had not been heard, as the muffled sounds of conversation continued to rise unbrokenly from the supper room. He tiptoed lightly across the room and gazed in surprise at the document fixed to the wall.

It was certainly not the copy of a birth or marriage certificate nor anything connected with a claim to a barony! It was a sheet of tracing linen some fifteen inches high by twelve wide, covered with little circles spaced irregularly and without any apparent plan, like the keys of a typewriter gone mad. Some of these circles contained numbers and others letters, also arranged without apparent plan. The only thing he could read about the whole document was a phrase, written in a circle from the center like the figures on a clock dial: "England expects every man to do his duty."

Cheyne stared in amazement, but soon realizing that his time might be short, he silently removed the drawing pins, folded the tracing and thrust it into his pocket. Then turning to the camera, he withdrew the dark slide, opened first one and then the other of its shutters, closed them again and replaced it in the camera. A few seconds sufficed to open and close the shutters of the other slide lying on the table. With a hurried glance round to make sure that no other paper was lying about which might also have formed part of the contents of Price's envelope, he tiptoed back to the window and prepared to make his escape.

But as he laid his hand on the blind he was halted by a sound from below. Someone had opened what was evidently the back door of the house and had stepped out on the ground below the window. Then Sime's voice came, grumbling and muffled: "Where the blazes do you keep the darned stuff? How can I find it in the dark?" There was a moment's pause, then in a changed voice a sudden sharp call of "Here, James! Look here quickly! What's this?"

He had seen the ladder! Cheyne realized that his retreat was cut off!

A sudden tumult arose downstairs. Hasty feet ran towards the garden and voices spoke low and hurriedly beneath the window. Cheyne saw that his only hope lay in instant action. He silently hurried across the room, tore the door open and ran to the head of the stairs. His hope was that he might slip down and out of the door while the others were still at the back of the house.

But he was just too late. As he reached the stairs he heard steps approaching the hall below. His retreat was cut off in this direction also.

There remained only one thing to do and he did it almost without thought. Opening the next door to that of the sitting room, he stepped noiselessly inside, closing the door save for a narrow chink through which he could hear and see what was happening.

Two of the men had raced up to the sitting room, and peeping out, Cheyne saw that they were Blessington and Sime. In a moment they were out again and running down, shouting: "It's gone, James! The tracing's gone!" Sounds indicative of surprise and consternation arose from below, but Cheyne could no longer hear the words. Then through the window, which also looked out over the garden, he heard Dangle's voice: "Keep guard of the house, Susan and Blessington. Come with me, Sime," and the sound of two pairs of feet rushing away towards the lane.

Instinctively Cheyne realized that his chance had come. It was now or never. If he could not escape while two of the conspirators were away, he would have no chance when all four were present.

He came out of his hiding-place and peeped through the well down into the hall. The electric light had been turned on and the hall was brilliantly illuminated. In it stood Blessington, glancing alternately up the stairs and out through a door to the back. In his hand he held an automatic pistol, and from the look of fury and desperation on his face Cheyne had no doubt that he would not hesitate to use it if he saw him.

"They must have only just gone!" Blessington cried through the door with a lurid oath, and Susan's voice answered with another equally vivid string of blasphemy.

Cheyne stood tense, scarcely daring to breathe and on the *qui vive* to take advantage of any chance that might offer. But Blessington wasn't going to give chances. He stood there with his pistol raised, and unarmed as Cheyne was, he recognized the hopelessness of trying to rush him.

He thought there might be a chance of escape from some of the other rooms, and silently crept about in the hope of finding a window or skylight from which he might perhaps obtain access to a downspout. But so far as he could ascertain in the dark there was nothing of the kind, and after a few minutes had passed he retraced his steps and set himself to watch Blessington.

He wondered whether he could make some noise with the ladder which would attract the two watchers to the garden and thus enable him to make a bolt for the front door, but while he was considering this he heard other voices which revealed the fact that Dangle and Sime had returned. Then Dangle's voice sounded in the hall: "'Fraid they've got away, but we'd better search the house again to make sure. You stick at the stairs, Susan, while we do the lower rooms."

Steps sounded below as the men moved from room to room. Cheyne's heart was pounding as it had done on different occasions before his ship had gone into action during the war, but he was calm and collected and determined to take the least chance that offered.

Presently he heard the men joining Susan in the hall. Now was the only chance he was likely to get and at all costs he must make the most of it. He hurried back to the sitting room window, and setting his teeth, lifted the blind and silently crawled out.

So far he had not been seen, and as rapidly as he dared he climbed down the ladder. Another five seconds and he would have got clear away, but at that moment the alarm was given. One of the men, looking out of a window, saw him in the now fairly clear light of the moon. Hurried steps sounded and Blessington appeared at the open door.

Fearful of his pistol, Cheyne leaped for his life. He landed on his feet, staggered, recovered himself and darted like a hare across the flower beds. With any ordinary luck he should have got clear away, but Blessington had picked up a broom as he ran, and this he threw with fatal aim. It caught Cheyne between the legs and he fell headlong. Other steps came hurrying up. By the light streaming from the back door he saw an arm raised. It fell and something crashed with a sickening thud on his head.

He saw a vivid shower of sparks, there was a roaring in his ears, great dark waves seemed to rise up and encompass him, and he remembered no more.

CHAPTER VII

Miss Joan Merrill

AFTER what seemed ages of forgetfulness a confused sense of pain began to make itself felt in Maxwell Cheyne's being, growing in force and definition as he gradually struggled back to consciousness. At first his whole body ached sickeningly, but as time passed the major suffering concentrated itself in his head. It throbbed as if it would burst, and he felt a terrible oppression, as if the weight of the universe rested upon it. So on the border line of consciousness he hovered for still further ages of time.

Presently by gradual stages the memory of his recent

adventure returned to him, and he began vaguely to realize that the murderous attempt which had been made on him had failed and that he still lived.

Encouraged by this reassuring thought, he hesitatingly essayed the feat of opening his eyes. For a time he gazed, confused by the dim shapes about him, but at last he came more fully to himself and was able to register what he saw.

It was almost dark, indeed most of the arc over which his eyes could travel was perfectly so. But here and there he noticed parallelograms of a less inky blackness, and after some time the significance of these penetrated his brain and he knew where he was.

He was lying on his back on the ground in the half-built house from which he had taken the ladder, and the parallelograms were the openings in the walls into which doors and windows would afterwards be fitted. Against the faint light without, which he took to be that of the moonlit sky, he could see dimly the open joists of the floor above him, a piece of the herringbone strutting of which cut across the space for one of the upstairs windows.

Feeling slightly better he tried his pocket, to find, as he expected, that the tracing was gone. Presently he attempted some more extensive movement. But at once an intolerable pang shot through him, and, sick and faint, he lay still. With a dawning horror he wondered whether his back might not be broken, or whether the blow on his head might not have produced paralysis. He groaned aloud and sank back once more into unconsciousness.

After a time he became sentient again, sick and giddy, but more fully conscious. While he could not think collectedly, the idea became gradually fixed in his mind that he must somehow get away from his present position, partly lest his enemies might return to complete their work, and partly lest, if he stayed, he might die before the workmen came in the morning. Therefore, setting his teeth, he made a supreme effort and, in spite of the terrible pain in his head, succeeded in turning over on to his hands and knees.

In this new position he remained motionless for some time, but presently he began to crawl slowly and painfully out towards the road. At intervals he had to stop to recover himself, but at length after superhuman efforts he succeeded in reaching the paling separating the lot from Hopefield Avenue. There he sank down exhausted and for some time lay motionless in a state of coma.

Suddenly he became conscious of the sound of light but rapid footsteps approaching on the footpath at the other side of the paling, and once more summoning all his resolution he nerved himself to listen. The steps drew nearer until he judged their owner was just passing and then he cried as loudly as he could: "Help!"

The footsteps stopped and Cheyne gasped out: "Help! I've hurt my head: an accident."

There was a moment's silence and then a girl's voice sounded.

"Where are you?"

"Here," Cheyne answered, "at the back of the fence." He felt dimly that he ought to give some explanation of his predicament, and went on in weak tones: "I was looking through the house and fell. Can you help me?"

"Of course," the girl answered. "I'll go to the police station in Cleeve Road—it's only five minutes—and they will look after you in no time."

This was not what Cheyne wanted. He had not yet decided whether he would call in the police and he was too much upset at the moment to consider the point. In the meantime, therefore, it would be better if nothing was said.

"Please not," he begged. "Just send a taxi to take me to a hospital."

The girl hesitated, then replied: "All right. Let me see first if I can make you a bit more comfortable."

The effort of speaking and thinking had so overcome

Cheyne that he sank back once more into a state of coma, and it was only half consciously that he felt his head being lifted and some soft thing like a folded coat being placed beneath. Then the girl's pleasant voice said: "Now just stay quiet and I shall have a taxi here in a moment." A further period of waiting ensued and he felt himself being lifted and carried a few steps. A jolting then began which so hurt his head that he fainted again, and for still further interminable ages he remembered no more.

When he finally regained his faculties he found himself in bed, physically more comfortable than he could have believed possible, but utterly exhausted. He was content to lie motionless, not troubling as to where he was or how he came there. Presently he fell asleep and when he woke he plucked up energy enough to open his eyes.

It was light and he saw that he was in hospital. Several other beds were in the ward and a nurse was doing something at the end of the room. Presently she came over, saw that he was awake, and smiled at him.

"Better?" she said cheerily.

"I think so," he answered weakly. "Where am I, nurse?"

"In the Albert Edward Hospital. You've had a nasty knock on your head, but you're going to be all right. Now you're to keep quiet and not talk."

Cheyne didn't want to talk and he lay motionless, luxuriating in the complete cessation of effort. After a time a doctor came and looked at him, but it was too much trouble to be interested about the doctor, and in any case he soon disappeared. Sometimes when he opened his eyes the nurse was there and sometimes she wasn't, and other people seemed to drift about for no very special reason. Then it was dark in the ward, evidently night again. The next day the same thing happened, and so for many days.

He had been troubled with the vague thoughts of his mother and sister, and on one occasion when he was feeling a little less tired than usual he had called the nurse and asked her to write to his sister, saying that he had met with a slight accident and was staying on in town for a few days. Miss Cheyne telegraphed to know if she could help, but the nurse, without troubling her patient, had replied: "Not at present."

At last there came a time when Cheyne began to feel more his own man and able, without bringing on an intolerable headache, to think collectedly about his situation. And at once two points arose in his mind upon which he felt an immediate decision must be made.

The first was: What answer should he return to the inevitable questions he would be asked as to how he met with his injury? Should he lodge an information against Messrs. Dangle, Sime and Co., accuse them of attempted murder and put the machinery of the law in motion against them? Or should he stick to his tale that an accident had happened, and keep the affair of Hopefield Avenue to himself?

After anxious consideration he decided on the latter alternative. If he were to tell the police now he would find it hard to explain why he had not done so earlier. Moreover, with returning strength came back the desire which he had previously experienced, to meet these men on their own ground and himself defeat them. He remembered how exceedingly nearly he had done so on this occasion. Had it not been for the accident of something being required from the garden or outhouse he would have got clear away, and he hoped for better luck next time.

A third consideration also weighed with him. He was not sure how far he himself had broken the law. Housebreaking and burglary were serious crimes, and he had an uncomfortable feeling that others might not consider his excuse for these actions as valid as he did himself. In fact he was not sure how he stood legally. Under the circumstances would his proper course not have been to lodge an information against Dangle and Sime immediately on getting ashore from the *Enid,* and let the police with a search warrant recover Price's letter? But he saw at once that that would have been useless. The men would have denied the theft, and he could not have proved it. His letter to his bank manager would have been evidence that he had handed it over to them of his own free will. No, to go to the police would not have got him anywhere. In his own eyes he had been right to act as he had, and his only course now was to pursue the same policy and keep the police out of it.

When, therefore, a couple of days later the doctor, who had been puzzled by the affair, questioned him on it, he made up a tale. He replied that he had for some time been looking for a house in the suburbs, that the outline of that in question had appealed to him, and that he had climbed in to see the internal accommodation. In the semidarkness he had fallen, striking his head on a heap of bricks. He had been unconscious for some time, but had then been able to crawl to the street, where the lady had been kind enough to have him taken to the hospital.

This brought him back to the second point which had been occupying his mind since he had regained the power of consecutive thought: the lady. What exactly had she done for him? How had she got him to the hospital and secured his admission? Had she taken a taxi, and if so, had she herself paid for it? Cheyne felt that he must see her to learn these particulars and to thank her for her kindness and help.

He broached the subject to the nurse, who laughed and said she had been expecting the question. Miss Merrill had brought him herself to the hospital and had since called up a couple of times to inquire for him. The nurse presumed the young lady had herself paid for the taxi, as no question about the matter had been raised.

This information seemed to Cheyne to involve communication with Miss Merrill at the earliest possible moment. The nurse would not let him write himself, but at his dictation she sent a line expressing his gratitude for the lady's action and begging leave to call on his leaving the hospital.

In answer to this there was a short note signed "Joan

Merrill," which stated that the writer was pleased to hear that Mr. Cheyne was recovering and that she would see him if he called. The note was headed 17 Horne Terrace, Burton Street, Chelsea. Cheyne admired the hand and passed a good deal of his superabundant time speculating as to the personality of the writer and wondering what a Chelsea lady could have been doing in the Hendon suburbs after midnight on the date of his adventure. When, therefore, a few days later he was discharged from the hospital, he betook himself to Chelsea with more than a little eagerness.

Horne Terrace proved to be a block of workers' flats, and inquiries at No. 17 produced the information that Miss Merrill occupied Flat No. 12—the top floor on the left-hand side. Speculating still further as to the personality of a lady who would choose such a dwelling, Cheyne essayed researches into the upper regions. A climb which left him weak and panting after his sojourn in bed brought him to the tenth floor, on which one of the doors bore the number he sought. To recover himself before knocking he felt constrained to sit down for a few moments on the stairs, and as he was thus resting the door of No. 12 opened and a girl came out.

She was of middle height, slender and willowy, though the lines of her figure were somewhat concealed by the painter's blue overall which she wore. She was not beautiful in the classic sense, yet but few would have failed to find pleasure in the sight of her pretty, pleasant, kindly face, with its straightforward expression, and the direct gaze of her hazel eyes. Her face was rather thin and her chin rather sharp for perfect symmetry, but her nose tilted adorably and the arch of her eyebrows was delicacy itself. Her complexion was pale, but with the pallor of perfect health. But her great glory was her hair. It covered her head with a crown of burnished gold, and though in Cheyne's opinion it lost much of its beauty from being shingled, it gave her an aureole like that of a medieval saint in a stained glass window. Like a saint, indeed, she seemed to Cheyne; a very human and approachable saint, it is true, but a saint for all that. Seated on the top step of the stairs he was transfixed by the unexpected vision, and remained staring over his shoulder at her while he endeavored to collect his scattered wits.

The sight of a strange young man seated on the steps outside her door seemed equally astonishing to the vision, and she promptly stopped and stood staring at Cheyne. So they remained for an appreciable time, until Cheyne, flushed and abashed, stumbled to his feet and plunged into apologies.

As a result of his somewhat incoherent explanation a light dawned on her face and she smiled.

"Oh, you're Mr. Cheyne," she exclaimed. She looked at him very searchingly, then invited: "But of course! Won't you come in?"

He followed her into No. 12. It proved to be a fair-sized room fitted up partly as a sitting room and partly as a studio. A dormer window close to the fireplace gave on an expanse of roofs and chimneys with, in a gap between two houses, a glimpse of the lead-colored waters of the river. In the partially covered ceiling was a large skylight which lit up a model's throne, and an easel bearing a half-finished study of a woman's head. Other canvases, mostly figures in various stages of completion, were ranged round the walls, and the usual artist's paraphernalia of brushes and palettes and color tubes lay about. Drawn up to the fire were a couple of easy-chairs, books and ash-trays lay on an occasional table, while on another table was a tea equipage. A door beside the fireplace led to what was presumably the lady's bedroom.

"Can you find a seat?" she went on, indicating the larger of the two armchairs. "You have come at a propitious moment. I was just about to make tea."

"That sounds delightful," Cheyne declared. "I came at the first moment that I thought I decently could. I was discharged from the hospital this morning and I thought I couldn't let a day pass without coming to try at least to express my thanks for what you did for me."

Miss Merrill had filled an aluminum kettle from a tap at a small sink and now placed it on a gas stove.

"We'll suppose the thanks expressed, all due and right and proper," she answered. "But I'll tell you what you can do. Light the stove! It makes such a plop I hate to go near it."

Cheyne, having duly produced the expected plop, returned to his armchair and took up again the burden of his tale.

"But that's all very well, Miss Merrill; awfully good of you and all that," he protested, "but it doesn't really meet the case at all. If you hadn't come along and played the good Samaritan I should have died. I was—"

"If you don't stop talking about it I shall begin to wish you had," she smiled. "How did the accident happen? I should be interested to hear that, because I've thought about it and haven't been able to imagine any way it could have come about."

"I want to tell you." Cheyne looked into her clear eyes and suddenly said more than he had intended. "In fact, I should like to tell you the whole thing from the beginning. It's rather a queer tale. You mayn't believe it, but I think it would interest you. But first—please don't be angry, but you must let me ask the question—did you pay for the taxi or whatever means you took to get me to the hospital?"

She laughed.

"Well, you are persistent. However, I suppose I may allow you to pay for that. It was five and six, if you must know, and a shilling to the man because he helped to carry you and took no end of trouble." She blushed slightly as if recognizing the unconscious admission. "A whole six and six you owe me."

"Is that all, Miss Merrill? Do tell me if there was anything else."

"There was nothing else, Mr. Cheyne. That squares everything between us."

85

"By Jove! That's the last thing it does! But if I mustn't speak of that, I mustn't. But please tell me this also. I understood from the nurse that you came with me to hospital. I am horrified every time I think of your having so much trouble, and I should like to understand how it all happened."

"There's not much to tell," Miss Merrill answered. "It was all very simple and straightforward. There happened to be a garage in the main street, quite close, and I went there and got a taxi. It was very dark, and when the driver and I looked over the fence we could not see you, but the driver fortunately had a flash lamp for examining his engine, and with its help we saw that you had fainted. We found you very awkward to get out." She smiled and her face lighted up charmingly. "We had to drag you round to the side of the building where there was a wire paling instead of the close sheeted fence in front. I held up the wires and the cabby dragged you through. Then when we got you into the cab I had to go along too, because the cabby said he wouldn't take what might easily be a dead body—a corp, he called it—without someone to account for its presence. He talked of you as if you were a sack of coal."

Cheyne was really upset by the recital.

"Good Lord!" he cried. "I can't say how distressed I am to know what I let you in for. I can't ever forget it. All right, I won't," he added as she held up her hand. "Go on, please. I want to hear it all."

Miss Merrill's hazel eyes twinkled as she continued:

"By the time we got to the hospital I was sure that nothing would save me from being hanged for murder. But there was no trouble. I simply told my story, left my name and address, and that was all. Now tell me what really happened to you; or rather wait until we've had tea."

Cheyne sat back in his chair admiring the easy grace with which she moved about as she prepared the meal. She was really an awfully nice looking girl, he thought; not perhaps exactly pretty, but jolly looking, the kind of girl it is a pleasure just to sit down and watch. And as they chatted over tea he discovered that she had a mind of her own. Indeed, she showed a nimble wit and a shrewd if rather quaint outlook on men and things.

"You mentioned Dartmouth just now," she remarked presently. "Do you know it well?"

"Why, I live there."

"Do you really? Do you know people there called Beresford?"

"Archie and Flo? Rather. They live on our road, but about half a mile nearer the town. Do you know them?"

"Flo only. I've been going to stay with them two or three times, though for one reason or another it has always fallen through. I was at school with Flo—Flo Salter, she was then."

"By Jove! Archie is rather a pal of mine. Comes out yachting sometimes. A good sort."

"I've never met him, but I used to chum with Flo. Congratulations, Mr. Cheyne."

Cheyne stared at her and she smiled gaily across.

"You haven't said that the world is very small after all," she explained.

Cheyne laughed.

"I didn't think of it or I should," he admitted. "But I hope you will come down to the Beresfords. I'd love to take you out in my yacht—that is, if you like yachting."

"That's a promise," the girl declared. "If I come I shall hold you to it."

When tea was removed and cigarettes were alight she returned to the subject of his adventure.

"Yes," Cheyne answered, "I should like to tell you the whole story if it really wouldn't bore you. But," he hesitated for a second, "you won't mind my saying that it is simply desperately private. No hint of it must get out."

Her face clouded.

"Oh," she exclaimed, "I don't want to hear it if it's a secret. It doesn't concern me anyway."

"Oh, but it does—now," Cheyne protested. "If I don't

87

tell you now you will think that I am a criminal with something to hide, and I think I couldn't bear that."

"No," she contradicted, "you think that you are in my debt and bound to tell me."

He laughed.

"Not at all," he retorted, "since contradiction is the order of the day. If that was it I could easily have put you off with the yarn I told the doctor. I want to tell you because I think you'd be interested, and because it really would be such a relief to discuss the thing with some rational being."

She looked at him keenly as she demanded: "Honor bright?"

"Honor bright," he repeated, meeting her eyes.

"Then you may," she decided. "You may also smoke a pipe if you like."

"The story opens about six weeks ago with a visit to Plymouth," he began, and he told her of his adventure in the Edgecombe Hotel, of the message about the burglary, of his ride home and what he found there, and of the despondent detective and his failure to discover the criminals. Then he described what took place on the launch *Enid*, his search of the coast towns and discovery of the trail of the men, his following them to London and to the Hopefield Avenue house, his adventure therein, the blow on his head, his coming to himself to find the tracing gone, his crawl to the fence and his relief at the sound of her footsteps approaching.

She listened with an ever-increasing eagerness, which rose to positive excitement as he reached the climax of the story.

"My word!" she cried with shining eyes when he had finished. "To think of such things happening here in sober old London in the twentieth century! Why, it's like the *Arabian Nights!* Who would believe such a story if they read it in a book? *What* fun! And you have no idea what the tracing was?"

"No more than you have, Miss Merrill."

"It was a cipher," she declared breathlessly. "A cipher telling where there was buried treasure! Isn't that all that is wanted to make it complete?"

"Now you're laughing at me," he complained. "Don't you really believe my story?"

"Believe it?" she retorted. "Of course I believe it. How can you suggest such a thing? I think it's perfectly splendid! I can't say how splendid I think it. It *was* brave of you to go into that house in the way you did. I can't think how you had the nerve. But now what are you going to do? What is the next step?"

"I don't know. I've thought and thought while I was in that blessed hospital and I don't see the next move. What would you advise?"

"I? Oh, Mr. Cheyne, I couldn't advise you. I'm thrilled more than I can say, but I don't know enough for that."

"Would you give up and go to the police?"

"Never." Her eyes flashed. "I'd go on and fight the gang. You'll win yet, Mr. Cheyne. Something tells me."

A wild idea shot into Cheyne's mind and he sat for a moment motionless. Then swayed by a sudden impulse, he turned to the girl and said excitedly:

"Miss Merrill, let's join forces. You help me." He paused, then went on quickly: "Not in the actual thing, I mean, of course. I couldn't allow you to get mixed up in what might turn out to be dangerous. But let me come and discuss the thing with you. It would be such a help."

"No!" she said, her eyes shining. "I'll join in if you like—I'd love it! But only if I share the fun. I'm either in altogether or out altogether."

He stood up and faced her.

"Do you mean it?" he asked seriously.

"Of course I mean it," she answered as she got up also.

"Then shake hands on it!"

Solemnly they shook hands, and so the firm of Cheyne and Merrill came into being.

CHAPTER VIII

A Council of War

CHEYNE returned to his hotel that afternoon in a jubilant frame of mind. He had been depressed from his illness and his failure at the house in Hopefield Avenue and had come to believe he was wasting his time on a wild-goose chase. But now all his former enthusiasm had returned. Once again he was out to pit his wits against this mysterious gang of scoundrels, and he was all eagerness to be once more in the thick of the fray.

Miss Merrill had told him something about herself before he had left. It appeared that she was the daughter of a doctor in Gloucester who had died some years previously. Her mother had died while she was a small child, and she was now alone in the world save for a sister who was married and living in Edinburgh. Her father had left her enough to live on fairly comfortably, but by cutting down her expenditure on board and lodging to the minimum she had been able to find the wherewithal necessary to enable her to take up seriously her hobby of painting. She was getting on well with that. She had not yet sold any pictures, but her art masters and the dealers to whom she had shown her work were encouraging. She also made a study of architectural details—moldings, string courses, capitals, etc.—which, having photographed them with her half-plate camera and flashlight apparatus, she worked into decorative panels and head and tail pieces for magazine illustration and poster work. With these also she was having fair success.

Cheyne was enthused by the idea of this girl starting out thus boldly to carve, singlehanded, her career in the world, and he spent as much time that evening thinking of her pluck and of her chances of success as of the mysterious affair in which now they were both engaged.

His first visit next day was to a man called Hake, whom he had met during the war and who was now a clerk in one of the departments of the Admiralty. From him he received definite confirmation that the whole of the Hull barony story was a fabrication of James Dangle's nimble brain. No such diplomat as St. John Price had ever existed, though it was true that Arnold Price had at the time in question been third officer of the *Maurania*. Hake added a further interesting fact, though whether it was connected with Cheyne's affair there was nothing to indicate. Price, the real Arnold Price through whom the whole mystery had arisen, had recently disappeared. He had left his ship at Bombay on a few days' leave and had not returned. At least he had not returned up to the latest date of which Hake had heard. Cheyne begged his friend to let him know immediately if anything was learned as to Price's fate, which the other promised to do.

In the afternoon Cheyne once more climbed the ten flights of stairs in No. 17 Horne Terrace, but this time he took the ascent slowly enough to avoid having to sit down to recover at the top. Miss Merrill opened to his knock. She was painting and a girl sat on the throne, the original of the picture he had seen the day before. He was told that he might sit down and smoke so long as he kept perfectly quiet and did not interrupt, and for half an hour he lay in the big armchair watching the face on the canvas grow more and more like that of the model. Then a little clock struck four silvery chimes, Miss Merrill threw down her brushes and palette and said "Time!" and the model relaxed her position. Both girls disappeared into the bedroom and emerged presently, the model in outdoor garb and Miss Merrill without her overall. The model let herself out with a "Good-afternoon, Miss Merrill," while the lady of the house took up the aluminum kettle and began to fill it.

"Gas stove," she said tersely.

Cheyne produced the expected plop, then stood with his back to the fire, watching his hostess's preparations for tea. The removal of the overall had revealed a light green knitted jumper of what he believed was artificial silk, with a skirt of a darker shade of the same color. A simple dress, he thought, but tremendously effective. How splendidly it set off the red gold of her hair, and how charmingly it revealed the graceful lines of her slender figure! With her comely, pleasant face and her clear, direct eyes she looked one who would make a good pal.

"Well now, and what's the program?" she said briskly when tea had been disposed of.

Cheyne began to fill his pipe.

"I scarcely know," he said slowly. "I'm afraid I've not any cut and dried scheme to put up except that I already mentioned: to get into that house somehow and have a look around."

She moved nervously.

"I don't like it," she declared. "There are many objections to it."

"I know there are, but what can you suggest?"

"First of all there's the actual danger," she went on, continuing her own train of thought and ignoring his question. "These people have tried to murder you once already, and if they find you in their house again they'll not bungle it a second time."

"I'll take my chance of that."

"But have you thought that they have an easier way out of it than that? All they have to do is to hand you over to the nearest policeman on a charge of burglary. You would get two or three years or maybe more."

"They wouldn't dare. Remember what I could tell about them."

"Who would believe you? They, the picture of injured innocence, would deny the whole thing. You would say they attempted to murder you. They would ridicule the idea. And—there you are."

"But I could prove it. There was my injured head, and you found me at that house."

"And what did you yourself tell the doctor had happened to you? No, you wouldn't have the ghost of a case."

"But Susan Dangle was at our house for several weeks. She could be identified."

"How would that help? She would of course admit being there, but would deny everything else. And you couldn't prove anything. Why, the gang would point out that it was Susan's presence at your house that had suggested the whole story to you."

Cheyne shook his head.

"I'm not so sure of that," he declared. "There would be a good deal of corroborative evidence on my side. And then there was Blessington at the hotel at Plymouth. He could be identified by the staff."

"That's true," she admitted. "But even that wouldn't help you much. He would deny having drugged you and you couldn't prove he had. No, the more I think of it the better their position seems to be."

"Well, then, what's the alternative?"

She shook her head and for a moment silence reigned. Then she went on:

"I've been thinking about the gang since you told me the story—it's another point, of course—but it occurs to me they must have had a fine old shock on the morning after your visit."

Cheyne looked up sharply.

"What do you mean?" he asked.

"Why, they must have been worried to death to know what had happened to you. Your dead body wasn't found —they'd soon have heard of it if it had been. And no information was given to the police about the affair— they'd soon have heard of that too. And you haven't struck at them. Probably they've made inquiries at Dartmouth and found you haven't gone home. They'll absolutely be scared into fits to know whether you're alive or dead, or what blow may not be being built up against them. Though they richly deserve it, I don't envy them their position."

This was a new idea to Cheyne.

"I hadn't thought of that," he returned, then he laughed. "Yes, it didn't work out quite as they wanted, did it? But I expect they know all about me. Don't you think that under the circumstances they would have gone round making discreet inquiries at the hospitals?"

"Well, that is at least something to be done. First job: find out if possible if anyone asked about you at the Albert Edward. If that fails, same question elsewhere."

"Right: that's an idea. But it is not enough." Cheyne shook his head to give emphasis to his remark. "We must do something more. And the only thing I can think of is to get into that house again and see what I can find. I'll risk the police."

Miss Merrill was evidently thrilled, but not converted.

"I shouldn't be in too great a hurry," she counseled. "How would it do if we went out there first and had a look around?"

"I don't see that we should gain much by looking at the outside of the house."

"You never know. Let's go as soon as it gets dark tonight. If we see nothing no harm is done."

Cheyne was not averse to the idea of an excursion in the company of his new friend, and he readily agreed, provided Miss Merrill gave her word not to run into any danger.

"I think you should put on a hat with a low brim and wear something with a high collar," he suggested. "I'll do the same, and in the dark we're not likely to be noticed even if any of the gang are about."

Miss Merrill pointed out that as she was unknown to the gang, it did not matter if her features were seen, but Cheyne was insistent.

"You don't know," he said. "We might both be seen, and then it would be as bad for you as for me. There'll be unavoidable risks enough in this job without taking on any we needn't."

They discussed their plans in detail, then Cheyne remarked: "Now that's settled, what's wrong with your coming and having a bit of dinner with me as a prelude to adventure?"

"That sounds bookish. Are you keen on books? I'll go and have dinner if I may pay my share, not otherwise."

Cheyne protested, but she was adamant. It appeared further she was a great reader, and they discussed books until it was time to go out. Then after dinner at an Italian restaurant in Soho they took the tube to Hendon and began to walk towards Hopefield Avenue.

The night was chilly for mid-May, but calm and dry. It would soon be quite dark out of the radius of the street lamps, as the quarter moon had not yet risen and clouds obscured the light of the stars. In the main street there was plenty of traffic, but Hopefield Avenue was deserted and their footsteps rang out loudly on the pavements.

"Let's walk past it," Miss Merrill suggested, "and perhaps we can hide and watch what goes on."

They did so. Laurel Lodge looked as before except that the lower front windows were lighted up. Building operations, however, had been much advanced in the six weeks since Cheyne's last visit. The almost completed walls of a house stood on the next lot, and the house in which the supposed dead body of Cheyne had been abandoned was practically complete.

"Half-finished houses are the stunt in this game," Cheyne observed. "Suppose we go back to that next door to our friends and see from there if anything happens."

Five minutes later they had passed along the lane at the back of the houses and taken up their positions in what was evidently to be the hall of the new house. A small window looked out from its side, not forty feet from the hall door of Laurel Lodge. Cheyne made a seat of a plank laid across two little heaps of bricks and they sat down and waited.

They were so ignorant as to the steps usually taken by a detective in such a situation that their idea of watching the house was simply adopted in the Micawberish hope that somehow something might turn up to help them.

What that something might be they had no idea. But with the extraordinary luck which so often seems reserved for those who blindly plunge, they had not waited ten minutes before they received some really important information.

The unconscious agent was a postman. They saw him first pass near a lamp farther down the street, and then watched him gradually approach, calling in one house after another. Presently he reached the gate of Laurel Lodge, and opening it, passed inside.

From where they sat, the watchers, being in line with the front of the house, were not actually in sight of the hall door. But there was a heap of building material in front of their hiding place and Cheyne, slipping hurriedly out, crouched behind the pile in such a position that he could see what might take place.

In due course the postman reached the door, but instead of delivering his letters and retreating, he knocked and stood waiting. The door was opened by a woman, and her silhouette against the lighted interior showed she was not Susan Dangle. The woman was short, stout and elderly.

"Evening, ma'am," Cheyne heard the man say. "A parcel for you."

The woman thanked him and closed the door, while the postman crossed to a house on the opposite side of the street. As soon as his back was turned Cheyne left his hiding-place, and was strolling along the road when the postman again stepped on to the footpath.

"Good-evening, postman," said Cheyne. "I'm looking for people called Dangle somewhere about here. Could you tell me where they live?"

The postman stopped and answered civilly:

"They've left here, sir, or at least there were people of that name here till a few weeks ago. They lived over there." He pointed to Laurel Lodge.

Cheyne made a gesture of annoyance.

"Moved; have they? Then I've missed them. I suppose you couldn't tell me where they've gone?"

The postman shook his head.

"Sorry, sir, but I couldn't. If you was to go to the post office in Hendon they might know. But I couldn't say nothing about it."

Nor could the postman remember the exact date of the Dangles' departure. It was five or six weeks since or maybe more, but he couldn't say for sure.

Cheyne returned to Miss Merrill with his news. A sudden flitting on the Dangles' part seemed indicated, born doubtless of panic at the disappearance of the supposed corpse, and if this was the cause of their move, no applications at the post office or elsewhere would bear fruit.

"We should have foreseen this," Cheyne declared gloomily. "If you think of it, to make themselves scarce was about the only thing they could do. If I was alive and conscious they couldn't tell how soon they might have a visit from the police."

"Well, we've got to find them," his companion answered. "I'll begin by making inquiries at the house. No," as Cheyne demurred, "it's my turn. You stay here and listen."

She slipped out on to the road, and passing through the gate of Laurel Lodge, rang the bell. The same elderly woman came to the door and Miss Merrill asked if Miss Dangle was at home.

The woman was communicative if not illuminating. No one called Dangle lived in the house, though she understood her predecessors had borne that name. She and her son had moved in only three weeks before, and they had only taken the house a fortnight before that. She did not know anything of the Dangles. Oh, no, she had not taken the house furnished. She had brought her own furniture with her. Indeed yes, moving was a horrible business and so expensive.

"That's something about the furniture," Miss Merrill said, when breathless and triumphant she had rejoined Cheyne. "If they took their furniture we have only to find out who moved it for them. Then we can find where it was taken."

"That's the ticket," Cheyne declared admiringly. "But how on earth are we going to find the removers? Have you any ideas?"

Miss Merrill looked at him quizzically.

"Just full of 'em," she smiled, "and to prove it I'll make you a bet. I'll bet you the price of our next dinner that I have the information inside half an hour. What time is it? Half-past nine. Very well: before ten o'clock. But the information may cost you anything up to a pound. Are you on?"

"Of course I'm on," Cheyne returned heartily, though in reality he was not too pleased by the trend of affairs. "Do you want the pound now?"

"No, I have it. But whatever the information costs me you may pay. Now *au revoir* until ten o'clock."

She glided away before Cheyne could reply, and for some minutes he sat alone in the half-built porch wondering what she was doing and wishing he could smoke. It was cold sitting still in the current of chilly air which poured through the gaping brickwork. He felt tired and despondent, and realized against his will that he had been severely shaken by his experiences and was by no means as yet completely recovered. If it was not for this splendid girl he would have been strongly tempted to throw up the sponge, and he thought with longing of the deep arm-chairs in the smoking room at the hotel, or better still, in Miss Merrill's studio.

Presently he saw her. She was crossing the street in front of Laurel Lodge. She was directly in the light of a lamp and he could not but admire her graceful carriage and the dainty way in which she tripped along.

She pushed open the gate of a house directly opposite and disappeared into the shadow behind its encircling hedge. In a moment she was out again and had entered the gate of the next house. There she remained for some time; indeed the hands on the luminous dial of Cheyne's watch showed three minutes to the hour before she reappeared. She recrossed the road and presently Cheyne heard her whisper: "That was a near squeak for my dinner! It's not after ten, is it?"

"Half a minute before," breathed Cheyne, continuing eagerly: "Well, what luck?"

"Watterson & Swayne. Vans came the day after your adventure."

Cheyne whistled below his breath.

"My word!" he whispered, "but you're simply It! How in all this earthly world did you find that out?"

She chuckled delightedly.

"Easy as winking," she declared. "Got it fifth shot. I called at five of the houses overlooking the Laurel gate, and pretended to be a woman detective after the Dangles. I was mysterious about the crimes they had committed and got the servants interested. There were servants at three of the houses—the others I let alone. I offered the servants five shillings for the name of the vans which had come to take the stuff, and the third girl remembered. I gave her the five shillings and told her I was good for another five if she could tell me the date of the moving, and after some time she was able to fix it. She remembered she had seen the vans on the day of a party at her sister's, and she found the date of that from an old letter."

"Good for you! I say, Miss Merrill, if you're going to carry on like this we shall soon have all we want. What's the next step now? Inquiries at Watterson & Swayne's?"

"No," she said decidedly, "the next step for you is bed. You're not really well enough yet for this sort of thing. We've done enough for tonight. We'll go home."

Cheyne protested, but as, apart from his health, it was obvious that inquiries could not at that hour be instituted at the furniture removers, he had to agree.

"I shall go round and see them tomorrow morning," he remarked as they walked back along Hopefield Avenue. "I suppose you couldn't manage to come at that time? Or shall I wait until the afternoon?"

She shook her head.

"Neither," she answered. "I shall be busy all day and you must just carry on."

Cheyne felt a surprisingly keen disappointment.

"But mayn't I come and report progress in the afternoon?" he begged.

"Not until after four. I shall be painting up till then."

He wanted to see her home, but this she would not hear of, and soon he was occupying one of these deep chairs in the hotel smoking room whose allure had seemed so strong to him in the draughty porch of the half-built house. As he sat he thought over the turn which this evening's inquiry had given to the affair in which he was engaged. It was clear enough now that Miss Merrill's view had been correct and that the Dangles were scared stiff by the absence of information about the finding of his body. As he put himself in their place, he saw that flight was indeed their only course. What he marveled at was that they should have taken time to remove their furniture. From their point of view it must have been a horrible risk, and it undoubtedly left, through the carrying contractor, a certain clue to their whereabouts.

But when Cheyne began his inquiries on the following morning he rapidly became less impressed with the certainty of the clue. A direct request at the firm's office for Dangle's address was met by a polite *non possumus,* and when during the dinner hour Cheyne succeeded in bribing a junior clerk to let him have the information, at a further interview the lad declared he could not find it. It was not until after five hours' inquiry among the drivers of the various vans which entered and left the yard that he learned anything, and even then he found himself no further on. The furniture, which had been collected from an unoccupied house, had been stored and still remained in Messrs. Watterson & Swayne's warehouses.

It was a weary and disgruntled Cheyne who at six o'clock that evening dragged himself up the ten flights to Miss Merrill's room. But when he was seated in her big armchair with his pipe going and had consumed a whisky and soda which she had poured out for him he began to feel that all was not necessarily lost and that life had compensations for failures in the role of amateur detective.

She listened carefully to his tale of woe, finally dropping a word of sympathy with his disappointment and of praise for his efforts which left him thinking she was certainly the good pal he expected her to be.

"But that's not the worst," he went on gloomily. "It's bad enough that I have failed today, but it's a great deal worse that I don't know how I am going to do any better. Those Watterson & Swayne people simply *won't* give away any information, and I don't see how else it's to be got."

"There's not much to go on certainly," she admitted. "That's where the police have the pull. They could go into that office and demand the Dangles' address. You can't. What about the others, that Sime and that Blessington? Could you trace them in any way?"

Cheyne moved lazily in his chair.

"I don't see how," he answered slowly. "We have little enough information about the Dangles, but there is less still about the others. We have practically nothing to go on. I wonder what a real detective would do in such a case. I feel perfectly certain he would find all four in a few hours."

"Ha! That gives me an idea." She sat up and looked at him eagerly, and then in answer to his question went on: "What about that detective who was already engaged on the case, the one the manager of the Plymouth hotel recommended? Why not get hold of him and see what he can do? He was a private detective, wasn't he—not connected with the police?"

"He was, and I have his name and address. By Jove, Miss Merrill, it's an idea! I'll go round and see him in the morning. He's a man I didn't take to personally, but what does that matter if he's good at his job?"

Though Cheyne thus enthusiastically received his companion's suggestion, he was not greatly enamored of the idea. As he said, he had not liked the man personally, and he would have preferred to have kept the affair in his own hands. But he felt bankrupt of ideas for carrying on the inquiry, and if a professional was to be brought in, this man whom he knew and who was vouched for by the manager of the Edgecombe should be as good as another. He decided, however, that he would not employ the fellow on the case as a whole. His job should be to find the quartet, and if and when he did that he could be paid his money and sent about his business. Cheyne felt that at this stage at all events he was not going to share the secret of the linen tracing.

But Cheyne, like many another before him, was to learn the difficulties which beset the path of him who makes half confidences.

CHAPTER IX

Mr. Speedwell Plays His Hand

NEXT morning Cheyne called at the offices of Messrs. Horton & Lavender's Private Detective Agency and asked if their Mr. Speedwell was within. By good fortune Mr. Speedwell was, and a few seconds later Cheyne was ushered into the room of the quiet, despondent-looking man whom he had interviewed at Warren Lodge nearly two months earlier.

"Glad to see you're better, sir," the detective greeted him. "I was expecting you would look in one of these days. You had my letter?"

"No," said Cheyne, considerably surprised, "and I should like to know why you were expecting me and how you know I was ill."

The man smiled deprecatingly.

"If I was really up to my job I suppose I'd tell you that

detectives knew everything, or at least that I did, but I never make any mystery between friends, leastwise when there isn't any. I knew you were ill because I was down at Warren Lodge a month ago looking for you and Miss Cheyne told me, and I was expecting you to call because I wrote asking you to do so. However, if you didn't get my letter, why then it seems to me I owe the pleasure of this visit to something else."

"You're quite right," said Cheyne. "You do. But before we get on to that, tell me what you called and wrote about."

"I'll do so, sir. I called because I had got some information for you, and when I didn't see you I wrote for the same reason asking you to look in here."

The man spoke civilly and directly, but yet there was something about him which rubbed Cheyne up the wrong way—something furtive in his manner, by which instinctively the other was repelled. It was therefore with rather less than his usual good-natured courtesy that Cheyne returned: "Well, here I am then. What is your information?"

"I'll tell you, sir. But first let me recall to your mind what I—acting for my firm—was asked to find out." He stressed the words "acting for my firm," and as he did so shot a keen questioning glance at Cheyne. The latter did not reply, and Speedwell, after pausing for a moment, went on:

"I was employed—or rather my firm was employed"— what his point was Cheyne could not see, but he was evidently making one—"my firm was employed by the manager of the Edgecombe Hotel to investigate a case of alleged drugging which had taken place in the hotel. That was all, wasn't it?"

"That or matters arising therefrom," Cheyne replied cautiously.

The detective smiled foxily.

"Ah, I see you have taken my meaning, Mr. Cheyne. That or matters arising directly therefrom. That, sir, is quite correct. Now, I have found out something about that. Not much, I admit, but still something. Though whether it is as much as you already are cognizant of is another matter."

Cheyne felt his temper giving way.

"Look here," he said sharply. "What are you getting at? I can't spend the day here. If you've anything to say, for goodness' sake get along and say it and have done with this beating about the bush."

Speedwell made a deprecating gesture.

"Certainly, sir; as you will. But"—he gave a dry smile—"have you not overlooked the fact that you called in to consult me?"

"I shall not do it now," Chayne said angrily. "Give me the information that you're being paid for and that will complete our business."

"No, sir, but with the utmost respect that will only begin it. I'll give you the information right away, but first I'd like to come to an understanding about this other business."

"What under the sun are you talking about? What other business?"

"The breaking and entering." Speedwell spoke now in a decisive, businesslike tone. "The breaking and entering of a house in Hopefield Avenue—Laurel Lodge, let us call it—on an evening just six weeks ago—on the fifth of April to be exact. I should really say the burglary, because there was also the theft of an important document. The owners of that document would be glad of information which would lead to the arrest of the thief."

This astounding statement, made in the calm matter-of-fact way in which the man was now speaking, took Cheyne completely aback. For a moment he hesitated. His character was direct and straightforward, but for the space of two seconds he was tempted to prevaricate, to admit no knowledge of the incidents referred to. Then his hot temper swept away all considerations of what might or might not be prudent, and he burst out: "Well, Mr. Speedwell, what of it? If you are so well informed as you pretend, you'll be aware that the parties lost no document on that night. I don't know what you're after, but it looks uncommonly like an attempt at blackmail."

Mr. Speedwell seemed pained at the suggestion. He assured Cheyne that his remarks had been misinterpreted, and deprecated the fact that such an unpleasant word had been brought into the discussion. "All the same," he concluded meaningly, "I am glad to have your assurance that the document in question was not stolen from the house."

Cheyne was not only mystified, but a trifle uneasy. He saw now that he had been maneuvered into a practical admission that he had committed burglary, and there was something in the way the detective had made his last remark that seemed vaguely sinister.

"Well, what business of yours is it?" he said brusquely. "What do you hope to get out of it?"

Speedwell nodded as he looked at the other out of his close-set furtive eyes.

"Now, sir," he answered approvingly, "that's what I like. That's coming to business, that is. I thought perhaps I could be of service to you, that's all. Here are these parties looking for you to make a prosecution for burglary, and here you are looking for them for a paper they have. And here am I," his face was inexpressibly sly, "in a position to help either party, as you might say. There's an old saying, sir, that knowledge is power, and many a time I've thought it's a true one."

"And you want to sell your knowledge?"

"Isn't it reasonable, *and* natural? It's my business to get knowledge, and I have to work hard to get it too. You wouldn't have me give away the fruits of my work? It's all I have to live by."

"Your knowledge belongs to your firm."

"No, sir, not in this case it doesn't. All this work was done in my own time; it was my hobby, so to speak. Besides, my firm didn't ask for the information and doesn't want it."

"What do you want for it?"

A momentary gleam appeared in Mr. Speedwell's eyes,

but he replied quietly and without emotion: "Two hundred pounds. Two hundred pounds and you shall hear all I know, and have my best help in whatever you want to do into the bargain. And in that case I won't be able to tell the other parties where you are to be found, so being as their question was addressed to me and not to my firm."

"Two hundred pounds!" Cheyne cried. "I'll see you far enough first. Confound your impertinence!" His anger rose and he almost choked. "Don't you imagine you are going to blackmail me! But I'll tell you what I am going to do. I'm going right in now to the head of your firm to let him know the way you conduct his business. Two hundred pounds. I don't think!"

He flung himself out of the room and called the girl in the outer office.

"I want to see the principal of the firm," he shouted. "It's important. Either Mr. Horton or Mr. Lavender will do. As soon as possible, please."

The girl seemed half startled and half amused. *"Who* did you want to see?" she asked.

"Mr. Horton or Mr. Lavender," Cheyne repeated firmly, fixing her with a wrathful stare.

"I—I'm afraid I don't know where they are," she stammered, the corners of her mouth twitching. Yes, she *was* laughing at him. Confound her impertinence also!

"You don't know?" he shouted furiously. "When will they be in?"

The girl looked scared, then her amusement evidently overcame her apprehension and she giggled.

"Not today, I'm afraid," she answered. "You see Mr. Horton has been dead over ten years and Mr. Lavender at least five."

Cheyne glared at her as he asked thickly:

"Then who is the present principal?"

"Mr. Speedwell."

"Damn," said Cheyne: then as he looked at the smiling face of the pretty clerk he suddenly felt ashamed of himself.

"I'm sure I beg your pardon," he said, and as he saw how neatly he had got his desserts he laughed ruefully himself. This confounded temper of his, he thought, was always putting him into the wrong. He was just determining for the thousandth time that he would be more careful not to give way to it in future when Mr. Speedwell's melancholy voice fell on his ears.

"Ah, that is better, sir. Won't you come back and let us resume our discussion?"

Cheyne re-entered the private room.

"I'm sorry I lost my temper," he said, "but really your proposition was so very—I may say, amazing, that it upset me. Of course you were not serious in what you said?"

Mr. Speedwell leaned forward and became the personification of suave amiability.

"I sell my wares in the best market, Mr. Cheyne," he declared. "You couldn't blame me for that; it's only business. But I don't want to drive a hard bargain with you. I would rather have an amicable settlement. I'm always one for peace and goodwill. An amicable settlement, sir; that's what I suggest." He beamed on Cheyne and rubbed his hands genially together.

"If you have information which would be useful to me I am prepared to pay its full value. As a matter of fact I called for that purpose. But you couldn't have any worth two hundred pounds or anything like it."

"No? Well, just what do you want to know?"

"Dangle's address."

"I can give you that. Anything else?"

Cheyne hesitated. Should he ask for all the information he could get about the sinister quartet and their mysterious activities? He had practically admitted the burglary. Should he not make the most of his opportunity? In for a penny, in for a pound.

"Did you ever hear of a man called Sime?" he asked.

"Of course, sir. Number Three of the quartet."

"I should like his address also."

"I can give it to you. And Blessington's?"

"Yes, Blessington's too."

Cheyne was amazed by the knowledge of this Speedwell. He would give a good deal to find out how he had obtained it.

"What are the businesses of these men?"

"That," said Mr. Speedwell, "is three questions. First: What is Dangle's business? Second: What is Sime's business? Third: What is Blessington's business? Yes, sir, I can answer these questions also."

"How did you find all that out?"

Mr. Speedwell smiled and shook his head.

"There, sir, you have me. I'm afraid I can't tell you that. You see, if we professional detectives were to give away our little methods to you amateur gentlemen we should soon be out of business. You, sir, will appreciate the position. It would be parting with our capital, and no business man can afford to do that. Anything else, Mr. Cheyne?"

"You mentioned a paper?"

"Yes, sir?"

"Where is it?"

"That I can answer partially."

"What is it about?"

"I do not know."

"Ah, then there is something you do not know. What is the enterprise these men are going into in connection with the paper?"

"That, Mr. Cheyne, I do not know either. You see I am perfectly open with you. I have been conducting a sort of desultory inquiry into these men's affairs, partly because I was interested, partly because I thought I could turn my information into money. I have reached the point indicated in my answers. I can proceed with the investigation and learn the rest of what you wish to know, assuming of course that we come to suitable terms. You can have the information I have already gained now, with of course the same proviso."

"What are your terms?"

"Twenty pounds a question. You have asked six questions to which I can give complete answers and one which I can answer partially; say six twenties and one ten— total, one hundred and thirty pounds."

"But it's iniquitous, scandalous, extortionate! I shouldn't think of paying such a sum."

"No, sir? That's a matter for yourself alone. It seems to me, then, that our business is completed." The man paused, then as Cheyne made no move continued confidentially. "You see, sir, I needn't tell a gentleman like yourself that value is relative and not absolute. If I hadn't another party willing to pay for my information about you I couldn't perhaps afford to refuse what you might be pleased to offer. But if I don't get my hundred and thirty from you I'll get it from the other party. It's a matter of £. s. d. for me."

"But how do I know you won't get my hundred and thirty and then go to the other party for his?"

Mr. Speedwell smiled craftily.

"You don't know, sir. In these matters one person has to take the other's word. You pay your money and you get the information you ask for. You don't pay and. I keep it. It's for you to say what you'll do."

Cheyne sat in thought. It was evident this man could give him valuable information, and he was well aware that if he had employed him to obtain it it might easily have cost him more than the sum asked. He did not doubt, either, that the quartet had asked for information about himself. When his dead body had not been found it would have been a likely move. But he was surprised that they should have asked under their own names. But then again, they mightn't have. Speedwell might have found these out. It was certainly an extraordinary coincidence that himself and the gang should have consulted the same private detective, though of course there was nothing inherently impossible in it.

On the whole he felt disposed to pay the money. He was comfortably enough off and he would scarcely feel it. The payment would not commit him to anything or put him in any way in the power of this detective. Moreover, the man was evidently skillful at his job and it might be useful enough to have him on his side. And last, but not least, after his failure of the day before it would be a pleasure to go back to Miss Merrill and tell her how well he had succeeded on this occasion.

"Look here," he said. "I don't think you can expect me to believe that these people came and asked you to find the burglar who had made off with their confidential paper, so that they might prosecute. That's rather tall, you know. Why didn't they go direct to the police?"

"I'm only telling you what they said. I'm not saying I believed it was really what they wanted." Speedwell paused. "As a matter of fact I don't mind telling you what I think," he went on presently. "I believe they are scared about you, and they want to find you to finish up the job they bungled. That's what I think, but I may be wrong."

"And if I pay you your hundred and thirty you'll give me your pledge not to give them the information?"

Mr. Speedwell looked pained.

"I don't think I said that, sir. It was two hundred that was mentioned. But see here. I don't want to be grasping. If you make it the even hundred and fifty I'll answer your questions and not theirs. Is it a bargain, sir?"

"Yes," said Cheyne. "I have my check-book here and I'll fill you in a check for the money as soon as I get your replies."

Mr. Speedwell beamed.

"Excellent, sir. An amicable settlement. That's what I like. Well, sir, I can trust you to keep your word. Here are the answers to your questions." He took a bulky note-book from his pocket and continued:

"First question, Dangle's present address: Earlswood, Dalton Avenue, Wembley." He waited while Cheyne wrote the address, then went on: "Second question, Sime's present address: 12 Colton Street, Putney." Again a pause and then: "Third question, Blessington's present address: Earlswood, Dalton Av—"

"The same as Dangle's?"

"The same as Dangle's, or rather, to be strictly accurate, Dangle's is the same as Blessington's. Blessington lives at this place and has for several years; Dangle joined him about six weeks ago, to be precise, on the day after the incident which I have just forgotten."

Cheyne nodded with a rueful smile.

"Well, then, these men's occupations?"

Mr. Speedwell was not to be hurried.

"Fourth question," he proceeded methodically, "Dangle's occupation. Dangle, Mr. Cheyne, is just an ordinary town sharp. He has a bit of money and adds to it in the usual ways. He's in with a cardsharping gang and helps them in their stunts—for a consideration. He frequents a West End gaming room, and if there is any fat pigeon around he'll lend a hand in the plucking. The sister helps as a decoy. They're a warm pair and I should think are watched by the police. They'll not want their dealings with you to come into the limelight anyway, so you've a pull over them there."

"Has Dangle no ostensible profession?"

"Not that I know of, unless you call billiard playing a profession."

"You might give me the address of the gaming rooms."

"27 Greenway Lane, Knightsbridge."

"What about Sime?"

"Sime is another of the same kidney. He does the night club end and brings likely mugs on to the gaming rooms. A plausible ruffian, Sime. A man without scruple and bad to be up against. He has no ostensible business, either."

"And Blessington?"

"Blessington is, in my opinion, the worst of the three. He has ten times the brains of the other two put together and is an out and out scoundrel. He's well enough off in a small way and is supposed to have made his money by systematic blackmail. He's supplying the cash for this little do of yours, whatever it may be. He is believed at Wembley to be something in the city, but I don't think he has any job. Lives on the interest of his money, I should think."

Cheyne noted the replies, marveling how the detective had come to learn so much. Then he asked his seventh question.

"Where is the paper?"

"That, sir, I can only answer partially. It is, or was up till quite lately, in Blessington's possession. Whether he carries it about with him or keeps it in his house or in his bank I don't know. He may even have lent it to one of the others, but he is the chief of the enterprise and it appears to belong to him."

"That's all right," Cheyne admitted. "Now what were you going to tell me apart from these questions—the information you wrote about?"

"Simply, sir, that the man who drugged you in the Edgecombe Hotel in Plymouth was named Stewart Blessington, that he lived at Wembley, and that he drugged you in order to ascertain if you carried on your person a certain paper of which he was in search."

"You can't tell me how he did it?"

"No, sir. Some simple trick of course, but I had no chance to find it out. I might perhaps suggest that he had two similar flasks, one innocent and the other drugged, and that he changed them by sleight of hand while attracting your attention elsewhere."

Cheyne shook his head. He had thought of this explanation before, but it was not satisfactory. He had been watching the man and he was satisfied he had not played any such trick. Besides, this would not explain why no trace of a drug was found in the food. Speedwell, however, could make no further suggestion.

Cheyne put away his notebook.

"There's another thing I should like to know," he said, "and that is how you have learned all this. I suppose you won't tell me?"

Speedwell smiled as he shook his head.

"Some day, sir, when the case is over. You see, if I were

to show you my channels of information you would naturally use them yourself, and then where should I come in? A man in my job soon learns where to pick up a bit of knowledge. It's partly practice and partly knowing the ropes."

"And there's another thing I wish," Cheyne went on as if he had not heard the other, "and that is that you had gone a bit further in your researches and learned what that paper was and what game that gang is up to."

The detective's manner became more eager.

"That's what I was coming to myself, Mr. Cheyne. If you want that information I can get it for you. But it may cost you a bit of money. It would depend on the time I should have to spend on it and the risks I should have to run. If you would like me to take it on for you I could do so. But of course it's a matter for yourself altogether."

Cheyne reflected. This Speedwell had certainly done an amazing amount of work already on the case, and his success so far showed that he was a shrewd and capable man. To engage him to complete the work would probably be the quickest way of bringing the matter to a head, and the easiest, so far as he himself was concerned. But then he would lose all the excitement and the fun. He had pitted his wits against these men, and to hand the affair over to Speedwell would be to confess himself beaten. Moreover, he would have to admit his failure to Miss Merrill and to forego any more alarms and excursions in her company. No, he would keep the thing in his own hands for the present at all events.

He therefore said that he was obliged for the other's offer, which later on he might be glad to accept, but that for the moment he would not make any further move.

"Right, sir. Whatever you say," Speedwell agreed amicably. "I might add what indeed you'll be able to guess for yourself from what I've told you, that this crowd is a pretty shrewd crowd, and they'll not, so to speak, be beating the air in this job of yours. They're going for something, and you may take it from me that something will be worth their going for. At least, if not, I'll eat my hat."

"I quite agree with you," Cheyne returned, fumbling in his pocket. "It now remains for me to write my check and then we shall be square."

Cheyne counted the hours until four o'clock, and as soon as he dared he set off for No. 17 Horne Terrace. Indeed, he timed his visit so well that as he reached the top of the tenth flight of steps, the door of room No. 12 opened and the model emerged. She held the door open for him, and ten minutes later he was seated in the big armchair drinking the usual cup of fragrant China tea.

Miss Merrill listened with close attention to his story, but she was not so enthusiastic at his success as he could have wished. She made no comment until he had finished and then her remark was, if anything, disparaging.

"I don't quite like it, you know," she said slowly. "From your description of him it certainly looks as if that detective was playing a game of his own. It doesn't sound straight. Do you think you can trust him?"

"Not as far as I can see him, but how can I help myself? I expect the addresses he gave are all correct, but I'm not at all satisfied that he won't go straight to the gang and tell them he has found me and get their money for that."

"And you think you wouldn't be wiser to back out yourself and instruct him to carry on for you?"

Cheyne sat up and took his pipe out of his mouth.

"I'm damned if I will," he declared hotly. "It might be a lot wiser and all that, but I'm just not going to."

"You're quite sure? I couldn't persuade you?" she went on demurely, without looking at him.

"I can't imagine you trying, Miss Merrill. But in any case I'm going on."

"Good!" she cried, and her eyes lit up as she smiled at him. "You're quite mad, but I sometimes like mad people. Then if, in spite of all I can say, you're going on, what about a visit to Wembley tonight?"

"The very ticket!" Cheyne was swept by a wave of delight and enthusiasm. "It is jolly of you to suggest it. And you will come out to dinner and I may pay my bet!"

"As it's a bet—all right. But you must go away now. I have some things to attend to. I'll meet you when and where you say."

"What about the Trocadero at seven? A leisurely dinner and then we for Wembley?"

"Right-o," she laughed and vanished into the other room, while Cheyne, full of an eager excitement, went off to telephone orders to the restaurant as to the reservation of places.

CHAPTER X

The New Firm Gets Busy

CHEYNE and Joan Merrill took a Wembley Park train from Baker Street shortly before nine that evening, and a few minutes later alighted at the station whose name was afterwards to become a household word throughout the length and breadth of the British Empire. But at that time the Exhibition was not yet thought of, and the ground, which was later to hum with scores of thousands of visitors from all parts of the world, was now a dark and deserted plain.

When the young people left the station and began to look around them, they found that they had reached the actual fringe of the metropolis. Towards London were the last outlying rows of detached and semidetached houses of the standard suburban type. In the opposite direction, towards Harrow, was the darkness of open country. Judging by the number of lights that were visible, this country was extraordinarily sparsely inhabited.

Guarded inquiries from the railway officials had evoked the information that Dalton Road lay some ten minutes' walk from the station in a northeasterly direction, and thither the two set off. They passed along with circumspection, keeping as far as possible from the street lamps and with their coat collars turned up and the brims of their hats pulled down over their eyes. But the place was deserted. During the whole of their walk they met only one person—a man going evidently to the station, and he strode past with barely a glance.

Dalton Road proved, save for its street lamps and footpath, to be little more than a lane. It led somewhat windingly in an easterly direction off the main road. The country at this point was more thickly populated and there was quite a number of houses in view. All were built in the style of forty years ago, and were nearly all detached, standing in small grounds or lots. Here and there were fine old trees which looked as if they must have been in existence long before the houses, and most of the lots were well supplied with shrubs and with high and thick partition hedges.

Nearly all the gates bore names, and as the two young people walked along, they had no difficulty in identifying Earlswood. There was a lamp at the other side of the road which enabled them to read the white letters on their green ground. Without pausing they glanced around, noting what they could of their surroundings.

A narrow lane running north and south intersected Dalton Road at this point, and in each of the four angles were houses. That in the southwest corner was undergoing extension, the side next the lane showing scaffolding and half-built brick walls. The two adjoining corners were occupied by houses which presented no interesting features, and in the fourth corner, diagonally opposite that of the building operations, stood Earlswood. All four houses were surrounded by unusually large lots containing plenty of trees. Earlswood was particularly secluded, the hall door being almost hidden from both road and lane by hedges and shrubs.

"Lucky it's got all those trees about it," Cheyne whispered as they passed on down Dalton Road. "If we have to burgle it we can do it without being overlooked by the neighbors."

They continued on their way until they found that Dalton Road debouched on a wide thoroughfare which inquiries showed was Walting Street, the main road between London and St. Albans. Then retracing their steps to Earlswood, they followed the cross lane, first south, which brought them back to Wembley, and north, which after about a mile brought them out on the Harrow Road. Having thus learned the lie of the land so as to know where to head in case a sudden flight became necessary, they returned once more to Earlswood to attempt a closer examination of the house.

They had noticed when passing along the cross lane beside the house to which the extension was being made that a gap had been broken in the hedge for the purpose of getting in the building materials. This was closed only by a wooden slat. With one consent they made for the gap, slipped through, and crouching in the shadow of the shrubs within, set themselves to watch Earlswood.

No light showed in any of the front windows, and as soon as Miss Merrill was seated on a bundle of brushwood sheltered from the light but rather chilly wind, Cheyne crept out to reconnoiter more closely. Making sure that no one was approaching, he slipped through the hedge, and then crossing both road and lane diagonally, passed down the lane at the side of Earlswood.

There was no gap in the Earlswood hedge, but just as in the case of that other similarly situated house which he had investigated, a narrow lane ran along at the bottom of the tiny garden behind. Cheyne turned into this and stood looking at the back of the house. The whole proceeding seemed familiar, a repetition of his actions on the night he traced the gang to Hopefield Avenue.

But the back of this house was in darkness, and pushing open a gate, he passed from the lane to the garden and silently approached the building. A path led straight from gate to door, a side door evidently, as the walled-in yard was on his left hand. Another path to the right led round the house to the hall door in the front.

Cheyne walked slowly round, examining doors and windows. All of these were fastened and he did not see how without breaking the glass he could force an entrance. But he found a window at the back, the sash of which was loose and easy fitting, and decided that in case of need he would operate on this.

Having learned everything he could, he retraced his steps to his companion and they held a whispered consultation. Cheyne was for taking the opportunity of the house being empty to make an attempt then and there to get in. But Miss Merrill would not hear of it. Such a venture, she said, would require very careful thought as well as apparatus which they had not got. "Besides," she added, "you've done enough for one night. Remember you're not completely well yet."

"Oh, blow my health; I'm perfectly all right," he whispered back, but he had to admit her other arguments were sound and the two, cautiously emerging from their hiding-place, walked back to Wembley and took the next train to town.

She was silent during the journey, but as they reached Baker Street she turned to him and said: "Look here, I believe I've got an idea. Bring a long-burning electric torch with you tomorrow afternoon and whatever tools you want to open the window, and perhaps we'll try our luck." She would not explain her plan nor would she allow him to accompany her to the studio, so with rather a bad grace he said good night and returned to his hotel.

The next day he spent in making an assortment of purchases. These were in all a powerful electric torch, guaranteed to burn brightly for a couple of hours, a short, slightly bent lever of steel with a chisel point at one end, a cap, a pair of thin gloves, a glazier's diamond, some twenty feet of thin rope and a five-inch piece of bright steel tubing with a tiny handle at one side. These, when four o'clock came, he took with him to Horne Terrace and spread in triumph on Miss Merrill's table.

"Good gracious!" cried the young lady as she stared wonderingly at the collection. "Whatever are these? Another expedition to Mount Everest?"

"Torch: takes the place of the old dark lantern," Cheyne answered proudly, pointing to the article in question. "Jemmy for persuading intractable doors, boxes and drawers; cap that will not drop or blow off; gloves to keep one's fingerprints off the furniture; diamond for making holes in panes of glass; penknife for shooting back snibs of windows; rope for escaping from upstairs windows, and this"—he picked up the bit of tube and levelled it at her—"what price this for bluffing out of a tight place? If the light's not too good it's a pretty fair imitation. Also"—he pointed to his feet—"rubber-soled shoes for silence."

She gave a delightful little ripple of laughter, then became serious.

"Have you no anklets?" she asked anxiously. "Don't say you have forgotten your anklets!"

"Anklets?" he repeated. "What d'you mean? I don't follow."

"To guard against the bites of sharks, of course," she declared. "Don't you remember the White Knight had them for his horse?"

Cheyne was so serious and eager that he felt somewhat dashed, but he joined in the laugh, and when they had had tea they settled down to talk over their arrangements. Then it seemed that she really had a plan, and when Chayne heard it he became immediately enthusiastic. Like all good plans it was simple, and soon they had the details cut and dry.

"Let's try tonight," Cheyne cried in excitement.

"Yes, I think we should. If these people have some scheme on hand every day's delay is in their favor and against you."

"Against us, Joan, not against me," he cried, then realizing what he had said, he looked at her anxiously. "I may call you Joan, mayn't I?" he pleaded. "You see, we're partners now."

She didn't mind, it appeared, what he called her. Any old name would do. And she didn't mind calling him Maxwell either. She hadn't noticed that Maxwell was so frightfully long and clumsy, but she supposed Max *was* shorter. So that was that. They returned to the Plan. Though they continued discussing it for nearly an hour neither was able to improve on it, except that they decided that the first thing to be done if they got hold of the tracing was to copy their adversaries and photograph it.

"Drat this daylight saving," Cheyne grumbled. "If it wasn't for that we could start a whole hour earlier. As it is there is no use going out there before nine." He paused and then went on: "Queer thing that these two houses should be so much alike—this Earlswood and the one in Hopefield Avenue. Both at cross roads, both with lanes behind them, and both surrounded by gardens and hedges and shrubs."

"Very queer," Joan admitted, "especially as there probably aren't more than a hundred thousand houses of that type in London. But it's all to the good. You'll feel at home when you get in."

They sparred pleasantly for some time, then after a leisurely dinner they tubed to Baker Street and took the train to Wembley Park. It was darker than on the previous evening, for the sky was thickly overcast. There had been some rain during the day, but this had now ceased, though the wind had turned east and it had become cold and raw.

Turning into Dalton Road, they reached the cross-lane at Earlswood, passed through the gap in the hedge and took up their old position among the shrubs. They had seen no one and they believed they were unobserved. From where they crouched they could see that Earlswood was again in darkness, and presently Cheyne slipped away to explore.

He was soon back again with the welcome news that
the rear of the house was also unlighted and that the Plan
might be put into operation forthwith. In spite of Joan's
ridicule he had insisted on bringing his complete outfit,
and he now stood up and patted himself over to make
sure that everything was in place. The cap, the gloves, and
the shoes he was wearing, the rope was coiled round his
waist beneath his coat, and the other articles were stowed
in his various pockets. He turned and signified that he
was ready.

Joan opened the proceedings by passing out through the
gap in the hedge, walking openly across to the Earlswood
hall door, and ringing. This was to make sure that the
house really was untenanted. If any one came she would
simply ask if Mrs. Bryce-Harris was at home and then
apologize for having mistaken the address.

But no one answered, and the demonstration of this was
Cheyne's cue. When he had waited for five minutes after
Joan's departure and no sound came from across the road,
he in his turn slipped out through the gap in the hedge,
and after a glance round, crossed Dalton Road, and passing down by the side of Earlswood, turned into the lane at
the back. On this occasion he could dimly see the gate into
the garden, which was painted white, and he passed
through, leaving it open behind him, and reached the
house.

The point upon which Joan's plan hinged was that,
owing to the shrubs in front of the building, it was possible
to remain concealed in the shadows beside the porch,
invisible from the road. She proposed, therefore, to stay at
the door while Cheyne was carrying on operations within,
and to ring if any one approached the house, adding a
double knock if there was urgent danger. She would hold
the newcomer with inquiries as to the whereabouts of the
mythical Mrs. Bryce-Harris, thus insuring time for her
companion to beat a retreat. She herself also would have
time in which to vanish before her victims realized what
had happened.

Feeling, therefore, that he would have a margin in which to withdraw if flight became necessary, Cheyne set to work to force an entrance. He rapidly examined the doors and windows, but all were fastened as before. Choosing the window with the loose sash upon which he had already decided, he took his knife and tried to open the catch. The two sashes were "rabbitted" where they met, but he was able to push the blade up right through the overhanging wood of the upper sash and lever the catch round until it snapped clear. Then withdrawing the knife, he raised the bottom sash. A moment later he was standing on the scullery floor.

His first care was to unlock and throw open the back door, so as to provide an emergency exit in case of need. Then he closed and refastened the scullery window, darkening with a pencil the wood where the knife had broken a splinter. As he said to himself, there was no kind of sense in calling attention to his visit.

He crossed the hall and silently opened the front door to see that all was right with Joan. Then closing it again, he began a search of the house.

The building was of old-fashioned design, a narrow hall running through its center from back to front. Five doors opened off this hall, leading to the dining room and the kitchen at one side, a sitting room and a kind of library or study at the other, and the garden at the back. Upstairs were four bedrooms—one unoccupied—and a servant's room.

Cheyne rapidly passed through the house searching for likely hiding places for the tracing. Soon he came to the conclusion that unless some freak place had been chosen, it would be in one of two places: either a big roll-top desk in the library or an old-fashioned escritoire in one of the bedrooms. Both of these were locked. Fortunately there was no safe.

He decided to try the desk first. A gentle application of the jemmy burst its lock and he threw up the cover and sat down to go through the contents.

Evidently it belonged to Blessington, and evidently also Blessington was a man of tidy and businesslike habits. There were but few papers on the desk and these from their date were clearly current and waiting to be dealt with. In the drawers were bundles of letters, accounts, receipts, and miscellaneous papers, all neatly tied together with tape and docketed. In one of the side drawers was a card index and in another a vertical numeralpha letter file. Through all of these Cheyne hurriedly looked, but nowhere was there any sign of the tracing.

A few measurements with a pocket rule showed that there were no spaces in the desk unaccounted for, and closing the top, Cheyne hurried upstairs to the escritoire. It was a fine old piece and it went to his heart to damage it with the jemmy. But he remembered his treatment aboard the *Enid,* and such a paroxysm of anger swept over him that he plunged in the point of his tool and ruthlessly splintered open the lid.

The drawers were fastened by separate locks, and each one Cheyne smashed with a savage satisfaction. Then he began to examine their contents.

This was principally bundles of old letters, tied up in the same methodical way as those downstairs. Cheyne did not read anything, but from the fragments of sentences which he could not help seeing there seemed ample corroboration of Speedwell's statements that Blessington lived by professional blackmail. He felt a wave of disgust sweep over him as he went through drawer after drawer of the obscene collection.

But here also no luck met his efforts, and with a sinking heart he took out his rule to measure the escritoire. And then he became suddenly excited as he found that the thickness of the wood at the back of the drawers, which normally should have been about half an inch, measured no less than four inches. Here, surely, there must be a secret drawer.

He examined the woodwork, but nowhere could he see the slightest trace of an opening. He pressed and pulled and pushed, but still without result: no knob would slide, no panel depress. But of the existence of the space there was no doubt. There was room for a receptacle six inches by twelve by three, and, moreover, all six sides of it sounded hollow when tapped.

There was nothing for it but force. With a sharp stroke he rammed the point of the jemmy into the side. It penetrated, he levered it down, and with a grinding, cracking sound the wood split and part of it was prised off. Eagerly Cheyne put the torch to the opening, and he chuckled with satisfaction as he saw within the familiar lilac gray of the tracing.

Once again he inserted the point of the jemmy to prise off the remainder of the side, but the heavy wood at the top of the piece prevented his getting a leverage. He withdrew the tool to find a fresh purchase, but as he did so, the front door bell rang—several sharp, jerky peals. Frantically he jammed in the jemmy, intending by sheer force to smash out the wood, but his position was hampered, and it cracked, but did not give. As he tried desperately for a fresh hold an urgent double knock sounded from below. Sweating and tugging with the jemmy he heard voices outside the window. And then with a resounding crack the panel gave, he plunged in his hand, seized the tracing, thrust it and the jemmy into his pocket and rushed out of the room.

But as he did so he heard the front door open and Dangle's voice from below: "It sounded in the house. Didn't you think so?" and Susan's: "Yes, upstairs, I thought."

Cheyne looked desperately round for a weapon. Near the head of the stairs stood a light cane chair, and this he seized as he dashed down. As he turned the angle of the stairs Dangle switched on the light in the hall, and with a startled oath ran forward to intercept him. With all his might Cheyne hurled the chair at the other's head. Dangle threw up his arms to protect his face, and by the time he recovered himself Cheyne was in the hall, doubling round the newel post. Both Dangle and Susan clutched at the flying figure. But Cheyne, twisting like an eel, tore himself free and made at top speed for the back door. This he slammed after him, rushing as fast as he could down the garden. He slackened only to pull the gate to as he passed through it, then sped along the lane, and turning at its end away from Dalton Road, tore off into the night.

These proceedings were not in accordance with the Plan. The intention had been that on either recovering the tracing or satisfying himself that it was not in the house, Cheyne would close the back door, and letting himself out by the front, would meet Joan, pull the door to after them, walk round the house and quietly disappear via the garden and lane. But the possibility of an unexpected flight had been recognized. It had been decided that in such a case the first thing would be to get rid of the tracing, so that in the event of capture, the fruits of the raid would at least be safe. Therefore, on all the routes away from Earlswood hiding places had been fixed on, from which Joan would afterwards recover it. Along the lane the hiding place was the back of a wall approaching a culvert, and over this wall Cheyne duly threw the booty as he rushed along.

By this time Dangle was out on the road and running for all he was worth. But Cheyne had the advantage of him. He was lighter and an experienced athlete, and, except for his illness, was in better training. Moreover, he was more lightly clad and wore rubber shoes. Dangle, though Cheyne did not know it, was hampered by an overcoat and patent leather boots. He could not gain on the fugitive, and Cheyne heard his footsteps dropping farther and farther behind, until at last they ceased altogether.

Cheyne slacked to a walk as he wiped the perspiration from his forehead. So far as he was concerned he had now only to make his way back to town and meet Joan at her studio. He considered his position and concluded his best and safest plan would be to go on to Harrow and take an express for Marylebone—if he could get one.

He duly reached Harrow, but he found there that he would have nearly an hour to wait for a non-stop train for London. He decided, however, that this would be better than risking a halt at Wembley Park, and he hung about at the end of the platform until the train came along. On reaching town he took a taxi to Horne Terrace and hurried up to No. 12. Joan had not returned!

He waited outside her room for a considerable time, then coming down, began to pace the street in front of the house. Every moment he became more and more anxious. It was now half past twelve o'clock and she should have been back over an hour ago. What could be keeping her? Merciful Heavens! If anything could have happened to her.

He wrote a note on a leaf of his pocketbook saying he would return in the morning, and going once more up to her flat, pushed it under the door. Then hailing a belated taxi, he offered the man a fancy price to drive him to Wembley Park.

Some half-hour later he climbed over the wall across which he had thrown the tracing. A careful search showed that it was no longer there; moreover it revealed the print of a dainty shoe with a rather high heel, such as he had noticed Joan wearing earlier in the evening. He returned to the shrubs at the gap where they had waited, but there he could find no trace of her at all. Then he walked all round Earlswood, but it was shrouded in darkness. Finally, his taximan having refused to wait for him and all traffic being over for the day, he set out to walk to London, which he reached between three and four o'clock.

He had some coffee at a stall and then returned to his hotel, but by seven he was once more at Horne Terrace. Eagerly he raced up the steps and knocked at No. 12. There was no answer.

Suddenly a white speck below the door caught his eye, and stooping, he saw the note he had pushed in on the previous evening. Joan evidently had not yet returned.

CHAPTER XI

Otto Schulz's Secret

CHEYNE, faced by the disquieting fact that Joan Merrill had failed to reach home in spite of her expressed intention to return there immediately, stood motionless outside her door, aghast and irresolute. With a growing anxiety he asked himself what could have occurred to delay her. He knew her well enough to be satisfied that she would not change her mind through sudden caprice. Something had happened to her, and as he considered the possibilities, he grew more and more uneasy.

The contingency was one which neither of them had foreseen, and for the moment he was at a loss as to how to cope with it. First, in his hot-blooded way he thought of buying a real pistol, returning to Earlswood, and shooting Blessington and Dangle unless they revealed her whereabouts. Then reason told him that they really might not know, that Joan might have met with an accident or for some reason have gone to friends for the night, and he thought of putting the matter in Speedwell's hands. But he soon saw that Speedwell had not the means or the organization to deal adequately with the affair and his thoughts turned to Scotland Yard. He was loath to confess his own essays in illegality in such an unsympathetic *milieu,* but of course no hesitation was possible if Joan's safety was at stake.

Still pondering the problem, he turned and slowly descended the stairs. He would wait, he thought, for an hour or perhaps two—say until nine. If by nine o'clock she had neither turned up nor sent a message he would go to Scotland Yard, no matter what the consequences to himself might be.

Thinking that he should go back to his hotel in case she telephoned, he strode off along the pavement. But he had scarcely left the doorway when he heard his name called from behind, and swinging round, he gazed in speechless amazement at the figure confronting him. It was James Dangle!

For a moment they stared at one another, and then Cheyne saw red.

"You infernal scoundrel!" he yelled, and sprang at the other's throat. Dangle, stepping back, threw up his hands to parry the onslaught, while he cried earnestly:

"Steady, Mr. Cheyne; for heaven's sake, steady! I have a message for you from Miss Merrill."

Cheyne glared wrathfully, but he pulled himself together and released his hold.

"Don't speak her name, you blackguard!" he said thickly. "What's your message?"

"She is all right," Dangle answered quickly, "but the rest of it will take time to tell. Let us get out of this."

Some passers-by, hearing the raised voices, had stopped, and a small crowd, eager for a row, had collected about the two men. Dangle seized Cheyne's wrist and hurried him down the street and round the corner.

"Let's go to your hotel, Mr. Cheyne, or anywhere else we can talk," he begged. "What I have to say will take a little time."

Cheyne snatched his wrist away.

"Keep your filthy hands to yourself," he snarled. "Where is Miss Merrill?"

"I am sorry to say she has met with a slight accident," Dangle replied, speaking quickly and with placatory gestures; "not in any way serious, only a twisted ankle. I found her on the road on my way back from chasing you, leaning up against the stone wall which runs along the lane at the back of Blessington's house. She had hurt herself in climbing down to get the tracing which you threw over. I called my sister and we helped her into the house, and Susan bathed and bound up her ankle and fixed her up comfortably on the sofa. It is not really a sprain, but it will be painful for a day or two."

Cheyne was taken aback not only by his enemy's knowledge, but also by being talked to in so friendly a fashion, and in his relief at the news he felt his anger draining away.

"You've got the tracing again, I suppose?" he said ruefully.

Dangle smiled.

"Well, yes, we have," he agreed. "But I have to admit it was the result of two lucky chances; first, my sister's and my return just when we did, and second, Miss Merrill's unfortunate false step over the wall. But your scheme was a good one, and with ordinary luck you would have pulled it off."

Cheyne grunted, and Dangle, turning towards him, went on earnestly: "Look here, Mr. Cheyne, why should we be on opposite sides in this affair? I have spoken to my partners, and we are all agreed. You are the kind of man we want, and we believe we could be of benefit to one another. In fact, to make a long story short, I am authorized to lay before you a certain proposition. I believe it will appeal to you. It is for that purpose I should like to go somewhere where we could talk. If not to your hotel, I know a place a few hundred yards down this street where we could get a private room."

"I want to go out and see Miss Merrill."

"Of course you do. But Miss Merrill was asleep when I left and most probably will sleep for an hour or two yet, so there is time enough. I beg that you will first hear what I have to say. Then we can go out together."

"Well, come to my hotel," Cheyne said ungraciously, and the two walked along, Dangle making tentative essays in conversation, all of which were brought to nought by the uncompromising brevity of his companion's responses.

"You'd better come up to my bedroom," Cheyne growled when at last they reached their goal. "These dratted servants are cleaning the public rooms."

In silence they sought the lift and Cheyne led the way to his apartment. Bolting the door, he pointed to a chair, stood himself with his back to the empty fireplace and remarked impatiently: "Well?"

Dangle laughed lightly.

"I see you're not going to help me out, Mr. Cheyne, and I suppose I can scarcely wonder at it. Well, I'll get ahead without further delay. But, as I've a good deal to say, I should suggest you sit down, and if you don't mind, I'll smoke. Try one of these Coronas; they were given to me, so you needn't mind taking one. No? I wonder would you mind if I rang and ordered some coffee and rolls? I've not breakfasted yet and I'm hungry."

With a bad grace Cheyne rang the bell.

"Coffee and rolls for two," Dangle ordered when an attendant came to the door. "You will join me, won't you? Even if my mission comes to nothing and we remain enemies, there's no reason why we should make our interview more unpleasant than is necessary."

Cheyne strode up and down the room.

"But I don't want the confounded interview," he exclaimed angrily. "For goodness' sake get along and say what you have to say and clear out. I haven't forgotten the *Enid*."

"No, that was illegal, wasn't it? Almost as bad as breaking and entering, burglary and theft. But now, there's no kind of sense in squabbling. Sit down and listen and I'll tell you a story that will interest you in spite of yourself."

"I shouldn't wonder," Cheyne said with sarcasm as he flung himself into a chair, "but if it's going to be more lies about St. John Price and the Hull succession you may save your breath."

Dangle smiled whimsically. "It was for your sake, Mr. Cheyne; perhaps not quite legitimate, but still done with the best intention. I told him that yarn—I admit, of course, it was a yarn—simply to make it easy for you to give up the letter. I knew that nothing would induce you to part with it if you thought it dishonorable; hence the story."

Cheyne laughed harshly.

"And what will be the object of the new yarn?"

"This time it won't be a yarn. I will tell you the truth."

"And you expect me to believe it?"

Dangle leaned forward and spoke more earnestly.

"You will believe it, not, I'm afraid, because I tell it, but because it is capable of being checked. A great portion of it can be substantiated by inquiries at the Admiralty and elsewhere, and your reason will satisfy you as to the remainder."

"Well, go on and get it over anyway."

Dangle once more smilingly shrugged his shoulders, lit his cigar and began:

"My tale commences as before with our mutual friend, Arnold Price, and once again it goes back to the year 1917. In February of '17 Arnold Price was, as you know, third mate of the *Maurania,* and I was on the same ship in command of her bow gun—she had guns mounted fore and aft. I hadn't known Price before, but we became friends—not close friends, but as intimate as most men who are cooped up together for months on the same ship.

"In February '17, as we were coming into the Bay on our way from South Africa, we sighted a submarine. I needn't worry you with the details of what followed. It's enough to say that we tried to escape, and failing, showed fight. As it chanced, by a stroke of the devil's own luck we pumped a shell into her just abaft the conning tower after she rose and before she could get her gun trained on us. She heeled over and began to sink by the stern. I confess that I'd have watched those devils drown, as they had done many of our poor fellows, but the old man wasn't that way inclined and he called for volunteers to get out one of the boats. Price was the first man to offer, and they got a boat lowered away and pulled for the submarine. She disappeared before they could get up to her, and we could see her crew clinging to wreckage. The men in the boat pulled all out to get there before they were washed away, for there was a bit of a sea running, the end of a southwester that had just blown itself out. Well, some of the crew held on and they got them into the boat; others couldn't stick it and were lost. The captain was there clinging on to a lifebelt, but just as the boat came up he let go and was sinking, when Arnold Price jumped overboard and caught him and supported him until they got a rope round him and pulled him aboard. I didn't see that myself, but I heard about it afterwards. The captain's name was Otto Schulz, and when they got him aboard the *Maurania* and fixed up in bed they found that he had had a knock on the head that would probably do for him. But all the same Price had saved his life, and what was more, had saved it at the risk of his own. That is the first point in my story."

Dangle paused and drew at his cigar. As he had foretold, Cheyne was already interested. The story appealed to him, for he knew that for once he was not being told a yarn. He had already heard of the rescue; in fact he had himself congratulated Price on his brave deed. He remembered a curious point about it. A day or two later Price had been hit in an encounter with another U-boat, and he and Schulz had been sent to the same hospital—somewhere on the French coast. There Schulz had died, and from there Price had sent the mysterious tracing which had been the cause of all these unwonted activities.

"We crossed the Bay without further adventures," Dangle resumed, "but as we approached the Channel we sighted another U-boat. We exchanged a few shots without doing a great deal of harm on either side, and when a destroyer came on the scene Brother Fritz submerged and disappeared. But as luck would have it one of his shells burst over our fo'c'sle. Both Price and I were there, I at my gun and he on some job of his own, and both of us got knocked out. Price had a scalp wound and I a bit of shell in my thigh; neither very serious, but both stretcher cases.

"We called at Brest that night and next morning they sent us ashore to hospital. Schulz was sent with us. By what seems now a strange coincidence, but what was, I suppose, ordinary and natural enough, we were put into adjoining beds in the same ward. That is the second point of my story."

Again Dangle paused and again Cheyne reflected that so far he was being told the truth. He wondered with a growing thrill if he was really going to learn the contents of Price's letter to himself and the meaning of the mysterious tracing, as well as the circumstances under which it was sent. He nodded to show he had grasped the point and Dangle went on:

"Price and I soon began to improve, but the blow on Schulz's head turned out pretty bad and he grew weaker and weaker. At last he got to know he was going to peg out, as you will see from what I overheard.

"I was lying that night in a sort of waking dream, half asleep and half conscious of my surroundings. The ward was very still. There were six of us there and I thought all the others were asleep. The night nurse had just had a look round and had gone out again. She had left the gas lit, but turned very low. Suddenly I heard Schulz, who was in the next bed, calling Price. He called him two or three times and then Price answered. 'Look here, Price,' Schulz said, 'are those other blighters asleep?' He talked as good English as you or me. Price said 'Yes,' and then Schulz went on to talk.

"Now, I don't know if you'll believe me, Mr. Cheyne, but though as a matter of fact, I overheard everything he said, I didn't mean to listen. I was so tired and dreamy that I just didn't think of telling him I was awake, and indeed if I had thought of it, I don't believe I should have had the energy to move. You know how it is when you're not well. Then when I did hear it was too late. I just couldn't tell him that I had learned his secret."

As Dangle spoke there was a knock at the door and a waiter arrived with coffee. Dangle paid him, and without further comment poured some out for Cheyne and handed it across. Cheyne was by this time so interested in the tale that his resentment was forgotten, and he took the cup with a word of thanks.

"Go on," he added. "I'm interested in your story, as you said I should be."

"I thought you would," Dangle answered with his ready smile. "Well, Schulz began by telling Price that he knew he wasn't going to live. Then he went on to say that he felt it cruelly hard luck, because he had accidentally come on a secret which would have brought him an immense fortune. Now he couldn't use it. He had been going to let it die with him, but he remembered what he owed to Price and had decided to hand over the information to him. 'But,' he said, 'there is one condition. You must first swear to me on your sacred honor that if you make anything out of it you will, after the war, try to find my wife and hand her one-eighth of what you get. I say one-eighth, because if you get any profits at all they will be so enormous that one-eighth will be riches to Magda.'

"I could see that Price thought he was delirious, but to quiet him he swore the oath and then Schulz told of his discovery. He said that before he had been given charge of the U-boat he had served for over six months in the Submarine Research Department, and that there, while carrying out certain experiments, he had had a lucky accident. Some substances which he had fused in an electric furnace had suddenly partially vaporized and, as it were, boiled over. The white-hot mass poured over the copper terminals of his furnace, with the result that the extremely high voltage current short-circuited with a corona of brilliant sparks. He described the affair in greater detail than this, but I am not an electrician and I didn't follow the technicalities. But they don't matter, it was the result that was important. When the current was cut off and the mass cooled he started in to clean up. He chipped the stuff off the terminals, and he found that the copper had fused and run. And then he made his great discovery: the copper had hardened. He tested it and found it was, roughly speaking, as hard as high carbon steel and with an even greater tensile strength! Unintentionally he had made a new and unknown alloy. Schulz knew that the ancients were able to harden copper and he supposed that he had found the lost art.

"At once he saw the extraordinary value of this discovery. If you could use copper instead of steel you would revolutionize the construction of electrical machinery; copper conduits could be lighter and be self-supporting—in scores of ways the new metal would be worth nearly its weight in gold. He could not work at the thing by himself, so he told his immediate superior, who happened also to be a close personal friend. The two tried some more experiments, and to make a long story short, they discovered that if certain percentages of certain minerals were added to the copper during smelting, it became hard. The minerals were cheap and plentiful, so that practically the new metal could be produced at the old price. This meant, for example, that they could make parts of machines of the new alloy, which would weigh—and therefore cost—only about one-quarter of those of ordinary copper. If they sold these at half or even three-quarters of the old price they would make an extremely handsome profit. But their idea was not to do this, but to sell their discovery to Krupps or some other great firm who, they believed, would pay a million sterling or more for it.

"But they knew that they could not do anything with it until after the war unless they were prepared to hand it over to the military authorities for whatever these chose to pay, which would probably be nothing. While they were still considering their course of action both were ordered back to sea. Schulz's friend was killed almost immediately, Schulz being then the only living possessor of the secret. Panic-stricken lest he too should be killed, he prepared a cipher giving the whole process, and this he sealed in a watertight cover and wore it continuously beneath his clothes. He now proposed to give it to Price, partly in return for what Price had done, and partly in the hope of his wife eventually benefiting. I saw him hand over a small package, and then I got the disappointment of my life, and so, I'm sure, did Price. Schulz was obviously growing weaker and he now spoke with great difficulty. But he made a final effort to go on; 'The key to the cipher—' he began and just then the sister came back into the room. Schulz stopped, but before she left he got a weak turn and fell back unconscious. He never spoke again and next day he was dead."

In his absorption Dangle had let his cigar go out, and now he paused to relight it. Cheyne sat, devouring the story with eager interest. He did not for a moment doubt it. It covered too accurately the facts which he already knew. He was keenly curious to hear its end: whether Dangle, having obtained the cipher, had read it, and what was the nature of the proposal the man was about to make.

"Next day I approached Price on the matter. I said I had involuntarily overheard what Schulz had told him, and as the affair was so huge, asked him to take me into it with him. As a matter of fact I thought then, and think now, that the job was too big for one person to handle. However, Price cut up rough about it: wouldn't have me as a partner on any terms and accused me of eavesdropping. I told him to go to hell and we parted on bad terms. I found out—I may as well admit by looking through the letters in his cabin while he was on duty—that he had sent the packet to you, and when I had made inquiries about you I was able to guess his motive. You, humanly speaking, were a safe life; you were invalided out of the service. He would send the secret to you to keep for him till after the war or to use as you thought best if he were knocked out.

"You will understand, Mr. Cheyne, that though keenly interested in the whole affair, while I was in the service I couldn't make any move in it. But directly I was demobbed I began to make inquiries. I found you were living at Dartmouth, and it was evident from your way of life that you hadn't exploited the secret. Then I found out about Price, learned that he was on one of the Bombay-Basrah troopships and that though he had applied to be demobbed there were official delays. The next thing I heard about him was that he had disappeared. You knew that?" Dangle seemed to have been expecting the other to show surprise.

"Yes, I knew it. I learned it at the same time that I learned St. John Price was a myth."

"Well, it's quite true. He left his ship at Bombay on a few days' leave to pay a visit up country and was never heard of again. Presumably he is dead. And now, Mr. Cheyne," Dangle shifted uneasily in his seat and glanced deprecatingly at the other, "now I come to a part of my story which I should be glad to omit. But I must tell you everything so that you may be in a position to decide on the proposal I'm going to make. At the time I was financially in very low water. My job had not been kept for me and I couldn't get another. I was pretty badly hit, and worse still, I had taken to gambling in the desperate hope of getting some ready money. One night I had been treated on an empty stomach, and being upset from the drink, I plunged more than all my remaining capital. I lost, and then I was down and out, owing fairly large sums to two men—Blessington and Sime. In despair I told them of Schulz's discovery. They leaped at it and said that if my sister Susan and myself would join in an attempt to get hold of the secret they would not only cancel the debts, but would offer us a square deal and share and share alike. Well, I shouldn't have agreed, of course, but—well, I did. It was naturally the pressure they brought to bear that made me do it, but it was also partly due to my resentment at the way Price had turned me down. We thought that as far as you were concerned, you were probably expecting nothing and would therefore suffer no disappointment, and we agreed unanimously to send both Frau Schulz and Mrs. Price equal shares with ourselves. I don't pretend any of us were right, Mr. Cheyne, but that's what happened."

"I can understand it very well," said Cheyne. He was always generous to a fault and this frank avowal had mollified his wrath. "But you haven't told me if you read the cipher."

"I'm coming to that," Dangle returned. "We laid our plans for getting hold of the package and with some forged references Susan got a job as servant in your house. She told us that so far as she could see the package would either be about your person or in your safe, and as she couldn't ascertain the point we laid our plans to find out. As you know, they drew blank, and then we devised the plant on the *Enid*. That worked, but you nearly turned the tables on us in Hopefield Avenue. How you traced us I can't imagine, and I hope later on you'll tell me. That night we didn't know whether we had killed you or not. We didn't want to and hadn't meant to, but we might easily have done so. When your body was not found in the morning we became panicky and cleared out. Then there came your attempt of last night. But for an accident it would have succeeded. Now we have come to the conclusion that you are too clever and determined to have you for an enemy. We are accordingly faced with an alternative. Either we must murder you and Miss Merrill or we must get you on to our side. The first we all shrink from, though"—and here Dangle's eye showed a nasty gleam—"if it was that or our failure we shouldn't hesitate, but the second is what we should all prefer. In short, Mr. Cheyne, will you and Miss Merrill join us in trading Schulz's secret: all, including Frau Schulz and Mrs. Price, to share equally? We think that's a fair offer and we extremely hope you won't turn us down."

"You haven't told me if you've read the cipher."

"I forgot that. I'm sorry to say that we have not, and that's another reason we want you and Miss Merrill. We want two fresh brains on it. But the covering letter shows that the secret is in the cipher and it must be possible to read it."

Cheyne did not reply as he sat considering this unexpected move. If he were satisfied as to Arnold Price's death and if the quartet had been trustworthy he would not have hesitated. Frau Schulz would get her eighth and Mrs. Price would get a quite unexpected windfall. Moreover, the people who worked the invention were entitled to some return for their trouble. No, the proposal was reasonable; in fact it was too reasonable. It was more reasonable than he would have expected from people who had already acted as these four had done. He found it impossible to trust in their *bona fides*. He would like to have Joan Merrill's views before replying. He therefore temporized.

"Your proposal is certainly attractive," he said, "but before coming to a conclusion Miss Merrill must be consulted. She would be a party to it, same as myself. Suppose we go out and see her now, and then I will give you my answer."

Dangle's face took on a graver expression.

"I'm afraid you can't do that," he answered slowly. "You see, there is more in it than I have told you, though I hoped to avoid this side of it. Please put yourself in our place. I come to you with this offer. I don't know whether you will accept it or turn it down. If you turn it down there is nothing to prevent you, with the information I have just given you, going to the police and claiming the whole secret and prosecuting us. Whether you would be likely to win your case wouldn't matter. You might, and that would be too big a risk for us. We have therefore in self-defense had to take precautions. And the precautions we have taken are these. Earlswood has been evacuated. Just as we left Hopefield Avenue so we have left Dalton Road. Our party—and Miss Merrill"—he slightly stressed the "and" and in his voice Cheyne sensed a veiled threat— "have taken up their quarters at another house some distance from town. In self-defense we must have your acceptance *before* further negotiations take place. You must see this for yourself."

"And if I refuse?"

Dangle lowered his voice and spoke very earnestly.

"Mr. Cheyne, if you refuse you will never see Miss Merrill alive!"

CHAPTER XII

In the Enemy's Lair

WITH some difficulty Cheyne overcame a sudden urge to leap at his companion's throat.

"You infernal scoundrel!" he cried thickly. "Injure a hair of Miss Merrill's head and you and your confounded friends will hang! I'll go to Scotland Yard. Do you think I mind about myself?"

Dangle gave a cheery smile.

"Right, Mr. Cheyne," he answered briskly, "by all means. Just do go to Scotland Yard and make your complaint. And what are you going to tell them? That Miss Merrill is in the hands of a dangerous gang of ruffians, and must be rescued immediately? And the present address of this gang is—?" He looked quizzically at the other. "I don't think so. I'm afraid Scotland Yard would be too slow for you. You see, my friends are waiting for a telephone message from me. If that is not received or if it is unsatisfactory—well, don't let us discuss unpleasant topics, but Miss Merrill will be very, very sorry."

Cheyne choked with rage, but for the moment he found himself unable to reply. That he was being bluffed he had no doubt, and in any other circumstances he would have taken a stronger line. But where Joan Merrill was concerned he could run no risks. It was evident that she really was in the power of the gang. Dangle could not possibly have known about the throwing of the tracing over the wall unless he really had found her as he had described.

A very short cogitation convinced Cheyne that these people had him in their toils. Application to Scotland Yard would be useless. No doubt the police could find the conspirators, but they could not find them in time. So far as retaliation or a constructive policy was concerned, he saw that he was down and out.

His thoughts turned to the proposal Dangle had made him. It was certainly fair—too fair, he still thought—but if it was a genuine offer, he need have no qualms about accepting it. Frau Schulz, Mrs. Price, Joan and himself were all promised shares of the profits. A clause could be put in covering Price, if he afterwards turned out to be alive. The gang might be a crowd of sharpers and thieves —so at least the melancholy Speedwell had said—but, as Cheyne came to look at it, they had not really broken the law to a much greater extent than he had himself. His case to the authorities—suppose he were to lay it before them —would not be so overwhelmingly clear. Something could be said for—or rather against—both sides.

If he had to give way he might as well give way with a good grace. He therefore choked down his rage, and turning to Dangle, said quietly:

"I see you've won this trick. I'll accept your offer and go with you."

Dangle, evidently delighted, sprang to his feet.

"Splendid, Mr. Cheyne," he cried warmly, holding out his hand. "Shake hands, won't you? You'll not repent your action, I promise you."

But this was too much for Cheyne.

"No," he declared. "Not yet. You haven't satisfied me of your *bona fides*. I'm sorry, but you have only yourselves to thank. When I find Miss Merrill at liberty and see Schulz's cipher, I'll be satisfied, and then I will join with you and give you all the help I can."

Dangle seemed rather dashed, but he laughed shortly as he answered: "I suppose we deserve that after all. But you will soon be convinced. There is just a formality to be gone through before we start. Though you may not believe my word, we believe yours, and we have agreed that all that we want before taking you further into our confidence, is that you swear an oath of loyalty to us. You won't object to that, I presume?"

Cheyne hesitated, then he said:

"I swear on my sacred honor that I will loyally abide

by the spirit of the agreement which you have outlined in so far as you and your friends act loyally to me and to Miss Merrill, and to that extent only."

"That's reasonable, and good enough," Dangle commented. "Now, if you'll excuse me, I'll go and phone to the others. You will understand," he explained on his return, "that my friends are some distance away from Wembley, and it will therefore take them a little time to get in. If they start now they will be there as soon as we are."

It was getting towards ten o'clock when Cheyne and Dangle turned into the gateway of Earlswood. A yellow car stood at the footpath, at sight of which Dangle exclaimed: "See, they've arrived." His ring brought Blessington to the door, and the latter greeted Cheyne apologetically, but with the same charm of manner that he had displayed in the Edgecombe Hotel at Plymouth.

"I do hope, Mr. Cheyne," he declared, "that even after all that has passed, we may yet be friends. We admire the way you have fought your corner, and we feel that what we both up to the present have failed to do may well be accomplished if we unite our forces. Come in and see if you can make friends with Sime."

"I came to see Miss Merrill," Cheyne answered shortly. "If Miss Merrill is not produced and allowed to go without restraint our agreement is *non est*."

"Naturally," Blessington returned smoothly. "We understand that that is a *sine qua non*. And so Miss Merrill will be produced. She is not here; she is at our house in the country in charge of Miss Dangle, and that for two reasons. The first is this. She met with, as doubtless you know, a trifling accident last night, and her ankle being a little painful, she was kept awake for some time. This morning when we left she was still asleep. We did not therefore disturb her. That you will appreciate, Mr. Cheyne, and the other reason you will appreciate equally. We had to satisfy ourselves by a personal interview that you really meant to give us a square deal." He raised his hand as Cheyne would have spoken. "There's nothing in that to which you need take exception. It is an ordinary business precaution—nothing more or less."

"And when will Miss Merrill be set at liberty?"

"While I don't admit the justice of the phrase, I may say that as soon as we have all mutually pledged ourselves to play the game I will take the car back to the other house, and when Miss Merrill has taken the same oath will drive her to her studio. Perhaps you would write her a note that you have sworn it, as she mightn't believe me. There are a few preliminaries to be arranged with Dangle and Sime can fix up with you. If you are at the studio at midday you will be in time to welcome Miss Merrill."

This did not meet with Cheyne's approval. He wished to go himself to the mysterious house with Blessington, but the latter politely but firmly conveyed to him that he had not yet irrevocably committed himself on their side, and until he had done so they could not give away their best chance of escape should the police become interested in their movements. Cheyne argued with some bitterness, but the other side held the trumps, and he was obliged to give way.

This point settled, nothing could have exceeded the easy friendliness of the trio. If Arnold Price were alive he would share equally with the rest. Would Mr. Cheyne come to the study while the formalities were got through? Did he consider this oath—typewritten—would meet the case? Well, they would take it first, binding themselves individually to each other and to him. Each of the three swore loyalty to the remaining quintet, the oaths of Joan Merrill and Susan being assumed for the moment. Then Cheyne swore and they all solemnly shook hands.

"Now that's done, Mr. Cheyne, we'll prove our confidence in you by showing you the cipher. But first perhaps you would write to Miss Merrill. Also if any point is not quite clear to you please do not hesitate to question us."

Cheyne was by no means enamored of the way things had turned out. He had been forced into an association with men with whom he had little in common and whom he did not trust. Had it not been for the trump card they held in the person of Joan Merrill nothing would have induced him to throw in his lot with them. But now, contingent on their good faith to him, he had pledged his word, and though he was not sure how far an enforced pledge was binding, he felt that as long as they kept their part of the bargain, he must keep his. He therefore wrote his letter, and then turning to Blessington, answered him civilly:

"There is one thing I should like to know; I have thought about it many times. How did you drug me in that hotel in Plymouth without my knowledge and without leaving any traces in the food?"

Blessington smiled.

"I'll tell you that with pleasure, Mr. Cheyne," he answered readily, "but I confess I am surprised that a man of your acumen was puzzled by it. It depended upon prearrangement, and given that, was perfectly simple. I provided myself with the drug—if you don't mind I won't say how, as I might get someone else into trouble—but I got a small phial of it. I also took two other small bottles, one full of clean water, the other empty, together with a small cloth. Also I took my Extra Special Flask. Sime, like a good fellow, get my flask out of the drawer of my wrecked escritoire." He smiled ruefully at Cheyne. "Then I prepared for our lunch: the private room, the menu and all complete. I told them at the hotel we had some business to arrange, and that we didn't want to be disturbed after lunch. You know, of course, that I got all details of your movements from Miss Dangle?"

"Yes, I understand that."

As Cheyne spoke Sime re-entered the room, putting down on the table the flask which had figured in the scene at the hotel. Blessington handed it to Cheyne.

"Examine that flask, Mr. Cheyne," he invited. "Do you see anything remarkable about it?"

It seemed an ordinary silver pocket flask, square and flat, and with a screw-down silver stopper. It was chased on both sides with a plain but rather pleasing design, and the base was flat so that it would stand securely. But Cheyne could see nothing about it in any way unusual.

"Open it," Blessington suggested.

Cheyne unscrewed the stopper and looked down the neck, but except that there was a curious projection at one side, which reduced the passage down to half the usual size, it seemed as other flasks. Blessington laughed.

"Look here," he said, and seizing a scrap of paper, he drew the two sketches which I reproduce. "The flask is divided down the middle by a diaphragm C, so as to form

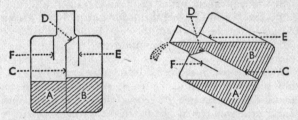

two chambers, A and B. In these chambers are put two liquids, of which one is drugged and the other isn't. E and F are two half diaphragms, and D is a very light and delicately fitted flap valve which will close the passage to either chamber. When you invert the flask, the liquid in the upper or B chamber runs out along diaphragm C, and its weight turns over valve D so that the passage to A chamber is closed. The liquid from B then pours out in the ordinary way. The liquid in A, however, cannot escape, because it is caught by the diaphragm F. If you want to pour out the liquid from A you simply turn the flask upside down, when the conditions as to the two liquids are reversed. You probably didn't notice that I used the flask in this way at our lunch. You may remember that I poured out your liqueur first—it was drugged, of course. Then I got a convenient fit of coughing. That gave me an excuse to set down the flask and pick it up again, but when I picked it up I was careful to do so by the other side, so that undrugged liqueur poured into my own cup. I drank my coffee at once to reassure you. Simple, wasn't it?"

"More than simple," Cheyne answered with unwilling admiration in his tone. "A dangerous toy, but I admit, deuced ingenious. But I don't follow even yet. That would have left the drugged remains in the cup."

"Quite so, but you have forgotten my other two bottles and my cloth. I poured the dregs from your cup into the empty bottle, washed the cup with water from the other, wiped it with my cloth, poured out another cup of coffee and drank it, leaving harmless grounds for any inquisitive analyst to experiment with."

"By Jove!" said Cheyne, then adding regretfully: "If we had only tried the handle of the cup for fingerprints!"

"I put gloves on after you went over."

Cheyne smiled.

"You deserved to succeed," he admitted ruefully.

"I succeeded in drugging you," Blessington answered, "but I did not succeed in getting what I wanted. Now, Mr. Cheyne, you would like to see the tracing. Show it to him, Dangle, while I go back to the other house for Miss Merrill."

Dangle left the room, returning presently with the blue-gray sheet which had been the pivot upon which all the strange adventures of the little company had turned. Cheyne saw at a glance it was the tracing which he had secured in the upper room in the house in Hopefield Avenue. There in the corners were the holes made by the drawing-pins which had fixed it to the door while it was being photographed. There were the irregularly spaced circles, with their letters and numbers, and there, written clockwise in a large circle, the words: "England expects every man to do his duty." Cheyne gazed at it with interest, while Dangle and Sime sat watching him. What on earth could it mean? He pondered awhile, then turned to his companions.

"Have you not been able to read any of it?" he queried.

Dangle shook his head.

"Not so much as a single word—not a letter even!" he declared. "I tell you, Mr. Cheyne, it's a regular sneezer! I wouldn't like to say how many hours we've spent—all of us—working at it. And I don't think there's a book on ciphers in the whole of London that we haven't read. And not a glimmer of light from any of them! Blessington had a theory that each of these circles was intended to represent one or more atoms, according to the number it contained, and that certain circles could be grouped to make molecules of the various substances that were to be mixed with the copper. I never could quite understand his idea, but in any case all our work hasn't helped us to find them. The truth is that we're stale. We want a fresh brain on it, and particularly a woman's brain. Sometimes a woman's intuition will lead her to a lucky guess. We hope it may in this case."

He paused, then went on again: "Another thing we tried was this. Suppose that by some system of numerical substitution each of these numbers represents a letter. Then groups of these letters together with the letters already in the circles should represent words. Of course it is difficult to group them, though we tried again and again. At first the idea seemed promising, but we could make nothing of it. We couldn't find any system either of substitution or of grouping which would give a glimmering of sense. No, we're up against it and no mistake, and when we think of the issues involved we go nearly mad from exasperation. Take the thing, Mr. Cheyne, and see what you and Miss Merrill can do. That is the original, but I have made a tracing of it, so that we can continue our work simultaneously."

Cheyne felt himself extraordinarily thrilled by this recital, and the more he examined the mysterious markings on the sheet the more interested he grew. He had always had a *penchant* for puzzles, and ciphers appealed to him as being perhaps the most alluring kind of puzzles extant. Particularly did this cipher attract him because of the circumstances under which it had been brought to his notice. He longed to get to grips with it, and he looked forward with keen delight to a long afternoon and evening over it with Joan Merrill, whose interest in it would, he felt sure, be no whit less than his own.

Certainly, he thought, his former enemies had made a good beginning. So far they were playing the game, and he began to wonder if he had not to some extent misjudged them, and if the evil characters given them by the gloomy Speedwell were not tinged by that despondent individual's jaundiced outlook on life in general.

Dangle had left the room, and he now returned with a bottle of whisky and a box of cigars.

"A drink and a cigar to cement our alliance, Mr. Cheyne," he proposed, "and then I think our business will be done."

Cheyne hesitated, while a vision of the private room in the Edgecombe Hotel rose in his memory. Dangle read his thoughts, for he smiled and went on:

"I see you don't quite trust us yet, and I don't know that I can blame you. But we really are all right this time. Examine these tumblers and then pour out the stuff yourself, and we'll drink ours first. We must get you convinced of our goodwill."

Cheyne hesitated, but Dangle insisting, he demonstrated to his satisfaction that his companions drank the same mixture as himself. Then Dangle opened the cigar box.

"These are specially good, though I say it myself. The box was given to Blessington by a rich West Indian planter. We only smoke them on state occasions, such as the present. Won't you take one?"

Cheyne felt it would be churlish to refuse, and soon the three were puffing such tobacco as Cheyne at all events had seldom before smoked. Sime then excused himself, explaining that though business might be neglected it could not be entirely ignored, and Cheyne, thereupon taking the hint, said that he too must be off.

"Tomorrow we shall be kept late in town," Dangle explained, as they stood on the doorstep, "but the next

evening we shall be here. Will you and Miss Merrill come
down and report progress, and let us have a council of
war?"

Cheyne agreed and was turning away, when Dangle
made a sudden gesture.

"By George! I was forgetting," he cried. "Wait a second, Mr. Cheyne."

He disappeared back into the house, returning a
moment later with a small purse, which he handed to
Cheyne.

"Do you happen to know if that is Miss Merrill's?" he
inquired. "It was found beside the chair in which we
placed her last night when we carried her in."

Cheyne recognized the article at once. He had frequently seen Joan use it.

"Yes, it's hers," he answered, to which Dangle replied
asking if he would take it for her.

Cheyne slipped the purse into his pocket, and next
moment he was walking along Dalton Road towards the
station, free, well, and with the tracing in his pocket. Until
that moment, in the inner recesses of his consciousness
doubt of the *bona fides* of the trio had lingered. Until
then the fear that he was to be the victim of some
plausible trick had dwelt in his heart. But now at last he
was convinced. Had the men desired to harm him they
had had a perfect opportunity. He had been for the last
hour entirely in their power. No one knew where he had
gone, and they could with the greatest ease have murdered him, and either hidden his body about the house or
garden or removed it in the car during the night. Yes, this
time he believed their story. It was eminently reasonable,
and as a matter of fact, it had been pretty well proved by
their actions, as well as by the facts that he had learned
at the Admiralty and elsewhere. They were at a standstill
because they couldn't read the cipher, and they really did
want, as they said, the help of his and Joan's fresh brains.
From their point of view they had done a wise thing in
thus approaching him—indeed, a masterly thing. Cheyne

was not conceited and he did not consider his own mental powers phenomenal, but he knew he was good at puzzles, and at the very least, he and Joan were of average intelligence. Moreover, they were the only other persons who knew of the cipher, and it was the soundest strategy to turn their antagonism into cooperation.

He reached North Wembley to find a train about to start for Town, and some half hour later he was walking up the platform at Euston. He looked at his watch. It was barely eleven. An hour would elapse before Joan would reach her rooms, and that meant that he had more than half an hour to while away before going to meet her. It occurred to him that in his excitement he had forgotten to breakfast, and though he was not hungry, he thought another cup of coffee would not be unacceptable. Moreover, he could at the same time have a look over the cipher. He therefore went to the refreshment room, gave his order, and sat down at a table in a secluded corner. Then drawing the mysterious sheet from his pocket, he began to examine it.

As he leaned forward over his coffee he felt Joan's purse in his pocket, and suddenly fearful lest in his eagerness to tell her his experiences he should forget to give it to her, he took it out and laid it on the table, intending to carry it in his hand until he met her. Then he returned to his study of the tracing.

There are those who tell us that in this world there are no trifles: that every event, however unimportant it may appear, is preordained and weighty as every other. On this bright spring morning in the first class refreshment room at Euston, Cheyne was to meet with a demonstration of the truth of this assertion which left him marveling and humbly thankful. For there took place what seemed to be a trifling thing, and yet that trifle proved to be the most important event that had ever taken place, or was to take place, in his life.

When he took his first sip of coffee he found that he had forgotten to put sugar in it, and when he looked at the sugar bowl he saw that by the merest chance it was empty. An empty sugar bowl. A trifle that, if ever there was one! And yet nothing of more supreme moment had ever happened to Cheyne than the finding of that empty bowl on his table at that moment.

The sugar bowl, then, being empty, he picked it up with his free hand and carried it across to the counter to ask the barmaid to fill it. Scarcely had he done so when there came from behind him an appalling explosion. There was a reverberating crash mingled with the tinkle of falling glass, while a sharp blast of air swept past him, laden with the pungent smell of some burned chemical. He wheeled round, the shrill screams of the barmaids in his ears, to see the corner of the room where he had been sitting, in complete wreckage. Through a fog of smoke and dust he saw that his table and chair were nonexistent, neighboring tables and chairs were overturned, the window was gone, hat-racks, pictures, wall advertisements were heaped in broken and torn confusion, while over all was spread a coat of plaster which had been torn from the wall. On the floor lay a man who had been seated at an adjoining table, the only other occupant of that part of the room.

For a moment no one moved, and then there came a rush of feet from without, and a number of persons burst into the room. Porters, ticket collectors, a guard, and several members of the public came crowding in, staring with round eyes and open mouths at the debris. Eager hands helped to raise the prostrate man, who appeared to be more or less seriously injured, while hurried questions were bandied from lip to lip.

It did not need the barmaid's half hysterical cry: "Why, it was your purse; I saw it go," to make clear to Cheyne what had happened, and as he grasped the situation his heart melted within him and a great fear took possession of his mind. Once again these dastardly scoundrels had hoaxed him! Their oaths, their protestations of friendship, their talk of an alliance—all were a sham! They were out to murder him. The purse they had evidently stolen from

Joan, filling it with explosives, with some time agent—probably chemical—to make it go off at the proper moment. They had given it to him under conditions which made it a practical certainty that at that moment it would be in his pocket, when he would be blown to pieces without leaving any clue as to the agency which had wrought his destruction. He suddenly felt sick as he thought of the whole hideous business.

But it was not contemplation of the fate he had so narrowly escaped that sent his heart leaping into his throat in deadly panic. If these unspeakable ruffians had tried to murder him with their hellish explosives, what about Joan Merrill? All the talk about driving her back to her rooms must have been mere eyewash. She must be in deadly peril—if it was not too late: if she was not already—Merciful Heaven, he could not frame the thought!—if she was not already *dead*! He burst into a cold sweat, as the idea burned itself into his consciousness. And then suddenly he knew the reason. He loved her! He loved this girl who had saved his life and who had already proved herself such a splendid comrade and helpmeet. His own life, the wretched secret, the miserable pursuit of wealth, victory over the gang—what were these worth? They were forgotten—they were nothing—they were less than nothing! It was Joan and Joan's safety that filled his mind. "Oh, God," he murmured in an agony, "save her, save her! No matter about anything else, only save her!"

He stood, leaning against the counter, overcome with these thoughts. Then the need for immediate action brought him to his senses. Perhaps it was not too late. Perhaps something might yet be done. Scotland Yard! That was his only hope. Instantly he must go to Scotland Yard and implore the help of the authorities.

He glanced round. Persons in authority were entering and pushing to the front of the now dense crowd. That surely was the stationmaster, and there was a policeman. Cheyne did not want to be detained to answer questions. He slipped rapidly into the throng, and by making way for those behind to press forward, soon found himself on its outskirts. In a few seconds he was on the platform and in a couple of minutes he was in a taxi driving towards Westminster as fast as a promise of double fare could take him.

He raced into the great building on the Embankment and rather incoherently stated his business. He was asked to sit down, and after waiting what seemed to him interminable ages, but what was really something under five minutes, he was told that Inspector French would see him. Would he please come this way.

CHAPTER XIII

Inspector French Takes Charge

CHEYNE was ushered into a small, plainly furnished room, in which at a table-desk was seated a rather stout, clean-shaven man with a cheerful, good humored face and the suggestion of a twinkle about his eye. He stood up as Cheyne entered, looked him over critically with a pair of very keen dark blue eyes, and then smiled.

"Mr. Maxwell Cheyne?" he said genially. "I am Inspector French. You wish to consult us? Now just sit down there and tell me your trouble, and we'll do what we can for you."

His manner was kindly and pleasant and did much to set Cheyne at his ease. The young man had been rather dreading his visit, expecting to be met with the harsh, incredulous, unsympathetic attitude of officialdom. But this inspector, with his easy manners, and his apparently human outlook, was quite different from his anticipation. He felt drawn to him and realized with relief that at least he would get a sympathetic hearing.

"Thank you," he said, trying to speak calmly. "It's very good of you, I'm sure. I'm in great trouble—not about myself, that is, but about my—my friend, a lady, Miss Joan Merrill. I'm afraid she is in terrible danger, if indeed it is not too late."

"Tell me the details." The man was all attention, and his quiet decisive manner induced confidence.

Curbing his impatience, Cheyne related his adventures. In the briefest outline he told of the drugging in the Plymouth hotel, of the burglary at Warren Lodge, of his involuntary trip on the *Enid,* of his journey to London and his adventure in the house in Hopefield Avenue. Then he described Joan Merrill's welcome intervention, his convalescence in the hospital, the compact between himself and Joan, his visit to Speedwell, and his burglary of Earlswood. He recounted Dangle's appearance as an envoy, the meeting with the gang, and the explosion at Euston, and finally voiced the terrible suggestion which this latter contained as to the possible fate of Joan.

Inspector French listened to his recital with an appearance of the keenest interest.

"You have certainly had an unusual experience, Mr. Cheyne," he remarked. "I don't know that I can recall a similar case. Now I think we may take it that Miss Merrill's safety is our first concern. We shall go out to this house, Earlswood, and see if we can learn anything about her there. The other activities of the gang must wait. Excuse me a moment." He gave some orders through his desk telephone, resuming: "I should think the house has probably been vacated: these people would cover their traces until they learned from the papers that you had been killed. However, we'll soon know that. Wait here until I arrange about warrants, and then we'll start."

He disappeared for some minutes, while Cheyne fretted and chafed and tried to control his impatience. Then he returned, and slipping an automatic pistol into his pocket, invited Cheyne to follow him.

He led the way downstairs and out into a courtyard in the great building. Two motorcars were just drawing up at the curb, while at the same moment no less than eight plain clothes men appeared from another door. The party having taken their places, the two vehicles slid out through a covered way into the traffic of the town.

"We shall go round to Chelsea first," French explained, "and make sure there is no news of Miss Merrill."

As they ran quickly through the busy streets, French asked a series of questions on points of Cheyne's statement upon which he desired further information. "If this trip draws blank, as I fear it will," he observed, "I shall want you to tell me your story again, this time with all the detail you can possibly put into it. For the moment there's not time for that."

At Horne Terrace there was no trace or tidings of Joan. It was by this time half past twelve, half an hour after the time at which Blessington had promised she should be there, and Cheyne felt all his forebodings confirmed. But he was not surprised, feeling but the more eager to push on to Wembley.

On the way French made him draw a sketch map of the position of Earlswood, and on nearing his goal he stopped the cars, and calling his men together, explained exactly what was to be done. Then telling Cheyne to sit with the driver and direct him to the front gate, they again mounted and went forward. At a good rate they swung into Dalton Road, and Cheyne pointing the way, his car stopped at the gate, while the other ran on down the cross-road to the lane at the back. The men sprang out, and in less time than it takes to tell, the house was surrounded.

Cheyne followed French as he hurried up to the door and gave a thundering knock. There was no answer, and walking round the house, the two men examined the windows. These being all fastened, French turned his attention to the back door, and after two or three minutes' work with a bunch of skeleton keys the bolt shot back, and followed by Cheyne and two of his men, he entered the house.

A short search revealed the fact that the birds had

flown, hurriedly, it seemed, as everything had been left exactly as during Cheyne's visit. On the table in the sitting room stood the glasses from which they had drunk their whisky, the box of cigars lay open beside them and the chairs were still drawn up to the table. But there was no sign of Sime or Dangle, and a hurried look round revealed no clue to their whereabouts.

"I feared as much," French commented, as he sent a constable to call in the men who were surrounding the house, "but we have still two strings to our bow." He turned to the others, and rapidly gave his orders. "You, Hinckston and Tucker, remain here and arrest any one who enters this house. Simmons, go to Locke Street, off Southampton Row, and find Speedwell, of Horton & Lavender's Detective Agency. You know him, don't you? Well, find him and tell him this affair has developed into attempted murder and abduction, and ask him can he give any information to the Yard. Tell him I'm in charge. The rest of you come with me to—what did Speedwell give you as Sime's address, Mr. Cheyne? . . . All right, I have it here—to 12 Colton Street, Putney. We shall carry out the same plan there, surround the house, and then enter and search it. All got that? Come along, Mr. Cheyne."

They hurried back to the cars and were soon running— somewhat over the legal speed—back to town. French, though he had shown energy enough at Earlswood, was willing to chat now in a pleasant, leisurely way, though he continued to interlard his remarks with questions on the details of Cheyne's story. Then he took over the tracing, and examined it curiously. "I'll have a go at this later," he said, as he put it in his pocket, "but I can scarcely believe they would have given you the genuine article."

Cheyne would have questioned this opinion, reminding his companion he had seen the tracing pinned up to be photographed in the house in Hopefield Avenue, but just then they swung into Colton Street, and the time for conversation had passed. Contrary to his expectation they ran past No. 12 without slackening, turned down the first side street beyond it, and there came to a stand.

"There's the end of the passage behind the house," French pointed when his men had dismounted. "Carter and Jones and Marshall go down there and watch the back. No doubt you counted and know it's the eighth house. You other two men and you, Mr. Cheyne, come with me."

He turned back into Colton Street and with his three followers strode rapidly up to No. 12. It was like its neighbors, a small two-storied single terrace house of old-fashioned design. Indeed the narrow road, with its two grimy rows of almost working-class dwellings, seemed more like one of those terrible streets built in the last century in the slum districts of provincial towns, than a bit of mid-London.

A peremptory knock from French producing no result, he had once more recourse to his skeleton keys. This door was easier to negotiate than the last, and in less than a minute it swung open and the four men entered the house.

On the right of the hall was a tiny sitting room, and there they found the remains of what appeared to have been a hastily prepared meal. Four chairs were drawn up to the small central table, on which were part of a loaf, butter, an empty sardine tin, egg shells, two cups containing tea leaves and two glasses smelling of whisky. French put his hand on the teapot. "Feel that, Mr. Cheyne," he exclaimed. "They can't be far away."

The teapot was warm, and when Cheyne looked into the kitchen adjoining, he found that the kettle on the gas ring was also warm, though the ring itself had grown cold. If the four lunchers were Blessington and Co., as seemed indubitable, they must indeed be close by, and Cheyne grew hot with eager excitement as he thought that French and he might be within reasonable sight of their goal.

Meanwhile French and his men had carried out a rapid search of the house, without result except to prove that once more the birds had flown. But as to the direction which their flight had taken there was no clue.

"I don't expect we'll see them back," French said to Cheyne, "but we must take no chances." He turned to his men. "Jones and Marshall, stay here in the house and arrest any one who enters. You, Carter, make inquiries in these houses to the right, and you, Hobbs, do the same to the left. Come, Mr. Cheyne, you and I will try the other side of the street."

They crossed to the house opposite, and French knocked. The door was opened by a young woman who seemed thrilled by French's statement that he was a police officer making inquiries about the occupiers of No. 12, but who was unable to give him any useful information about them. A man lived there—she believed his name was Sime—but she did not know either himself or anything about him. No, she hadn't seen any recent arrivals or departures. She had been engaged at the back of the house during the whole morning and had not looked out across the street. Yes, she believed Sime lived alone except for an elderly housekeeper. As far as she knew he was quite respectable, at least she had never heard anything against him.

Politely thanking her, French tried the next house. Here he found a small girl who said she had looked out some half an hour previously and had seen a yellow motor standing before No. 12. But she had not seen it arrive or depart, nor anyone get in or out.

French tried five houses without result, but at the sixth he had a stroke of luck.

In this house it appeared that there was a chronic invalid, a sister of the woman who opened the door. This poor creature was confined permanently to bed, and in the hope of relieving the tedium of the days, she had had the bed drawn close to her window, so as to extract what amusement she could from the life of the street. If there had been any unusual happenings in front of No. 12, she would certainly have witnessed them. Yes, the woman was sure her sister would see the visitors.

"Lucky chance, that," French said, as they waited to know if they might go up. "If this woman's eyes and brain are unaffected she'll have become an accurate observer, and we'll probably learn all there is to know."

In a moment the sister appeared beckoning, and going upstairs they found in a small front room a bed drawn up to the window, in which lay a superior looking elderly woman with a pale patient face, lined by suffering, in which shone a pair of large dark intelligent eyes. She was propped up the better to see out, and her face lighted up with interest at her unexpected callers, as she laid down among the books on the coverlet an intricate looking piece of fancy sewing.

Inspector French bowed to her.

"I'd like to say how much I appreciate your kindness in letting us come up, madam," he said with his pleasant kindly smile, "but when you hear that we are trying to find a young lady who we fear has been kidnaped, I am sure you will be glad to help us. The matter is connected with No. 12 opposite. Can you tell me if any persons arrived or left it this morning?"

"Oh, yes, I can," the invalid replied in cultivated tones —a lady born, though fallen on evil days, thought Cheyne —"I like to watch the people passing and I did notice arrivals and departures at No. 12. About, let me see— half past eleven, or perhaps a minute or two later a motor drove up to No. 12, a yellow car, fair size and covered in. Three men got out and went into the house. One was Mr. Sime, who lives there, the others I didn't know. Mr. Sime opened the door with his latch-key. In a couple of minutes one of the strangers came out again, got into the car, and drove off."

"That the car you saw outside Earlswood, Mr. Cheyne?" asked French.

"Certain to be," Cheyne nodded. "It was a yellow covered-in car of medium size, No. XL7305."

"I didn't observe the number," the lady remarked. "The bonnet was facing towards me."

"What was the driver like, madam?" queried Cheyne.

"One of Mr. Sime's companions drove. He was short and rather stout, with a round face, and what, I believe, is called a toothbrush mustache."

"That's Blessington all right. And was the third man of medium height and build, with a clean-shaven, somewhat rugged face?"

"Yes, that exactly describes him."

"And that's Dangle. There's no question about the party, Inspector."

"None. Then, madam, you saw—?"

"That, as I said, was about half-past eleven. About half-past one the man you have called Blessington came back with the car. He got out, left it, and went into the house. In about a quarter of an hour he came out again and started his engine. Then the other two men followed, assisting a young lady who appeared to be very weak and ill. She seemed scarcely able to walk, and they almost carried her. Another girl followed, who drew the door of the house after her."

Cheyne started on hearing these words, and looked with an agonized expression at the Inspector. "What were they like, these women?" he breathed through his dry lips.

But both men knew the answer. The girl assisted out by Sime and Dangle was undoubtedly Joan Merrill, and the other equally certainly was Susan Dangle.

"She was lame—the one you thought ill?" Cheyne persisted. "She had twisted her ankle."

"Perhaps so," the lady returned, "but I do not think so. She seemed to me to step equally well on each foot. It was more as if she was half asleep or very weak. Her head hung forward and she did not seem to notice where she was going."

Cheyne made a gesture of despair.

"Heavens above!" he cried hoarsely. "What have they done to her?"

"Drugged her," French answered succinctly. "But you

should take courage from that, Mr. Cheyne. It looks as if they didn't mean to do her a personal injury. Yes, madam?"

Before the invalid could speak Cheyne went on, a puzzled note in his voice.

"But look here," he said slowly, "I don't understand this. You say that the sick lady was wearing a fur coat?"

"Yes, a musquash fur."

"But—" He looked at French in perplexity. "Miss Merrill has a fur coat like that—I've seen it. But she wasn't wearing it last night. Can it be someone else after all?" His voice took on a dawning eagerness.

French shook his head.

"Don't build too much on that, Mr. Cheyne. They may have lent her a coat."

"Yes, but why should they? She had a coat last night, a perfectly warm coat of brown cloth. She wouldn't want another."

"Perhaps her own got muddy when she fell. We'll have to leave it at that for the moment. We'll consider it later. Let's get on now and hear what this lady can tell us. Yes, madam, if you please?"

"I am afraid there is not much more to be told. All five got into the car and drove off."

"In which direction?"

"Eastwards."

"That is to say, they have just left about half an hour. We were only fifteen minutes behind them, Mr. Cheyne."

He got up to go, but the lady motioned him back to his seat.

"There is one other thing I have just remembered," she said. "It may or may not have something to do with the affair. Last night—it must have been about half-past eleven—I heard a motor in the street. It stopped for about ten minutes, though the engine ran all the time, then went off again. I didn't look out, but now that I come to think about it it sounded as if it might be standing at No.

12. Of course you understand that is only a guess, but motorcars are somewhat rare visitors to this street, and there may have been some connection."

"Extremely probable, I should think, madam," French commented. He rose. "Now we must be off to act on what you have told us. I needn't say that you have placed us very greatly in your debt."

"It was but little I could do," the lady returned. "I do hope you may be able to help that poor girl. I should be so glad to hear that she is all right."

Cheyne was touched by this unexpected sympathy.

"You may count on my letting you know, madam," he said, and then thinking of the terribly monotonous existence led by the poor soul, he went on warmly: "I should like, if I might, to call and tell you all about it, but if I am prevented I shall certainly write. May I know what name to address to?"

"Mrs. Sproule, 17 Colton Street. I should be glad to see you if you are in this district, but I couldn't think of taking you out of your way."

A few moments later French had collected his three remaining men, and was being driven rapidly to the nearest telephone call office. There he rang up the Yard, repeated the descriptions of the car and of each of its occupants, and asked for the police force generally to be advised that they were wanted, particularly the men on duty at railway stations and wharves, not only in London, but in the surrounding country.

"Now we'll have a shot at picking up the trail ourselves," he went on to Cheyne when he had sent his message. He re-entered the car, calling to the driver: "Get back and find the men on point duty round about Colton Street."

Of the four men they interviewed, three had not noticed the yellow car. The fourth, on a beat in the thoroughfare at the eastern end of Colton Street, had seen a car of the size and color in question going eastwards at about the hour the party had left No. 12. There seeming nothing abnormal about the vehicle, he had not specially observed it or noted the number, but he had looked at the driver, and the man he described resembled Blessington.

"That's probably it all right," French commented, "but it doesn't help us a great deal. If they were going to any of the stations or steamers, or to practically anywhere in town, this is the way they would pass. Let us try a step further."

Keeping in the same general direction they searched for other men on point duty, but though after a great deal of running backwards and forwards, they found all in the immediate neighborhood that the car would have been likely to pass, none of them had noticed it.

"We've lost them, I'm afraid," French said at last. "We had better go back to the Yard. As soon as that description gets out we may have news at any minute."

A quarter of an hour later they passed once more through the corridors of the great building which houses the C.I.D., and reached French's room. There sitting waiting for them was the melancholy private detective, Speedwell. He rose as they entered.

"Afternoon, Mr. French. Afternoon, Mr. Cheyne," he said ingratiatingly, rubbing his hands together. "I got your message, Mr. French, and I thought I'd better call round. Of course I'll tell you anything I can to help."

French beamed on him.

"Now that was good of you, Speedwell; very good. I'll not forget it. Did Simmons tell you what had happened?"

"Not in detail—only that Blessington, Sime, and the Dangles were wanted."

"Well, Mr. Cheyne here and Miss Merrill were out there last night," he shook his head reproachfully at Cheyne while a twinkle showed in his eyes, "and your friends got hold of Miss Merrill and we can't find her. Mr. Cheyne they enticed into the house with a fair story. They led him to believe that Miss Merrill would be in her studio when he got back to town and gave him her purse, which they said she had dropped. It contained a time bomb, and only the merest chance saved Mr. Cheyne from being blown to bits. There are charges against the quartet of attempted murder of Mr. Cheyne, and of abduction of Miss Merrill. Can you help us at all?"

Speedwell shook his head.

"I doubt it, Mr. French, I doubt it, sir. I found out a little, not very much. But all the information I have is at your disposal."

Cheyne stared at him.

"But how can that be?" he exclaimed. "You were in their confidence—to some extent at all events. Surely you got some hint of what they were after?"

Speedwell made a deferential movement, and his smile became still more oily and ingratiating.

"Now, Mr. Cheyne, sir, you mustn't think too much of that. That was what we might call in the way of business." He glanced sideways at Cheyne from his little foxy close-set eyes. "You can't complain, sir, but what I answered your questions, and you'll admit you got value for your money."

"I don't understand you," Cheyne returned sharply. "Do you mean that that tale you told me was a lie, and that you weren't employed by these people to find the man who burgled their house?"

Speedwell rubbed his hands together more vigorously.

"A little business expedient, sir, merely an ordinary little business expedient. It would be a foolish man who would not display his wares to the best advantage. I'm sure, sir, you'll agree with that."

Cheyne looked at him fiercely for a moment.

"You infernal rogue!" he burst out hotly. "Then your tale to me was a tissue of lies, and on the strength of it you cheated me out of my money! Now you'll hand that £150 back! Do you hear that?"

Speedwell's smile became the essence of craftiness.

"Not so fast, sir, not so fast," he purred. "There's no need to use unpleasant language. You asked for a thing and agreed to pay a certain price. You got what you asked for, and you paid the price you agreed. There was no cheating there."

Cheyne was about to retort, but French, suave and courteous, broke in:

"Well, we can talk of that afterwards. I think, Mr. Cheyne, that Mr. Speedwell has made us a satisfactory offer. He says he will tell us everything he knows. For my part I am obliged to him for that, as he is not bound to say anything at all. I think you will agree that we ought to thank him for the position he is taking up, and to hear what he has to say. Now, Speedwell, if you are ready. Take a cigar first, and make yourself comfortable."

"Thank you, Mr. French. I am always glad, as you know, sir, to assist the Yard or the police. I haven't much to tell you, but here is the whole of it."

He lit his cigar, settled himself in his chair, and began to speak.

CHAPTER XIV

The Clue of the Clay-marked Shoe

"You know, Mr. French," said Speedwell, "about my being called in by the manager of the Edgecombe in Plymouth when Mr. Cheyne was drugged? Mr. Cheyne has told you about that, sir?" French nodded and the other went on: "Then I need only tell you what Mr. Cheyne presumably does not know. I may just explain before beginning that I came into contact with Mr. Jesse, the manager, over some diamonds which were lost by a visitor to the hotel and which I had the good fortune to recover.

"The first point that struck me about Mr. Cheyne's little affair was, How did the unknown man know Mr. Cheyne was going to lunch at that hotel on that day? I found out from Mr. Cheyne that he hadn't mentioned his visit to Plymouth to anyone outside of his own household, and I found out from Mrs. and Miss Cheyne that they hadn't either. But Miss Cheyne said it had been discussed at lunch, and that gave me the tip. If these statements were all O.K. it followed that the leakage must have been through the servants and I had a chat with both, just to see what they were like. The two were quite different. The cook was good-humored and stupid and easy going, and wouldn't have the sense to run a conspiracy with anyone, but the parlormaid was an able young woman as well up as any I've met. So it looked as if it must be her.

"Then I thought over the burglary, and it seemed to me that the burglars must have got inside help, and if so, there again Susan was the girl. Of course there was the tying up, but that would be the natural way to work a blind. I noticed that the cook's wrists were swollen, but Susan's weren't marked at all, so I questioned the cook, and I got a bit of information out of her that pretty well proved the thing. She said she heard the burglars ring and heard Susan go to the door. But she said it was three or four minutes before Susan screamed. Now if Susan's story was true she would have screamed far sooner than that, for, according to her, the men had only asked could they write a letter when they seized her. So that again looked like Susan. You follow me, sir?"

Again French nodded, while Cheyne broke in: "You never told me anything of that."

Speedwell smiled once more his crafty smile.

"Well, no, Mr. Cheyne, I didn't mention it certainly. It was only a theory, you understand. I thought I'd wait till I was sure.

"Well, gentlemen, there it was. Someone wanted some paper that Mr. Cheyne had—it was almost certainly a paper, as they searched his pocketbook—and Susan was involved. I hung about Warren Lodge, and all the time I was watching Susan. I found she wrote frequent letters and always posted them herself: so that was suspicious too. Then one day when she was out I slipped up to her room and searched around. I found a writing case in her box of much too good a kind for a servant, and a blotting-paper pad with a lot of ink marks. When I put the pad before a mirror I made out an address written several times: 'Mr. J. Dangle, Laurel Lodge, Hopefield Avenue, Hendon.' So that was that."

Speedwell paused and glanced at his auditors in turn, but neither replying, he resumed:

"I generally try to make a friend when I'm on a case: they're useful if you want some special information. So I chummed up with the housemaid at Mrs. Hazelton's—friends of Mr. Cheyne's—live quite close by. I told this girl I was on the burglary job, and that there would be big money in it if the thieves were caught, and that if she helped me she should get her share. I told her I had my suspicions of Susan, said I was going to London, and asked her would she watch Susan and keep me advised of how things went on. She said yes, and I gave her a couple of pounds on account, just to keep her eager, while I came back to town to look after Dangle."

In spite of the keen interest with which he was listening to these revelations, Cheyne felt himself seething with indignant anger. How he had been hoodwinked by this sneaking scoundrel, with his mean ingratiating smile and his assumption of melancholy! He could have kicked himself as he remembered how he had tried to cheer and encourage the mock pessimist. He wondered which was the more hateful, the man's deceit or the cynical way he was now telling of it. But, apparently unconscious of the antagonism which he had aroused, Speedwell calmly and, Cheyne thought disgustedly, a trifle proudly, continued his narrative.

"I soon found that James Dangle lived at Laurel Lodge. He was alone except for a daily char, but up till a short while earlier his sister had kept house for him. When I learned that his sister had left Laurel Lodge on the same day that Susan took up her place at Warren Lodge, I soon guessed who Susan really was.

"I thought that when these two would go to so much trouble, the thing they were after must be pretty well worth while, and I thought it might pay me if I could find out what it was. So I shadowed Dangle, and learned a good deal about him. I learned that he was constantly meeting two other men, so I shadowed them and learned they were Blessington and Sime. Blessington I guessed first time I saw him was the man who had drugged you, Mr. Cheyne, for he exactly covered your and the manager's descriptions. It seemed clear then that these three and Susan Dangle—if her real name was Susan—were in the conspiracy to get whatever you had."

"But what I would like to have explained," Cheyne burst in, "was why you didn't tell me what you had discovered. You were paid to do it. What did you think you were taking that hotel manager's money for?"

Speedwell made a gesture of deferential disagreement.

"I scarcely think that you can find fault with me there, Mr. Cheyne," he answered with his ingratiating smile. "I was investigating: I had not reached the end of my investigation. As you will see, sir, my investigation took a somewhat unexpected turn—a very unexpected turn, I might almost say, which left me in a bit of doubt as to how to act. But you'll hear."

Inspector French had been sitting quite still at his desk, but now he stretched out his hand, took a cigar from the box, and as he lit it, murmured: "Go on, Speedwell. Sounds like a novel. I'm enjoying it. Aren't you, Mr. Cheyne?"

Cheyne made noncommittal noises, and Speedwell, looking pleased, continued:

"One evening, nearly two months ago, I got back late from another job and I found a wire waiting for me. It was from Mrs. Hazelton's housemaid and it said: 'Maxwell Cheyne disappeared and Susan left Warren Lodge for London.' I thought to myself: 'Bully for you, Jane,' and then I thought: 'Susan will be turning to Brother James. I'll go out to Hopefield Avenue and see if I can pick anything up.' So I went out. It was about half-past ten when I arrived. I found the front of the house in darkness, but an upper window at the back was lighted up. There was a lane along behind the houses, you understand, Mr. French, and a bit of garden between them and the lane. The gate into the garden was open, and I slipped in and began to tiptoe towards the house. Then I heard soft steps coming in after me, and I turned aside and hid behind a large shrub to see what would happen. And then I saw something that interested me very much. A man came in very quietly and I saw in the faint moonlight that he was carrying a ladder." There was an exclamation from Cheyne. "He put the ladder to the lighted window and climbed up, and then I saw who it was. I needn't tell you, Mr. Cheyne, I was surprised to see you, and I waited behind the bush for what would happen. I saw and heard the whole thing: the party coming down to supper, your getting in, Sime coming out and seeing the ladder, the alarm, your coming out, and them getting you on the head in the garden. You'll perhaps think, Mr. Cheyne, that I should have come out and lent you a hand, but after all, sir, I don't know that you could claim that you had the right of it altogether, and besides, it all happened so quickly I had no chance to interfere. Well, anyhow they knocked you out and then they searched you and took a folded paper from your pocket. 'Thank goodness, we've got the tracing at all events,' Dangle said, speaking very softly, 'but now we're in the soup and no mistake. What are we going to do with the confounded fool's body?' They examined the ladder and saw from the contractor's name that it had been brought from the new house, then they whispered together and I couldn't hear what was said, but at last Sime said: 'Right, we'll fix it so that it will look as if he fell off the ladder.' Then the three men picked you up, Mr. Cheyne, and carried you out down the lane. Susan stood in the garden waiting, and I had to sit tight behind the bush. In about ten minutes the men came back and then Sime took the ladder and carried it away down the lane. The others whispered together and then Dangle said something to Susan, ending up: 'It's in the second left hand drawer.' She went indoors, but came out again in a moment with a powerful electric torch. Blessington and Dangle then searched for traces of your little affair, Mr. Cheyne. They found the marks of the ladder butts in the soft grass and smoothed them out, and they looked everywhere, I suppose, for footprints or something that you might have dropped when you fell. Then Sime came back and they all went in and shut the door."

Cheyne snorted angrily.

"It didn't occur to you, I suppose, to make any effort to help me or even find out if I was alive or dead? You weren't going to have any trouble, even if you did become an accessory after the fact?"

"I'm coming to that, Mr. Cheyne. All in good time, sir." Speedwell rubbed his hands unctuously. "You will understand that as long as the garden was occupied I couldn't come out from behind the bush. But directly the coast was clear I got out of the garden and turned along the lane where they had carried you. I wondered where they could have hidden you, and I started searching. I remembered what Sime had said about the ladder, so I went to the half-built house and had a look around, but I couldn't find you in it. Then I saw you lying back of the road fence, but just at that minute I heard footsteps, and I stopped behind a pile of bricks till the party would pass. But you called out and the lady stopped, and once again I couldn't interfere. I heard the arrangements about the taxi, and when the lady went away to get it I slipped out and hid where I could see it. In that way I got its number. Next day I saw the driver and got out of him where he had taken you, and I kept my eye on you and when you got better trailed you to Miss Merrill's. From other people living in the flats I found out about her." After a pause he concluded: "And I think, gentlemen, that's about all I have to tell you."

Inspector French slowly expelled a cloud of gray cigar smoke from his mouth.

"Really, Speedwell, you have surpassed yourself," he murmured. "Your story, as I told you, sounds like a novel. A pity though, that having gone so far you did not go a little farther. You did not find out, for example, what business this mysterious quartet were plotting?"

"I did not, Mr. French," the man returned earnestly. "I gathered that it was connected with 'the tracing' that Dangle spoke of, and I imagined the tracing was what they had been wanting from Mr. Cheyne, and evidently had got, but I didn't get a sight of it, and I have no idea of their game."

"And did you find out nothing that might be a help? Where did those three men spend their time? What did they do in the daytime?"

"Just what I told Mr. Cheyne, sir. I gave him perfectly correct information in everything. Dangle is a town sharp and helps run a gambling room in Knightsbridge. Sime is another of the same—collects pigeons in the night clubs for the others to pluck. Blessington, I got the hint, lived by blackmail, but I've no proof of this."

"Anything else?"

"No, Mr. French, not that I know. Unless"—he hesitated—"unless one thing. It may or may not be important; I don't know. It's this: Dangle, during these last three or four weeks, he's been away nearly half the time from London—on the Continent. I don't know to what country, but it must be France or Belgium or Holland, I should think—or maybe Ireland—because he has crossed over one night and crossed back the next. I know that because of a remark I overheard him make to Sime in a tube lift where I was standing just behind him. It was a Wednesday and he said: 'I'm crossing tonight, but I'll be back on Friday morning.'"

This seemed to be the sum total of Speedwell's

knowledge, or at least all he would divulge, and he presently departed, apparently cheered by French's somewhat
cryptic declaration that he would not forget the part the
other had played in the affair. He perhaps would not have
been so pleased had he heard French's subsequent com-
ments to Cheyne. "A dangerous man, Mr. Cheyne, for an
amateur to deal with, though he's too much afraid of the
Yard to try any monkeying with me. I may tell you in
confidence that he was dismissed from the force on suspicion of taking bribes to let a burglar get away—I
needn't say the thing couldn't be proved, or he would have
seen the inside of a convict prison, but there was no doubt
at all that he was guilty. Since that he has been caught
sailing rather close to the wind, but again he just managed to keep himself safe. But the result is, he would do
anything to curry favor here, and indeed once or twice he
has been quite useful. I shouldn't be at all surprised if he
had been blackmailing Blessington & Co. in connection
with your attempted murder."

"Ugh!" Cheyne made a gesture of disgust. "The very
sight of the man makes me sick." Then, his look of anxious
eagerness returning, he went on: "But, Inspector, his
story is all very well and interesting and all that, but I
don't see that it helps us to find Miss Merrill, and that is
the only thing that matters."

"The only thing to you, perhaps," French returned,
"but not the only thing to me. This whole business looks
uncommonly like conspiracy for criminal purposes, and if
so, it automatically concerns the Yard." He glanced at the
clock on the wall before his desk. "Let's see now, it's just
five o'clock. Before giving up for the day I should like to
have a look over Miss Merrill's room to settle that little
question of the fur coat, and I should like you to come
with me. Shall we go now?"

Cheyne sprang to his feet eagerly. Action was what he
wanted, and his heart beat more rapidly at the prospect of
visiting a place where every object would remind him of

the girl he loved, and whom, in spite of himself, he feared he had lost. Impatiently he waited while French put on his hat and left word where he could be found in case of need.

Some fifteen minutes later the two men were ascending the stairs of the house in Horne Terrace. The door of No. 12 was shut, and to Cheyne's knock there was no response.

"I'm afraid you needn't expect Miss Merrill to have got back," French commented. "I had better open the door."

He worked at it for a few moments, first with his bunch of skeleton keys, then with a bent wire, until the bolt shot back, and pushing open the door, they entered the room.

It was just as Cheyne had last seen it except that the kettle and tea equipage had been tidied away. French stood in the middle of the floor, glancing keenly round on the contents. Then he moved to the other door.

"This her bedroom?" he inquired, as he pushed it open and looked in.

As Cheyne followed him into the tiny apartment, he felt as a devout Mohammedan might, who through stress of circumstances entered fully shod into one of the holy places of his religion. It seemed nothing short of profanation for himself and this commonplace inspector of police to intrude into a place so hallowed by association with Her. In a kind of reverent awe he looked about him. There was the bed in which She slept, the table at which She dressed, the wardrobe in which Her dresses hung, and there—what were those? He stood, stricken motionless by surprise, staring at a tiny pair of rather high-heeled brown shoes which were lying on their sides on the floor in front of a chair.

French noted his expression.

"What is it?" he queried, following the direction of the other's eyes.

"Her shoes!" Cheyne said in a tone of wonder, as he might have said: "Her diamond coronet."

French frowned.

"Well, what's wonderful about that?" he asked with the nearest approach to sharpness in his tone that Cheyne had yet heard.

"Her shoes," Cheyne repeated. "Her shoes that she wore last night."

It was now French's turn to look interested.

"Sure of that?" he asked, picking up the shoes.

"Certain. I saw them on her in the train to Wembley. Unless she has two absolutely identical pairs, she was wearing those."

French had been turning the shoes over in his hand.

"You said you saw a mark of where someone had slipped on the bank behind the wall you threw the tracing over," he went on. "You might describe that mark."

"It was just a kind of scrape on the sloping ground, with the footprint below it. Her foot had evidently slipped down till it came to a firmer place."

"Right foot or left?"

"Right."

"And which way was the toe pointing: towards the bank or parallel with it?"

"Parallel. She had evidently climbed up diagonally."

"Quite so. Now another question. If you were standing in the field looking towards the bank, did she climb towards the right hand or the left?"

"The left."

"And the soil where the mark was; you might describe that."

"It was rather light in color, a yellowish brown. It was clayey, and the print showed clearly, as it would in stiff putty."

French nodded.

"Then, Mr. Cheyne, if all your data are right, and if the footprint was made by Miss Merrill when she was wearing these shoes, I should expect to find a mark of yellowish clay on the outside of the right shoe. Isn't that correct?"

Cheyne thought for a moment, then signified his assent.

"I turn up this shoe," French continued, suiting the

action to the word, "and I find here the very mark I was expecting. See for yourself. I think we may take it then, not only that Miss Merrill made the mark on the bank, and of course made it last night, but also that she was wearing these shoes when she made it. And that would coincide with your observation."

"But," cried Cheyne, "I don't understand. How did the shoes get here? Miss Merrill wasn't here since we left to go to Wembley."

"How do you know?"

"Well, there's what Dangle said. I don't mean of course that I believe Dangle. Everything else he's said to me has turned out to be a lie. But in this case the circumstances seem to prove this story. If he didn't see Miss Merrill how did he know of her getting over the wall for the tracing? And if he didn't capture her then why did she not return here? Or rather, suppose she did return, why should she go away again without leaving a note or sending me a message?"

French shook his head.

"I don't know," he answered. "I merely asked the question and your answer certainly seems sound. But now let us look about the coat." He opened the wardrobe door. "Is the cloth coat she was wearing last night here?"

A glance showed Cheyne the brown cloth, fur-trimmed coat Joan had worn on the previous evening.

"And you will see further," went on French when he had been satisfied on this point, "that there is no coat here of musquash fur. You say she had one?"

"Yes. I have seen her wearing it several times."

"Then I think Mrs. Sproule saw her wearing it today. We may take it, I think, either that she returned here last night and changed her clothes, or else that someone brought in her coat and shoes, left them here and took out her others."

"The latter, I should think," Cheyne declared.

"Why?"

"Because I don't think she would come here of her own

free will and leave again without sending me some message."

French did not reply. He had rather taken the view that if the girl was the prisoner of the gang the garments would not have been changed, and the more he thought over it the more probable this seemed. Rather he was inclined to believe that she had reached her rooms after the episode at Earlswood, possibly even with the tracing; that she had been followed there and by some trick induced to leave again, when in all probability she had been kidnaped and the tracing recovered by the gang. But he felt there was no use in discussing this theory with Cheyne, whose anxiety as to the girl's welfare had rendered his critical faculty almost useless. He turned back to the young man.

"I have no doubt that that shoe of Miss Merrill's made the mark you saw," he observed. "At the same time I want definite evidence. It won't take very long to run out to Wembley and try. Let us go now, and that will finish us for tonight."

They took a taxi and were soon at the place in question. The print was not so clear as when Cheyne had seen it first, but in spite of this French had no difficulty in satisfying himself. The shoe fitted it exactly.

That night after supper, as French stretched himself in his easy-chair, he decided he would have a preliminary look at the tracing. He recognized that the mere fact that it had been handed to Cheyne by Dangle involved the probability that it was not the genuine document but a faked copy. At the same time he was bound to make what he could of it, and it was with very keen interest he unfolded and began to study it.

It was neatly drawn, though evidently not by a professional draughtsman. The lettering of the words, "England expects every man to do his duty" was amateurish. He wondered what the phrase could mean. It did not seem to ring quite true. In his mind the words ran "England expects that every man this day will do his duty," but he rather thought this was the version in the song, and if so, the wording might have been altered from the original for metrical reasons. He determined to look up the quotation on the first opportunity. On the other hand it might have been condensed into eight words in order to fit round the sheet. It was spaced in a large circle among the smaller circles like the figures of a clock. It conveyed to him no idea whatever, except the obvious suggestion of Nelson. Could Nelson, he wondered, or Trafalgar, be the key word in some form of cipher?

As he studied the sheet he noted some points which Cheyne appeared to have missed, or which at all events he had not mentioned. While the circles were spaced without any apparent plan—absolutely irregularly, it seemed to French—there was some evidence of arrangement in their contents. Those nearer the edges of the tracing contained letters, while those more centrally situated bore numbers. There was no hard and fast line between the two, as letters and numbers appeared, so to speak, to overlap each other's territory, but broadly speaking the arrangement held. He noticed also a few circles which contained neither numbers nor letters, but instead tiny irregular lines. There were only some half dozen of these, but all of them so far as he could see occurred on the neutral territory between the number zone and the letter zone. These irregular lines represented nothing that he could imagine, and no two appeared of the same shape.

That the document was a cipher he could not but conclude, and in vain he puzzled over it until long past his usual bedtime. Finally, locking it away in his desk, he decided that when he had completed the obvious investigations which still remained, he would have another go at it, working through all the possibilities that occurred to him systematically and thoroughly.

But before French had another opportunity to examine it, further news had come in which had led him a dance of several hundred miles, and left him hot on the track of the conspirators.

CHAPTER XV

The Torn Hotel Bill

ON reaching the Yard next morning Inspector French began his day by compiling a list of the various points on which obvious investigations still remained to be made. He had already determined that these should be carried through with the greatest possible dispatch, leaving a general consideration of the case over until their results should be available.

The immediate questions were, of course: Was Joan Merrill alive? And if so, where was she? These must be solved as soon as possible. The further matters relating to the hiding-place and aims of the gang could wait. It was, however, likely enough that if French could find Joan, he would have at least gone a long way towards solving her captors' secret.

Perhaps the most promising of all the lines of inquiry open to him were the detailed searches of Blessington's and Sime's houses, and he decided he would begin with these. Accordingly, having called Sergeant Carter and a couple more men, he went out to Earlswood and set to work.

French was extraordinarily thorough. Nothing in that house, from the water cistern space in the roof to the floors of the pantries and the tool shed in the yard—nothing escaped observation. The furniture was examined, particularly the writing desk and the old escritoire, the carpets were lifted and the floors tested, the walls were minutely inspected for secret receptacles, the pages of the books were turned over, the clothes—of which a respectable wardrobe remained—were gone through, with special attention to the pockets. Nothing was taken for granted: everything was examined. Even the outside of the house and the soil of the garden were looked at, and at the end, some four hours after they had begun, French had to admit that his gains were practically nil.

The reservation was in respect of four objects, from one or more of which he might conceivably extract some information, though he was far from hopeful. The first was the top sheet of Blessington's writing pad. French, following his usual custom, had examined it through a mirror, but so completely covered was it with inkstains that he was unable to decipher even a single word. However, on chance he tore it off and put it in his pocket, in the hope that a future more detailed examination might reveal something of interest.

The second object was a scrap of crumpled paper which he found in the right-hand upper pocket of one of Dangle's waistcoats. It looked as if it had been crushed to the bottom of the pocket by some other article—such as an engagement book—being thrust down on the top of it. When the pockets had been cleared—as all had been—this small piece of paper had evidently been overlooked.

French straightened it out. It was the bottom portion of what was clearly a bill, apparently a French hotel bill. On the back was a note written in pencil, and as French read it, the thought passed through his mind that he could not have imagined any more unexpected or puzzling contents. It was in the form of a memorandum and read:

> . . . . . . ins.
> . . . . ators.
> Peaches—3 doz. tins.
> Safety Matches—6 doz. boxes.
> Galsworthy—The Forsyte Saga.
> Pencils and Fountain Pen Ink.
> Sou'wester.

The paper was torn across the first two items, so that only part of the words were legible. What so heterogeneous a collection could possibly refer to French could not imagine, but he put the fragment in his pocket with the blotting paper for future study.

The other two objects were photographs, and from the descriptions he had received from Cheyne he felt satisfied that one was of Blessington and the other of Dangle. These were of no help in themselves, but might later prove useful for identification purposes.

The search of Earlswood complete, French gave his men an hour for lunch, and then started a similar investigation of Sime's house. He was just as painstaking and thorough here, but this time he had no luck at all. Though Sime had not so carefully destroyed papers and correspondence, he could not find a single thing which seemed to offer help.

Sime's house being so much smaller than Blessington's, the search was finished in little over an hour. On its completion French sent two of his men back to the Yard, while with Sergeant Carter he drove to Horne Terrace. There he examined Joan Merrill's rooms, again without result.

The work ended about four, and then he and Carter began another job, quite as detailed and a good deal more wearisome than the others. He had determined to question individually every other person living in the house—that is, the inhabitants of no less than nine flats—in the hope that some one of them might have seen or heard Joan returning to her rooms on the night of her disappearance. In a way the point was not of supreme importance, but experience had taught French the danger of neglecting *any* clue, no matter how unpromising, and he had long since made it a principle to follow up every opening which offered.

For over two hours he worked, and at last, as he was beginning to accept defeat, he obtained just the information he required.

It appeared that about a quarter past eleven on the night in question, the fifteen-year-old daughter of a widow living on the third floor was returning home from some small jollification when she saw, just as she approached the door, three persons come out. Two were men, one tall, well built and clean-shaven, the other short and stout, with a fair toothbrush mustache. The third person was Miss Merrill. A street lamp had shone directly on their faces as they emerged, and the girl had noticed that the men wore serious expressions and that Miss Merrill looked pale and anxious, as if all three were sharers in some bad news. They crossed the sidewalk to a waiting motor. Miss Merrill and the taller man got inside, the second man driving. During the time the girl saw them, none of them spoke. She remembered the car. It was a yellow one with a coach body, and looked a private vehicle. Yes, she recognized the photograph the Inspector showed her—Blessington's. It was that of the driver of the car.

It did not seem worth while to French to try to trace the car, as he fancied he knew where it had gone. From Horne Terrace to Sime's house in Colton Street was about a ten minute run. Therefore if it left the former about 11:15, it should reach the latter a minute or two before the half-hour. This worked in with the time at which the invalid lady, Mrs. Sproule, had heard the motor stop in the street, and to French it seemed clear that Miss Merrill had been taken direct to Sime's, and kept there until 1:45 P.M. on the following day. What arguments or threats the pair had used to get her to accompany them French could not tell, but he shrewdly suspected that they had played the same trick on her as on Cheyne. In all probability they had told her that Cheyne had met with an accident and was conscious and asking for her. Once in the cab it would have been child's play for a powerful man like Sime to have chloroformed her, and having got her to the house, they could easily have kept her helpless and semi-conscious by means of drugs.

French returned on foot to the Yard, thinking over the affair as he walked. It certainly had a sinister look. These men were very much in earnest. They had not hesitated to resort to murder in the case of Cheyne—it was through, to them, an absolutely unforeseen accident that he escaped —and French felt he would not give much for Joan Merrill's chances.

When he reached his office he found that a piece of news had just come in. A constable who had been on point duty at the intersection of South and Mitchem

Streets, near Waterloo Station, had noticed about 2 P.M. on the day of the disappearance of the gang, a yellow motorcar pass close beside him and turn into Hackworth's garage, a small establishment in the latter street. Though he had not observed the vehicle with more than the ordinary attention such a man will give to the passing traffic, his recollection both of the car and driver led him to the belief that they were those referred to in the Yard circular. The constable was waiting to see French, and made his report with diffidence, saying that though he thought he was right, he might easily be mistaken.

"Quite right to let me know anyhow, Wilson," French said heartily. "If you've seen Blessington's car it may give us a valuable clue, and if you're mistaken, there's no harm done. We've nothing to lose by following it up." He glanced at his watch. "It's past my dinner hour, but I'll take a taxi and go round to this garage on my way home. You'd better come along."

Ten minutes later the two men reached Hackworth's establishment, and pushing open the door of the tiny office, asked if the manager was about.

"I'm John Hackworth. Yes, sir?" said a stout man in shabby gray tweeds. "Want a car?"

"I want a word with you, Mr. Hackworth," said French pleasantly. "Just a small matter of private business."

Hackworth nodded, and indicated a farther door.

"In here," he invited, and when French and the constable had taken the two chairs the room contained, he briskly repeated: "Yes, sir?"

At this hint not to waste valuable time, French promptly introduced himself and propounded his question. Mr. Hackworth looked impressed.

"You don't tell me that gent was a wrong 'un?" he said anxiously, then another idea seeming to strike him, he continued: "Of course it don't matter to me in a way, for I've got the car. I'll tell you about it."

French produced his photograph of Blessington.

"Tell me first if that's the man," he suggested.

Mr. Hackworth pushed the card up to the electric bulb. "It's him," he declared. "It's him and no mistake. He walked in here yesterday—no, the day before—about eleven and asked to see the boss. 'I've got a car,' he said when I went forward, 'and there's something wrong with the engine. Sometimes it goes all right and sometimes it doesn't. Maybe,' he said, 'you'll start it up and it'll run a mile or two well enough, then it begins to miss, and the speed drops perhaps to eight or ten miles. I don't know what's wrong.'

"What about your petrol feed?" I said. "Sounds like your carburetor, or maybe your strainer or one of your pipes choked."

" 'I thought it might be that,' he said, 'but I couldn't find anything wrong. However, I want you to look over it, that is, if you can lend me a car while you're doing it.'

"Well, sir, I needn't go into all the details, and to make a long story short, I agreed to overhaul the car and to lend him an old Napier while I was at it. He went away, and same day about two or before it he came back with his car, a yellow Armstrong Siddeley. It seemed to be all right then, but he said that that was just the trouble—it might be all right now and it would be all wrong within a minute's time. So I gave him the Napier—it was a done machine, worth very little, but would go all right, you understand. He asked me how long I would take, and I said I'd have it for him next day, that was yesterday. He had three or four suitcases with him and he transferred these across. Then he got into the Napier and drove away, and that was the last I saw of him."

"And what was wrong with his own car?"

"There, sir, you have me beat. Nothing! Or nothing anyhow that I could find."

"Was the Napier a four-seater?"

"Five. Three behind and two in front."

"A coach body?"

"No, but with a good canvas cover, and he put it up, too, before starting."

"Raining?"

"Neither raining nor like rain: nor no wind neither."

"How long was he here altogether?"

"Not more than five or six minutes. He left just as soon as he could change the cars."

French, having put a few more questions, got the proprietor to write out a detailed description of the Napier. Next, he begged the use of the garage telephone and repeated the description to the Yard, asking that it should be circulated among the force without delay. Finally he thanked the stout Mr. Hackworth for his help, and with Constable Wilson left the establishment.

"Now, Wilson," he said, "you've done a good day's work. I'm pleased with you. You may get along home, and if I want anything more I'll let you know in the morning."

But though it was so late, French did not follow his subordinate's example. Instead he stood on the sidewalk outside the garage, thinking hard.

As to the nature of the defect in the engine of the yellow car he had no doubt. What was wrong with it was just what Hackworth had said was wrong with it—nothing whatever. French could see that the whole episode was simply a plan on Blessington's part to change the car and thus cover up his traces. The yellow Armstrong-Siddeley was known to be his by many persons, and Blessington wanted one which, as he would believe, could not be traced. He would have seen from the papers that Cheyne had escaped the fate prepared for him, and he would certainly suspect that the outraged young man would put his knowledge at the disposal of the police. Therefore the yellow car was a danger and another must be procured in its place. The trick was obvious, and French had heard of something like it before.

But though the main part of the scheme was clear to French, the details were not. From the statement of Mrs. Sproule, the invalid of Colton Street, the yellow car had left Sime's house at about 1:45. According to this Hackworth it had reached the garage at a minute or so before two. Now, from Colton Street to the garage was a ten or twelve minutes' drive, therefore Blessington must have gone practically direct. Moreover, when he left Colton Street Joan Merrill and the other members of the gang were in the car, but when he reached the garage he was alone. Where had the others dismounted?

Another question suggested itself to French, and he thought that if he could answer it he would probably be able to answer the first as well. Why did Blessington select this particular garage? He did not know this Hackworth—the man had said he had never seen Blessington before. Why then this particular establishment rather than one of the scores nearer Sime's dwelling?

For some minutes French puzzled over this point, and then a probable explanation struck him. There, just a hundred yards or more away, was a place admirably suited for dropping his passengers and picking them up again—Waterloo Station. What more natural for Blessington than to pull up at the departure side with the yellow Armstrong-Siddeley and set them down? What more commonplace for him than to pick them up at the arrival side with the black Napier? While he was changing the cars, they could enter, mingle with the crowds of passengers, work their way across the station and be waiting for him as if they had just arrived by train.

Late as it was, French returned to the Yard and put a good man on to make inquiries at Waterloo in the hope of proving his theory. Then, tired and very hungry, he went home.

But when he had finished supper and, ensconced in his armchair with a cigar, had looked through the evening paper, interest in the case reasserted itself, and he determined that he would have a look at the scrap of paper which he had found in the pocket of one of Dangle's waistcoats.

As has been said, it was a list or memorandum of certain articles, written on the back of part of an old hotel bill. French reread the items with something as nearly

approaching bewilderment as a staid inspector of the Yard
can properly admit. Peaches, safety matches, the Forsyte
Saga, pencil, fountain pen ink, and a sou'wester! What in
the name of goodness could anyone want with such a
heterogeneous collection? And the quantities! Three dozen
tins of peaches, and six dozen boxes of matches! Enough
to do a small expeditionary force, French thought whimsically, though he did not see an expeditionary force
requiring the works of John Galsworthy, ink, and pencils.

And yet was this idea so absurd? Did not these articles,
in point of fact, suggest an expedition? Peaches, matches,
pencils, and ink—all these articles were commonplace and
universally obtainable. Did the fact that a quantity were
required not mean that Dangle or his friends were to be
cut off for some considerable time from the ordinary
sources of supply? It certainly looked like it. And as he
thought over the other articles, he saw that they too were
not inconsistent with the same idea. The Forsyte Saga was
distinguished from most novels in a peculiar and indeed a
suggestive manner. It consisted of a number of novels, each
full length or more than full length, but the point of interest was that the entire collection was published on thin
paper in this one volume. Where could one get a greater
mass of reading matter in a smaller bulk: in other words,
where could one find a more suitable work of fiction to
carry with one on an expedition?

The sou'wester also fitted from this point of view into
the scheme of things, but it added a distinctive suggestion
all its own: that of the sea. French's thoughts turned
towards a voyage. But it could not be an ordinary voyage
in a well-appointed liner, where peaches and matches and
novels would be as plentiful as in the heart of London.
Nor did it seem likely that it could be a trip in the *Enid*.
Such a craft could not remain out of touch with land for
so long a period as these stores seemed to postulate. French
could not think of anything that seemed exactly to meet
the case, though he registered the idea of an expedition as
one to be kept in view.

Leaving the point for the time being, he turned over the paper and began to examine its other side.

It formed the middle portion of an old hotel bill, the top and bottom having been torn off. The items indicated a stay of one night only being merely for bed and breakfast. The name of the hotel had been torn off with the bill head, and also all but a few letters of the green rubber receipt stamp at the bottom. French felt that if he could only ascertain the identity of the hotel it might afford him a valuable clue, and he settled down to study it in as close detail as possible.

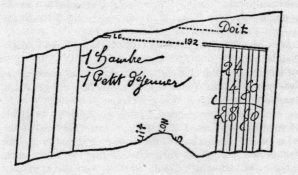

He recalled two statements that Speedwell had made about Dangle. First, the melancholy detective had said that commencing about a fortnight after the acquisition by the gang of Price's letter and the tracing, Dangle had begun paying frequent visits to the Continent or Ireland, and secondly, that in a tube lift he had overheard Dangle say that he was crossing on a given night, but would be back the next. French thought he might take it for granted that this bill had been incurred on one of these trips. He wondered if Dangle had always visited the same place, as, if so, the bill would refer to an hotel near enough to England to be visited in one day. Of none of this was there any evidence, but French believed that it was sufficiently probable to be taken as a working hypothesis. If it led nowhere, he could try something else.

Assuming then that one could cross to the place in one night and return the next, it was obvious that it must be comparatively close to England, and, the language on the bill being French, it must be in France or Belgium. He took an atlas and a Continental Bradshaw, and began to look out the area over which this condition obtained. Soon he saw that while the whole of Belgium and the north-west of France, bounded by a rough line drawn through Chalons, Nancy, Dijon, Angoulême, Chartres, and Brest, were within the *possible* limit, giving a reasonable time in which to transact business, it was more than likely the place did not lie east of Brussels and Paris.

He turned back to the torn bill. Could he learn nothing from it?

First, as to the charges. With the franc standing at eighty, twenty four francs seemed plenty for a single room, though it was by no means exorbitant. It and the 4.50 fr. for *petit déjeuner* suggested a fairly good hotel—probably what might be termed good second-class—not one of the great hotels de luxe like the Savoy in London or the Crillon or Claridge's in Paris, but one that ordinary people patronized, and which would be well known in its own town.

Of all the information available, the most promising line of research seemed that of the rubber stamp, and to that French now turned his attention. The three lines read:

> . . . uit
> . . . lon,
> . . . S.

French thought he had something that might help here. He rose, crossed the room, and after searching in his letter file, produced three or four papers. These were hotel bills he had incurred in France and Switzerland when he visited those countries in search of the murderer of Charles

Gething of the firm of Duke & Peabody, and he had brought them home with him in the hope that some day he might return as a holiday-maker to these same hotels. Now perhaps they would be of use in another way.

He spread them out and examined their receipt stamps. From their analogy the . . . uit on his fragment obviously stood for the words "Pour acquit," anglice: "paid." The middle line ending in . . . lon was unquestionably the name of the hotel, and the third, ending in S, that of its town. And here again was a suggestion as to the size of the establishment. A street was not included in the address. It must therefore be well known in its town.

It seemed to him moreover that this fact also conveyed a suggestion as to the size of the town. If the latter were Paris or Brussels—as he had thought not unlikely as both these names ended in s—a street address would almost certainly have been given. The names of the hotel and town alone pointed to a town of the same standing as the hotel itself—a large town to have so important an hotel, but not a capital city. In other words, there was a certain probability the hotel was situated in a large town comparatively near the English Channel, Paris and Brussels being excepted.

As French sat pondering over the affair, he saw suddenly that further information was obtainable from the fact that the lettering on a rubber stamp is always done symmetrically. Once more rising, he found a small piece of tracing paper, and placing this over the mutilated receipt stamp, he began to print in the missing letters of the first line. His printing was not very good, but he did not mind that. All he wanted was to get the spacing of the letters correct, and to this end he took a lot of trouble. He searched through the advertisements in several papers until he found some type of the same kind as that of the . . . uit, and by carefully measuring the other letters he at last satisfied himself as to just where the P of Pour acquit would stand. This, he hoped, would give him the number of letters in the names of both the hotel and the town.

Drawing a line down at right angles to the t of acquit, he found that the n of . . . lon projected slightly over a quarter inch farther along, while the S of the town was almost directly beneath. By drawing another line down from the P of Pour, and measuring these same distances from it, he found the lengths of the names of hotel and town, and by further careful examination and spacing of type, he reached definite conclusions. The name of the hotel, including the word hotel, contained from eighteen to twenty letters and that of the town six, more or less according to whether letters like I or W predominated.

He was pleased with his progress. Starting from nothing he had evolved the conception of an important hotel—the something-lon, in a large town situated in France or Belgium, and comparatively near the English Channel, the name of the town consisting of five, six, or seven letters of which the last one was S. Surely, he thought, such an hotel would not be hard to find.

If he was correct as to the size of the town, it was one which would be marked on a fairly small scale map, and taking his atlas, he began to make a list of all those which seemed to meet the case. He soon saw there were a number—Calais, Amiens, Beauvais, Étaples, Arras, Soissons, Troyes, Ypres, Bruges, Roulers, and Malines.

He had by this time become so excited over his quest that in spite of the hour—it was long past his bedtime—he telephoned to the Yard to send him Baedeker's Guides to Northern France and Belgium, and when these came he began eagerly looking up the hotels in each of the towns on his list. For a considerable time he worked on without result, then suddenly he laughed from sheer delight.

He had reached Bruges, and there, third on the list, was "Grand Hôtel du Sablon!" Moreover, this name exactly filled the required space.

"Got it in one," he chuckled, feeling immensely pleased with himself.

But French, if sometimes an enthusiastic optimist and again a down and out pessimist, was at all times thorough.

He did not stop at Bruges. He worked all the way through the list, and it was not until he had satisfied himself that no other hotel fulfilling the conditions existed in any of the other towns, that he felt himself satisfied. It was true there was an Hotel du Carillon in Malines, but this name was obviously too short for the space.

As he went jubilantly to bed, the vision of a trip to the historic city of Bruges bulked large in his imagination.

CHAPTER XVI

A Tale of Two Cities

NEXT morning French had an interview with his chief at the Yard at which he produced the torn hotel bill, and having demonstrated the methods by which he had come to identify it with the Grand Hôtel du Sablon in Bruges, suggested that a visit there might be desirable. To his secret relief Chief Inspector Mitchell took the same view, and it was arranged that he should cross as soon as he could get away.

On his return to his room he found Cheyne waiting for him. The young man seemed to have aged by years since his frenzied appeal to the Yard, and his anxious face and distrait manner bore testimony to the mental stress through which he was passing. Eagerly he inquired for news.

"None so far, I'm sorry to say," French answered, except that we have found that Miss Merrill did return to her rooms that night," and he told what he had learned of Joan's movements, as well as of his visit to Hackworth's garage, and of Blessington's exchange of cars. But of Bruges and the hotel bill he said nothing. Cheyne, he felt sure, would have begged to be allowed to accompany him to Belgium, and this he did not want. But in his kindly way he talked sympathetically to the young man reiterating his promise to let him know directly anything of importance was learned.

Cheyne having reluctantly taken his leave, French turned to routine business, which had got sadly behind during the last few days. At this he worked all the morning, but on his return from lunch he found that further news had come in.

Sergeant Burnett, the man he had put on the Waterloo Station job, was waiting for him, and reported success in his mission. He had, he said, spent the whole of the day from early morning at the station, and at last he had obtained what he wanted. A taximan on a nearby stand had been called to the footpath at the arrival side of the station at about 2:00 P.M. He had drawn up behind an old black car, which he had thought was a Napier. His own fare, a lady, kept him waiting for a few seconds while she took a somewhat leisurely farewell of the gentleman who was seeing her off, and during this time he had idly watched the vehicle in front. He had seen an invalid lady in a sable colored fur coat being helped in. There was a second lady with her, and a tall man. The three got in, and the car moved off at the same time as his own. Sargeant Burnett had questioned the man on the appearance of the travelers, and was pretty certain that they were Joan, Susan, and Sime. Dangle, so far as he could learn, was not with them.

French felt the sudden thrill of the artist who has just caught the elusive effect of light which he wanted, as he reflected how sound had been his deduction. He had considered it likely that these people would use Waterloo Station to effect the change of cars, and now it seemed that they had done so. Nothing like a bit of imagination, he thought, as he good-naturedly complimented the sergeant on his powers, and dismissed him.

Having too much to see to at the Yard to catch the 2:00 P.M. from Victoria for Ostend, he rang up and engaged a berth on the Harwich-Zeebrugge boat, and that night at 8:40 P.M. he left Liverpool Street for Belgium.

Apart from his actual business, he was looking forward with considerable keenness to the trip. Foreign travel had become perhaps his greatest pleasure, and he had never yet been in Belgium. Moreover he had always heard Bruges mentioned as the paradise of artists, and in a rather shame-faced way he admitted an interest in and appreciation of art. He had determined that if at all possible he would snatch enough time to see at least the more interesting parts of the old town.

They left the Parkeston Quay at 10:30, and by 6 next morning French was on deck. He was anxious to miss no possible sight of the approach of Zeebrugge. He had read with a thrilled and breathless interest the story of what was perhaps the greatest naval exploit of all time—as, indeed, who has not?—and as the long, low line of the famous mole loomed up rather starboard of straight ahead, his heart beat faster and a lump came in his throat. There, away to the right, round the curve of the long pier, must have been where *Vindictive* boarded, where in an inferno of fire her crew reached with their scaling ladders the top of the great sea wall, and climbing down on the inside, joined a hand-to-hand fight with the German defenders. And here, at the left hand end of the huge semicircle, was the lighthouse, which he was now rounding as *Thetis, Intrepid,* and *Iphigenia* rounded it on that historic night. He tried to picture the scene. The screen of smoke to sea, which baffled the searchlights of the defenders and from which mysterious and unexpected craft emerged at inter-vals, the flashing lights as guns were fired and shells burst over the mole, the sea, and the low-lying sand dunes of the coast behind. The din of hell in the air, fire, smoke, explosion, and death—and those three ships passing on; *Thetis* a wreck, struck and fiercely burning, forced aside by the destruction of her gear, but lighting her fellows straight to their goal—the mouth of the canal which led to the submarine base at Bruges. French crossed the deck and gazed at the spot with its swing bridge and stone side walls, as he thought how, had the desperate venture failed, history might have been changed and at that touch and go period of the war the Central Powers might have triumphed. It was with renewed pride and wonder in the men who conceived and carried out the wonderful enterprise that he crossed back over the deck and set himself to the business of landing.

A short run past the sandhills at the coast and across the flat Belgian fields brought the spires of Bruges into view, and slowly rounding a sharp curve through the gardens of the houses in the suburbs, they joined the main line from Ostend, and a few minutes later entered the station. Emerging on to the wide boulevard in front, French's eyes fell on a bus bearing the legend "Grand Hôtel du Sablon," and getting in, he was driven across the boulevard and a short way up a long, rather narrow and winding street, between houses some of which seemed to have stood unaltered—and doubtless had—for six hundred years, when Bruges, three times its present size, was the chief trading city of the Hanseatic League. As he turned into the hotel, chimes rang out—from the famous belfry, the porter told him—tinkling, high-pitched bells and silvery, if a trifle thin in the clear morning air.

He called for some breakfast, and as he was consuming it the anticipated delights of sight-seeing receded, and interest in the movements of James Dangle became once more paramount. He was proud of his solution of the problem of the torn hotel bill, and not for a moment had a doubt of the correctness of that solution entered his head.

It came upon him therefore as a devastating shock when the courteous manager of the hotel, with whom he had asked an interview, assured him not only that no such person as the original of the photograph he had presented had ever visited his establishment, but that the fragment of the bill was not his.

To French it seemed as if the bottom had fallen out of his world. He had been so sure of his ground; all his reasoning about the stamp, the size of the hotel and town and lengths of their names had seemed so convincing and unassailable. And the names Grand Hôtel du Sablon and Bruges had worked in so well! More important still, no other hotel seemed to fill the bill. French felt cast down to the lowest depths of despair, and for a time he could only stare speechlessly at the manager.

At last he smiled rather ruefully.

"That's rather a blow," he confessed. "I was pretty sure of my ground. Indeed, so sure was I, that if I might without offense, I should like to ask you again if there is no possibility that the man might have been here, say, during your absence."

The manager was sympathetic. He brought French a sample of his bill, stamped with his rubber receipt stamp, and French saw at once their dissimilarity with those he had been studying. Moreover, the manager assured him that neither had been altered for several years.

So he was no further on! French lit a cigar, and retiring to a deserted corner of the salon, sat down to think the thing out.

What was he to do next? Was he to return to London by the next boat, giving up the search and admitting defeat, or was there any possible alternative? He set his teeth as he swore great oaths that nothing short of the direct need would lead him to abandon his efforts until he had found the hotel, and learned Dangle's secret.

But heroics were all very well: what, in point of fact was he to do? He sat considering the problem for an hour, and at the end of that time he had decided to go to Brussels, borrow or buy a Belgian hotel guide, and go through it page by page until he found what he wanted. If none of the hotels given suited, he would go on to Paris and try a similar experiment.

This decision he reached only after long consideration, not because it was not obvious—it had instantly occurred to him—but because he was convinced that the methods he had already tried had completely covered the ground. He had proved that there was no hotel whose name ended

in . . . lon in a fair-sized town whose name ended
in . . . s in all the district in question, other than the
Grand Hôtel du Sablon at Bruges. There still remained,
however, the chance that it might be a southern French or
Swiss hotel, and he saw that he would have to make sure
of this before returning to London.

Still buried in thought, he walked slowly back to the
station to look up trains to Brussels. The fact that he was
in the most interesting town in Belgium no longer stirred
his pulse. His disappointment and anxiety about his case
drove all irrelevant matters from his mind, and he felt
that all he wanted now was to be at work again to
retrieve his error.

He reached the station, and began searching the huge
timetable boards for the train he wanted. He was interested to notice that the tables were published in two lan-
guages, French and what he thought at first was Dutch,
but concluded later must be Flemish. Idly he compared
the different spelling of the names of the towns. Brugge
and Bruges, Gent and Gand, Brussel and Bruxelles,
Oostende and Ostende, and then suddenly he came up
as it were all standing, and a sudden wave of excitement
passed over him as he stood regarding another pair of
names. Antwerpen and Anvers! Anvers! A six lettered
town ending in s! He cursed himself for his stupidity. He
had always thought of the place as Antwerp, but he ought
to have known its French name. Anvers! Once more he
was alert and full of eager optimism. Had he got it at
last?

He passed through on to the platform, and making for
a door headed "Chef de Gare," asked for the stationmaster. There, after a moment's delay, he was shown into the
presence of an imposing individual in gold lace, who, however, was not too important to listen to him carefully and
reply courteously in somewhat halting English. Monsieur
wished to know if there was an hotel whose name ended
in . . . lon in Antwerp? He could not recall one off hand,

but he would look up the advertisements in his guides and tourist programs. Ah, what was this? The Grand Hôtel du Carillon. Was that what monsieur required?

A name of twenty letters—which would exactly fill the space on the receipt stamp! It certainly was what monsieur required! The very idea raised monsieur to an exalted pitch of delighted enthusiasm. The stationmaster was gratified at the reception of his information.

"I haf been at the 'otel myself," he volunteered. "It is small, but vair' goot. It is in the Place Verte, near to the Cathedral. Does monsieur know Antwerp?"

Monsieur did not, but he expressed the pleasure it would give him to make its acquaintance, and thanking the polite official he returned to the timetables to look up the trains thither.

His most direct way, it appeared, was through Ghent and Termonde, but on working out the services he found he could get quicker trains via Brussels. He therefore booked by that route, and at 11:51 he climbed into a great through express from Ostend to Brussels, Aix-la-Chapelle, Strasbourg, and, it seemed to him, the whole of the rest of Europe. An hour and a half's run brought him into Brussels-Nord, and from there he wandered out into the Place Rogier for lunch. Then returning to the station he took an express for Antwerp, arriving in the central terminus of that city a few minutes after three o'clock.

He had bought a map of Antwerp at a bookstall in Brussels, from which he had learned that the Place Verte was nearly a mile away in the direction of the river. His traveling impedimenta consisting of a handbag only, he determined to walk, and emerging from the great marble hall of the station, he passed down the busy Avenue de Keyser, and along the Place de Meir into the older part of the town. As he walked he was immensely impressed by the fine wide streets, the ornate buildings, and the excellence of the shops. Everywhere were evidences of wealth and prosperity, and as he turned into the Place Verte, and

looked across at the huge bulk of the Cathedral with its
soaring spire, he felt that here was an artistic treasure of
which any city might well be proud.

The Grand Hôtel du Carillon was an old, quaint looking building looking out over the Place Verte. French,
entering, called for a bock in the restaurant, and after
he had finished, asked to see the manager. A moment later
a small, stout man with a humorous eye appeared, bowed
low, and said that he was M. Marquet, the proprietor.

"A word with you in private, M. Marquet," French
requested, when they had exchanged confidences on the
weather. "Won't you take something with me?"

The proprietor signified his willingness in excellent
English, and when further drinks had been brought, and
French had satisfied himself that they were alone, he went
on:

"I am a detective officer from the London police, and I
am trying to trace an Englishman called Dangle. I have
reason to suppose he stayed at this hotel recently. There is
his photograph. Can you help me at all?"

At the name Dangle, M. Marquet had nodded, and
when he saw the photograph he beamed and his whole
body became affirmation personified. But certainly, he
knew M. Dangle. For several weeks—he could not say
how many, but he could ascertain from his records—for
several weeks M. Dangle had been his guest at intervals.
Sometimes he had stayed one night, sometimes two, sometimes three. Yes, he was usually alone, but not always.
On three or four occasions he had been accompanied by
another gentleman—a tall, well-built, clean-shaven man,
and once a third man had come, a short man with a fair
mustache. Yes, that was the photograph of the short man,
M.—? Yes; Blessington. The other man's name he could
not remember, but it would appear in the register: Sile,
Site—something like that. Yes, Sime: that was it. No, he
was afraid he knew nothing about these gentlemen or
their business, but he would be glad to do everything in
his power to assist monsieur.

French, his enthusiasm and delight remaining at fever heat, was suitably grateful. He wished just to ask M. Marquet a few more questions. He would like to know the last occasion on which M. Dangle had stayed.

"Why," M. Marquet exclaimed, "he just left yesterday. He came here, let me see, on Tuesday night quite late, indeed it was nearly one on Wednesday morning when he arrived. He came, he said, off the English boat train which arrives here about midnight. He stayed here two days—till yesterday, Thursday. He left yesterday shortly after déjeuner."

"He was alone?"

"Yes, monsieur. This time he was alone."

French, metaphorically speaking, hugged himself on hearing this news. Through his brilliant work with the torn bill, he had added one more fine achievement to the long list of his successes. He could not but believe that the most doubtful and difficult step of the investigation had now been accomplished. With a trail only twenty four hours old, he should surely be able to put his hands on Dangle with but little delay. Moreover, from the fact that so many visits had been paid to Antwerp it looked as if the secret of the gang was hidden in the city. Greatly reassured, he proceeded to acquire details.

He began by obtaining from M. Marquet's records lists of the visits of the three men, and that gentleman's identification of the torn bill. Also he pressed him as to whether he could not remember any questions or conversations of the trio which might give him a hint as to their business, but without success. He saw and made a detailed search of the room Dangle had occupied during his last visit, but here again with no result. Dangle, M. Marquet said, had been out all day on the Wednesday, the day after his arrival, but on Thursday he had remained in the hotel until his departure about 2:00 P.M. M. Marquet had not seen him leave, but he had sent the waiter for his bill after déjeuner, and the proprietor believed he had gone a little later. Possibly the porter could give more information on the point.

The porter was sent for and questioned. He knew M. Dangle well and recognized his photograph. He had been present in the hall when the gentleman left on the previous day, shortly before two o'clock. M. Dangle had walked out of the hotel with his suitcase in his hand, declining the porter's offer to carry it for him or call a taxi. The trams, however, passed the door, and the porter had assumed M. Dangle intended to travel by that means. No, he had not noticed the direction he took. There was a "stillstand" or tramway halt close by. Dangle had not talked to the porter further than to wish him good-day when he met him. He had not asked questions, or given any hint of his business in the town.

Following his usual procedure under such circumstances, French next asked for interviews with all those of the staff who had come in any way in contract with his quarry, but in spite of his most persistent efforts he could not extract a single item of information as to the man's business or movements.

Baffled and weary from his journey, French took his hat and went out in the hope that a walk through the streets of the fine old city would clear his brain and bring him the inspiration he needed. Crossing beneath the trees of the Place Verte, he passed round the cathedral to the small square from which he could look up at the huge bulk of the west front, with its two unequal towers, one a climbing marvel of decoration, "lace in stone," the other unfinished, and topped with a small and evidently temporary spire. Then, promising himself a look round the interior before leaving the town, he regained the tramline from the Place Verte, and following it westwards, in two or three minutes came out on the great terraces lining the banks of the river.

The first sight of the Scheldt was one which French felt he would not soon forget. Well on to half a mile wide, it bore away in both directions like a great highway leading from this little Belgium to the uttermost parts of the earth. Large ships lay at anchor in it, as well as clustering along the wharves to the south. This river frontage of wharves and sheds and cranes and great steamers extended as far as the eye could reach; he had read that it was three and a half miles long. And that excluded the huge docks for which the town was famous. As he strolled along he became profoundly impressed, not only with the size of the place, but more particularly with the attention which had been given to its artistic side. In spite of all this commercial activity the city did not look sordid. Thought had been given to its design; one might almost say loving care. Why, these very terraces on which he was walking, with their cafés and their splendid view of the river, were formed on neither more nor less than the vast roofs of the dock sheds. French, who knew most of the English ports, felt his amazement grow at every step.

He followed the quays right across the town till he came to the Gare du Sud, then turning away from the river, he found himself in the Avenue du Sud. From this he worked back along the line of great avenues which had replaced the earlier fortifications, until eventually, nearly three hours after he had started, he once again turned into the Place Verte, and reached the Carillon.

He ordered a room for the night, and some strong tea, after which he sat on in his secluded corner of the comfortable restaurant, and smoked a meditative cigar. His walk had done him good. His brain had cleared, and the weariness of the journey, and the chagrin of his deadlock had vanished. His thoughts returned to his problem, which he began to attack in the new.

He puzzled over it for the best part of an hour, without making the slightest progress, and then he began to consider how far the ideas he had already arrived at fitted in with what he had since learned of Dangle's movements.

He had thought that the nature of the articles on Dangle's list suggested a sea expedition. He remembered the delight with which, many years earlier, he had read *The*

Riddle of the Sands, and he thought that had Dangle contemplated just such another cruise as that of the heroes of that fascinating book, he might well have got together the articles in question. But since these idea had passed through his mind, French had learned the following fresh facts:

1. From a fortnight after obtaining the tracing, Dangle had been paying frequent visits to Antwerp.

2. He had on these occasions put up at the Carillon.

3. His last visit had followed immediately on the failure to murder Cheyne, with its almost certain result of the calling in of Scotland Yard.

4. He had on this last visit remained at the Carillon for two days, leaving about 2:00 P.M. on the Thursday, the previous day.

5. He had carried his hand-bag from the hotel, without calling for a taxi.

At first French could not see that these additional facts had any bearing on his theory, but as he continued turning them over in his mind, he realized that all but one might be interpreted as tending in the same direction.

1. Dangle's visits to Antwerp. Supposing Dangle had been planning some secret marine expedition, where, French asked himself, could he have found a more suitable base from which to make his arrangements? Antwerp was a seaport: moreover, it was a great seaport, large enough for a secret expedition to set sail from without attracting notice. It was a foreign port, away from the inquisitive notice of the British police, but, on the other hand, it was the nearest great port to London. If these considerations did not back up his theory, they at least did not conflict with it.

2. Why had Dangle put up at the Carillon? The hotels near the station were the obvious ones for English visitors. Could it be because the Place Verte was close to the river and the shipping? This, French admitted to himself, sounded farfetched, and yet it might be the truth.

3. The dispersal and disappearance of the gang immedi-

ately on the probability of its activities becoming known to the police looked suspiciously like a flight.

4. Could it be that Dangle's arrival in Antwerp was ahead of schedule, that is, the flight brought him there two days before the expedition was to start? Or could it be that on his arrival he immediately set to work to organize the departure, but was unable to complete his arrangements for two days? At least, it might be so.

Lastly, had he carried his bag from the hotel for the same reason as he might have chosen the hotel: that he was going, not to the station, but the few hundred yards to the quays, thence to start on this maritime expedition? Again, it might be so.

French was fully aware that the whole of these elaborate considerations had the actual stability of a house of cards. Each and every one of his deductions might be erroneous and the facts might be capable of an entirely different construction. Still, there was at least a suggestion that Dangle might have left Antwerp by water shortly after two o'clock on the previous day. It was the one constructive idea French could evolve, and he decided that in the absence of anything better he would try to follow it up.

It was too late to do anything that night. After dinner, therefore, he had another walk, spent an hour in a cinema, and then went early to bed, so as to be fresh for his labors of the following day.

CHAPTER XVII

On the Flood Tide

FRENCH was astir betimes next morning, and over his coffee and rolls and honey he laid his plans for the day. As to the next step of his investigation he had no doubt. He must begin by finding out what vessels had left the city after 2:00 P.M. on the previous Thursday. That done, he could go into the question of the passengers each carried, in the hope of learning that Dangle was among them.

At the outset he was faced by the handicap of being a stranger in a strange land. If Antwerp had been an English port he would have known just where to get his information, but here he was unfamiliar with the ropes. He did not know if all sailings were published in any paper or available to the public at any office; moreover, his ignorance of both French and Flemish precluded his mixing with clerks or dock loafers from whom he might pick up information. Of course there were the Belgian police, but he did not wish to apply to them if he could carry out his job by himself.

However, this part of his problem proved easier of solution than he had expected. Inquiries at the post office revealed the fact that there was a shipping agency in the Rue des Tanneurs, and soon he had reached the place, found a clerk who spoke English, and put his question.

When French wished to be suave, as he usually did, he could, so to speak, have wheedled his best bone from a bulldog. Now, explaining in a friendly and confidential manner who he was and why he wanted the information, he begged the other's good offices. The clerk, flattered at being thus courteously approached, showed a willingness to assist, with the result that in ten minutes French had the particulars he needed.

He turned into a café, and calling for a bock, sat down to consider what he had learned. And of this the very first fact filled him with delight, as it seemed to fit in with the theory he had evolved.

On Thursday it had been high water at 2:30 P.M. By 2:30 the dock gates had been opened, and it appeared that, taking advantage of this, several steamers had left shortly after that hour.

This was distinctly encouraging, and French turned to

the list of ships with a growing hope that the end of his investigation might be coming into sight. In all, eleven steamers had left the port on the day in question, between the hours of 2:00 and 6:00 P.M., the period he had included in his inquiry.

There was first of all a Canadian Pacific liner, which had sailed from the quays at 3:00 P.M., and at 3:30 a small passenger boat had left for Oslo and Bergen. The remaining boats were tramps. There were four coasters, two for Newcastle, one for Goole, and one for Belfast, a 6,000 tonner for Singapore and the Dutch Islands, another slightly smaller ship for Genoa and Spezia, and another for Boston, U.S.A. Then there was a big five-masted sailing ship, bound with a general cargo for Buenos Aires and the River Platte, and finally there was a small freighter in ballast for Casablanca.

Of these eleven ships, the windjammer at once attracted French's attention. Here was a vessel on which, if you took a passage, you might easily require three dozen tins of peaches before you reached your journey's end. He determined to begin with this, taking the other ships in order according to the position of their offices. Fortunately in each case the clerk had given him the name of the owners or agents.

His first call, therefore, was at an old-fashioned office in a small street close to the Steen Museum. There he saw M. Leblanc, the owner of the windjammer, and explained his business. But M. Leblanc could not help him. The old gentleman had never heard of Dangle nor had any one resembling his visitor's photograph called or done any business with his firm. Moreover, no passengers had shipped on the windjammer, and the crew that had sailed was unchanged since the previous voyage.

This was not encouraging, and French went on to the next item on his program, the headquarters of the small freighter which had sailed in ballast for Casablanca. She was owned by Messrs. Merkel & Lowenthal, whose office

was farther down the Rue des Tanneurs, and five minutes
later he had pushed open the door and was inquiring for
the principal.

This was a more modern establishment than that of M.
Leblanc. Though small, the office ran to plate glass windows, teak furniture, polished brass fittings, and encaustic
tiles, while the two typists he could envisage through the
small inquiry window seemed unduly gorgeous as to
raiment and pert as to demeanor.

He was kept waiting for some minutes, then told that
M. Merkel, the head of the business, was away, but that
M. Lowenthal, the junior partner, would see him.

His first glance told French that M. Lowenthal was a
man to be watched. Seldom had he seen so many of the
tell-tale signs of roguery concentrated in the features of
one person. The junior partner had a mean, sly look, close-
set, shifty eyes which would not meet French's, and a large
mouth with loose, fleshy lips. His manner was in accord
with his appearance, now blustering, now almost ful-
somely ingratiating. French took an instant dislike to him,
and though he remained courteous as ever, he determined
not to lay his cards on the table.

"My name," he began, "as you will have seen from my
card, is French, and I carry out the business of a general
agent in London. I am trying to obtain an interview with
a friend, who has been staying here, off and on, for some
time. I came on here from Brussels in the hope of seeing
him, but he had just left. I was told that he had sailed
with your ship, the *L'Escaut,* on Thursday afternoon, and
if so I called to ask at which port I should be likely to get
in touch with him. His name is Dangle."

While French spoke he watched the other narrowly, on
his favorite theory that the involuntary replies to unexpected remarks—starts, changes of expression, sudden
pallors—were more valuable than spoken answers.

But M. Lowenthal betrayed no emotion other than a
mild surprise.

"That iss a very egstraordinary statement, sir," he said in heavy guttural tones. "I do not really know who could haf given you such misleading information. Your friend's name is quite unknown to me, and in any case we do not take passengers on our ships."

This seemed an entirely reasonable and proper reply, and yet to French's highly developed instincts it did not ring true. However, he could do nothing more, and after a little further conversation containing not a few veiled inquiries, all of which, he noted, were skillfully parried by the other, he apologized for his mistake and withdrew.

Though he was dissatisfied with the interview, he could only continue his program. He recognized that the secret might be located in Canada or the States, and that Dangle might have booked on the C.P.R. liner. Or he might have gone to Norway—indeed, for the matter of that, he might have signed on on any of the ships for any part of the world.

But after a tedious morning of calls and interviews, French had to confess defeat. He could get no farther. At none of the offices at which he applied had he obtained the slightest helpful hint. It began to look as if he had been mistaken as to Dangle's sea expedition, and if so, as he reminded himself with exasperation, he had no alternative theory to follow up.

He strolled slowly along the pleasant, sunlit streets, as he reviewed his morning's work. He was satisfied with all his interviews but the one. Everywhere save in M. Lowenthal's office he felt he had been told the truth. But instinctively he distrusted the junior partner. That the man had lied to him he had no reason to suspect, but he had no doubt that he would do so if it suited his book.

French felt that it was unsatisfactory to leave the matter in this state, and he presently thought of a simple subterfuge whereby it might be cleared up. It was almost the lunch hour, a suitable time for putting his project into operation. He hurried back to the Rue des Tanneurs, and turning into a café nearly opposite Messrs. Merkel & Lowenthal's premises, ordered a bock and selected a seat from which he could observe the office door.

He was only just in time. He had not taken his place five minutes when he saw M. Lowenthal emerge and walk off towards the center of the town. Three men clerks and the two rapid-looking typists followed, and lastly there appeared the person for whom he was waiting—the sharp-looking office boy who had attended to him earlier in the day.

The boy turned off in the opposite direction to his principal—towards a quarter inhabited by laborers and artisans, and French, getting up from his table, slipped quietly out of the café and followed him.

The chase continued for some ten minutes, when the quarry disappeared into a small house in a back street. French strolled up and down until some half an hour later the young fellow reappeared. As he approached French allowed a look of recognition and slight surprise to appear on his features.

"Ah," he said, pausing with a friendly smile, "you are the clerk who attended to me this morning in Messrs. Merkel & Lowenthal's office, are you not? A piece of luck meeting you! I wonder if you could give me a piece of information? I forgot to ask it of M. Lowenthal this morning, and as I am in a hurry, it would be worth five francs to me not to have to go back to your office."

The youth's eyes had brightened at the suggestion of financial dealings, and French felt he would learn all the other could tell him. He therefore continued without waiting for a reply.

"The thing is this: I am joining my friend, M. Dangle, aboard the *L'Escaut* at the first opportunity. It was arranged between us that one of us should take with him a couple of dozen of champagne. I want to know whether he took the stuff, or whether I am to. Can you help me at all?"

The clerk's English, though fairly good, was not quite equal to such a strain, and French had to repeat himself less idiomatically. But the boy grasped his meaning at last, and then at once dashed his hopes by saying he had never heard of any M. Dangle.

"There he is," French went on, producing his photograph. "You must have seen him scores of times."

And then French got the reward of his pertinacity. A look of recognition passed over the clerk's features, and he made a gesture of comprehension.

"*Mais oui, m'sieur;* yes, sir," he answered quickly," but that is not M. Danggalle. I know him: it is M. Charles."

"That's right," French returned, trying to keep the triumph out of his voice. "His name is Dangle Charles. I know him as M. Dangle, because he is one of four brothers at our works. But of course he would give his name here as M. Charles. But now, can you tell me anything about the champagne?"

The clerk shook his head. He had not known upon what business M. Charles had called at the office.

"Oh, well, it can't be helped," French declared. "I thought that perhaps when he was in with you last Wednesday you might have heard something about it. You don't know what luggage he took aboard the *L'Escaut?*"

The clerk had not been aware that M. Charles had embarked on the freighter, still less did he know of what his luggage had consisted. But as French talked on in his pleasant way, the following facts became apparent; first, that Dangle for some weeks past had been an occasional visitor at the shipping office; second, that on the previous Wednesday he had been closeted with the partners for the greater part of the day; third, that the *L'Escaut* had evidently sailed on an expedition of considerable importance and length, for a vast deal of stores had gone aboard her, about which both partners had shown very keen anxiety; fourthly, that not only had M. Merkel, the senior partner, himself sailed on her, but it was likely that he intended to be away some time as M. Lowenthal had moved into his room, and lastly, that the *L'Escaut* had come up from the firm's yard during the Wednesday night and had anchored in the river off the Steen until she left about 3:00 P.M. on the Thursday.

These admissions made it abundantly clear that French was once more on the right track, and he handed over his five francs with the feeling that he had made the cheapest bargain of his life.

He had no doubt that Dangle had sailed with the senior partner on the tramp, but he felt he must make sure, and he walked slowly back towards the quays, turning over in his mind possible methods for settling the point. One inquiry seemed promising. If the ship had lain at anchor out in the river, and if Dangle had gone aboard her, he must have had a boat to do so. French wondered could he find that boat.

He felt himself held up by the language difficulty. Up to the present he had had extraordinary luck in this respect, but then up to the present he had been interviewing educated persons whose business brought them in contact with foreigners. He doubted if he could make boatmen and loafers about the quays understand what he wanted.

A trial convinced him that his fears were well founded, and he lost a solid hour in finding the Berlitz School and engaging a young linguist with a reputation for discretion. Then, accompanied by M. Jules Renard, he returned to the quays and set systematically to work. He began by inquiring where boats might be hired, and where there were steps at which ships' boats might come alongside. Taking these in turn he asked had the boatmen taken a passenger out to the *L'Escaut* between 2:00 and 3:00 P.M. on the previous Thursday? Or had the loafer, stevedore, shunter, or constable, as the case might be, noticed if a boat had come ashore from the same vessel on the same date and at the same time?

Though the work was easy it bade fair to be tedious,

and therefore for more than one reason French felt a glow of satisfaction when at his fourth inquiry his question received an affirmative answer. A wizened old man, one of a small knot of longshoremen whom M. Renard addressed, separated himself from his companions and came forward. He said that he was a boatman, and that he had been hailed by a man—an Englishman, he believed—at the time stated, and had rowed him out to the ship.

"Ask him if that's the man," French directed, producing Dangle's photograph, though he felt there could be no doubt as to the reply.

He was therefore immensely dashed when the boatman shook his head. This was not the man at all. The traveler was a short, rather stout man with a small fair mustache.

French gasped. The description sounded familiar. Taking out Blessington's photograph he passed it over.

This time the boatman nodded. Yes, that was the man he had rowed out. He had no doubt of him whatever.

This was unexpected but most welcome news, though as French thought over it, he saw that it was not so surprising after all. If Dangle was in it, why not Blessington, and for the matter of that, why not Sime also? In this case he wondered where Susan could be, and more acutely, what had been the fate of Joan Merrill. Possibly, he thought, his inquiries about Dangle would solve these questions also.

Half an hour later he struck oil for the second time. Another boatman, a little further along the quays, had also rowed a passenger out to the *L'Escaut,* and this one, it appeared, was Dangle. But though French kept working steadily away, he could hear nothing of Sime.

In the end it was a suggestion of Renard's that put him once more on the trail. The interpreter proved an intelligent youth, and when he had grasped the point at issue, he stopped and pointed to the river.

"You say, monsieur, that the sheep, she lie there, opposite the Musée Steen, is it not so? *Bon!* We haf walked along all the quays near to that. Your friends would not haf

211

hired boat from farther on—it is too far. You say, too, they come from England secretly, is it not? *Bon!* They would come to the other side."

French did not understand.

"The other side?" he repeated questioningly.

"But yes, monsieur, the other side." The young fellow's eyes flashed in his eagerness. "Over there, La Gare de Waes." He pointed out across the great stream to its west bank.

"I didn't know there was a station across there," French admitted. "Where does the line go to?"

"Direct to Ghent. Your friends change trains at Ghent. It is a quiet railway. They come unseen."

"Good man," said French heartily. "We'll go and find out. How do you get to the blessed place?"

M. Renard smiled delightedly.

"Ah yes, monsieur. You weesh to cross? Is it not?" he cried. "This way. We take ferry from the Quai Van Dyck. It is near."

Half an hour later they had reached the Tête de Flandre —the low-lying western bank of the Scheldt. It bore a small but not unpicturesque cluster of old-fashioned houses, nestling about one of the historic Antwerp forts. Renard, now apparently quite as interested in the chase as French, led the way along the river bank from boatman to boatman, with the result that before very many minutes had passed French had obtained the information he wanted.

It appeared that about 1:00 P.M. on the day in question, a strapping young boatman had noticed three strangers approaching from the direction of the Waes Station, a hundred yards or more distant. They consisted of a tall, clean-shaven man of something under middle age and two women, both young. One was tall and strongly made and dark as to hair and eyes, the other was slighter and with red gold hair. The smaller one seemed to be ill, and was stumbling along between the other two, each of whom supported her by an arm. None of the trio could speak

French or Flemish, but they managed by signs to convey the information that they wanted to be put on board the *L'Escaut*, which was lying out in midstream. The man had rowed them out, and they had been received on board by an elderly gentleman with a dark beard.

Further questions produced the information that the fair lady appeared to be seriously ill, though whether it was her mind or body that was affected, the boatman couldn't be sure. She was able to walk, but would not do so unless urged on by the others. She had not spoken or taken any interest in the journey. She had not appeared even to look round her, but had sat gazing listlessly at nothing, with a vacant expression in her eyes. Her companions had had real difficulty in getting her up the short ladder on to the *L'Escaut's* deck.

The news was rather unexpected to French. About Joan Merrill it was both disconcerting and reassuring; the former because he could not see that the gang had anything but a sinister reason for inveigling the young girl aboard the ship—probably she will fall overboard at night, he thought; the latter because she was at least still alive, or had been two days ago. It was quite evident that she was drugged, probably with morphine or something similiar. It might, however, mean that while wishing Joan no harm, they were taking her with them on their expedition to insure her silence as to their movements.

As French returned across the ferry, he kept on puzzling as to Lowenthal's position. Could Lowenthal be arrested? Was he in league with the gang? If so, could he be held responsible for the abduction of Joan Merrill? French didn't think the evidence would justify drastic measures. He had, as a matter of fact, no actual evidence against Lowenthal. Of his complicity he was satisfied, but he doubted if he could prove it.

He got rid of the young interpreter, and strolling slowly along the quays, thought the matter out. No, he had not a good enough case with which to go to the Belgian police.

But he could do the next best thing. He could call on
M. Lowenthal for the second time, and try to bluff an
admission out of him.

As he walked to the Rue des Tanneurs, he felt his prospects were not rosy. But at least he had no difficulty in
obtaining his interview. M. Lowenthal seemed surprised to
see him so soon again, but received him politely, and asked
what he could do for him.

"I want to ask you another question, M. Lowenthal, if
you please," French answered in his pleasantest manner,
"and first I must tell you that the agency I hold is that
of Detective Inspector at New Scotland Yard in London.
My question is this: When you and M. Merkel entered
into relations with Blessington, Sime, and the Dangles, did
you know that they were dangerous criminals wanted by
the English police?"

In spite of the most evident efforts for self-control,
Lowenthal was so much taken aback that he could not for
some moments speak. His swarthy face turned a greenish
hue and little drops of sweat showed on his forehead. To
the other pleasant characteristics with which French had
mentally endowed him, he now added that of coward, and
his hopes of his bluff succeeding grew brighter. He sat
waiting in silence for the other to recover himself, then
said suavely:

"After that, M. Lowenthal, you will see for yourself that
you cannot plead ignorance of the affair. Let me advise
you for your own sake to be open with me."

The man pulled himself together. He wiped his brow as
he replied earnestly, but in somewhat shaky accents:

"That I haf met Blessington, Sime, and Dangle I do not
deny, though they were Merkel's friends—not mine. But I
do not know that they are criminal. Dangle, he called here
and asked Merkel to take him on the next"—he hesitated
for a word—"next work, next sail of the sheep. Merkel
said that Dangle iss a writer—he writes books. He weeshed
to see the sail to Casablanca to deescribe it in hiss book.

Merkel said he would haf to pay fare, the firm could not afford it unless. Dangle agreed. Merkel was going himself, and Dangle suggested Sime and Blessington go also to make party—to play cards. Of a second Dangle I know nothing. They went secretly—I admit it—because the law forbids to take passengers for sail without a certificate. That is all of the affair."

Not a single word of this statement did French believe, but he saw that unless he could get some further information, or surprise this Lowenthal into some more damaging admission, he could not have him arrested. After all, the story hung together. Merkel might conceivably be playing his own game, and have pitched the yarn of the author out for copy to his partner. The contravention of the shipping laws would undoubtedly account for the secrecy with which the start was made. Certainly there was no evidence to bring before a jury.

French proceeded to question the junior partner with considerable thoroughness, but he could not shake his statement. The only additional facts he learned were that the *L'Escaut* was going to Casablanca on the order of the Moroccan Government to load up a cargo of agricultural samples for the Italian market, and that M. Merkel was accompanying it simply as a holiday trip.

With this French had to be content, and he went to the post office, and got through on the long distance telephone to his chief at the Yard. To him he repeated the essentials of the tale, asking him to inquire from the Moroccan authorities as to the truth of their portion of it, as well as to endeavor to trace the *L'Escaut*.

On leaving the post office, it occurred to him that communication with the *L'Escaut* should be possible by wireless, and he returned to the Rue des Tanneurs to ascertain this point. There he was told that just after he had left M. Lowenthal had received a telephone call, requiring his immediate presence in Holland, and he had with a great rush caught the afternoon express for the Dutch capital.

"Skedaddled, by Jove!" said French to himself. "Guess that lets in the Belgian police."

He called at headquarters, and saw the officer in charge, and before he left to catch the connection for London, it had been arranged that the movements of the junior partner should be gone into, and a watch kept for the return of that enterprising weaver of fairy tales.

CHAPTER XVIII

A Visitor from India

WHEN French reached Victoria, the first person he saw on the platform was Maxwell Cheyne.

"They told me at the Yard that you might be on this train," the young man said excitedly as he elbowed his way forward. "Any news? Anything about Miss Merrill?"

He looked old and worn, and it was evident that his anxiety was telling on him. In his eagerness he could scarcely wait for the Inspector to dismount from his carriage, and his loud tones were attracting curious looks from the bystanders.

"Get a taxi," French answered quietly. "We can talk there."

A few seconds later they found a vehicle, and Cheyne, gripping the other by the arm, went on earnestly:

"Tell me. I can see you have learned something. Is she —all right?"

"I got news of her on Thursday last. She was all right then, though still under the influence of a drug. The whole party has gone to sea."

"To sea?"

"Yes, to sea in a small tramp. I don't know what they are up to, but there is no reason to suppose Miss Merrill is otherwise than well. Probably they took her with them to prevent her giving them away. They would drug her to get her to go along, but would cease it as soon as she was on board. I wired for inquiries to be made at the different signal stations, and news may be waiting for us at the Yard."

A few seconds sufficed to put Cheyne in possession of the salient facts which French had learned, and the latter in his turn asked for news.

"By Jove, yes!" Cheyne cried, "there is news. You remember that Arnold Price had disappeared? Well, yesterday I had a letter from him!"

"You don't say so?" French rejoined in surprise. "Where did he write from?"

"Bombay. He was shortly leaving for home. He expects to be here in about a month."

"And what about his disappearance?"

"He was ill in hospital. He had gone up to Agra on some private business and met with an accident—was knocked down in the street and was insensible for ages. He couldn't say who he was, and the hospital people in Agra couldn't find out, and he hadn't told the Bombay people where he was going to spend his leave."

"Did he mention the letter?"

"Yes, he thanked me for taking charge of it and said that when he reached home he would relieve me of further trouble about it. He little knows!"

"That's so," French assented.

Their taxi had been held up by a block at the end of Westminster Bridge, but now the mass cleared and in a few seconds they reached the Yard.

French's first care was to get rid of Cheyne. He repeated what he had learned about Joan Merrill, then, assuring him that the key of the matter lay in the cipher, he advised him to go home and try it once more. Directly any more news came in he would let him know.

Cheyne having reluctantly taken his departure, French made inquiries as to what had been done in reference to

his telephone from Antwerp. It appeared that the Yard
had not been idle. In the first place an application had
been made to the Moroccan Government, who had replied
that no ship had been chartered by them for freight at
Casablanca, nor was anything known of agricultural samples for the Italian market. Lowenthal's story must therefore have been an absolute fabrication. He had, however,
told it so readily that French suspected it had been made
up beforehand, so as to be ready to serve up to any inquisitive policeman or detective who might come along.

Next Lloyd's had been approached, as to the direction
the *L'Escaut* had taken, and a reply had shortly before
come in from them. It stated that up to noon on that day,
the vessel had not been reported from any of their stations.
But this, French realized, might not mean so much. If she
had gone south down the English Channel it would have
been well on to dark before she reached the Straits of Dover.
In any case, had she wished to slip through unseen, she
had only to keep out to the middle of the passage, when
in ordinary weather she would have been invisible from
either coast. On the other hand, had she gone north, she
would almost naturally have kept out of sight of land. It
was true that in either case she would have been likely to
pass some other vessel which would have spoken her, and
the fact that no news of such a recognition had come to
hand seemed to indicate that she was taking some unusual
course out of the track of regular shipping.

French wired this information to the Antwerp police,
and then, his chief being disengaged, went in and gave
him a detailed account of his adventures in Belgium.

Chief Inspector Mitchell was impressed by the story. He
sat back in his chair and treated French to a prolonged
stare as the latter talked. At the end of the recital he
remained sitting motionless for some moments, whistling
gently below his breath.

"Any theories?" he said at last.

French shook his head.

"Well, no, sir," he answered slowly. "It's not easy to see what they're after. And it's not easy to see, either, why the whole gang wanted to go. It looked at first as if they were just clearing out because of Cheyne's coming to the Yard, but it's more than that. The arrangements were made too long ago. They have been dealing with that Antwerp firm for several weeks."

"The hard copper was all a story?"

"Looks like it, sir. As a matter of fact every single statement those men made that could be tested has been proved false. Even when there didn't seem any great object in a yarn they pitched it. Lies seemed to come easier to them."

"Well, I've known a good few cases of that, and so have you, French. It's a habit that grows. Now, what's your next move?"

French hesitated.

"For the moment the outlook's not very cheery," he said at last. "All the same I can't believe that boat can go away out of the Scheldt and disappear. In my judgment she's bound to be reported before long, and I'm looking forward to getting word of her within the next day or so. Then I have no doubt that the tracing is some kind of cipher, and if we could read it we should probably get light on the whole affair."

"Why shouldn't you read it? Try it again."

"I intend to, sir. But I don't hope for much result, because I don't believe we've got the genuine document. I don't believe they would have handed it, nor a copy of it either, to a man they intended to murder, lest it should be found on his body. I'd state long odds they gave him a fake."

"I think you're probably right," the chief admitted. "Try at all events. You never know your luck."

He bent over his desk, and French, realizing that the interview had come to an end, quietly left the room. Then, seeing there was nothing requiring his attention urgently, and tired after his journey, he went home.

But contrary to his expectations, the next day passed without any news of the *L'Escaut,* and the next, and many days after that. Nor could all his efforts with the tracing throw any light on that mysterious document. As time passed he began to grow more and more despondent, and the fear that he was going to make a mess of the case grew steadily stronger. In vain he laid his difficulties before his wife. For once that final source of inspiration failed him. Mrs. French did not take even one illuminating notion. When the third week had gone by, something akin to despair seized upon the Inspector. The only possibility of hope now seemed to lie in the return of Arnold Price, and French began counting the days until his arrival.

One night about three weeks after his return from Belgium he settled down with a cigar after dinner, his thoughts running in their familiar groove: What were these people engaged on? Was there any way in which he could find out? Had he overlooked any evidence or any inquiries? Had he neglected any possible line of research?

The more he considered the affair in all its bearings, the more conscious he became of the soundness of the advice he had given to Cheyne, and which in his turn he had received from his chief. Unquestionably in the tracing lay the solution he required, and once again he racked his brains to see if he could not by any means devise a way to read its message.

On this point he concentrated, going over and over again everything he had learned about it. For perhaps an hour he remained motionless in his chair, while the smoke from his cigar curled up and slowly dissolved into the blue haze with which the room was becoming obscured. And then suddenly he sat up and with a dawning, tremulous eagerness considered an idea which had just leaped into his mind.

He had suddenly remembered a statement made by Cheyne when he was giving his first rather incoherent account of his adventures. The young man said that it had been arranged between himself and Joan Merrill that if either were lucky enough to get the tracing into his or her possession, the first thing he or she would do would be to photograph it. Now, in juxtaposition with that statement, French recalled the facts, first, that Joan must have reached her flat on the night of her abduction at least several minutes before Blessington and Sime arrived with their car; and secondly, that during those minutes she had the tracing with her—the genuine tracing, as there was every reason to believe. *Had Joan photographed it?*

French was overwhelmed with amazement and chagrin at his failure to think of this point before, nor could he acquit Cheyne of a like astounding stupidity. For himself he felt there was no excuse whatever. He had even specially noticed the girl's camera and the flashlight apparatus which she used for her architectural details when he was searching her rooms, but he had then, and since then up till this moment, entirely and completely forgotten the arrangement made between the partners.

Late as it was, French decided to go then and there to ascertain the point. The key of Joan's flat was at the Yard, and twenty minutes later he had obtained it and was in a taxi bowling towards Horne Terrace.

He kept the vehicle while he ran up the ten flights to No. 12 and secured the camera. Then hastening down, he was driven back to the Yard.

By a piece of good luck he found a photographer who had been delayed by other important work, and him he pressed into the service forthwith. With some grumbling the man returned to his dark room. French, too eager to await his report, accompanying him.

A few moments sufficed to settle the question. The camera contained a roll of films of which the first seven had been exposed, and a short immersion in the developer showed that numbers 5, 6, and 7 bore the hoped for impress.

Gone was French's despondency and the weariness

caused by his heavy day, and instead he was once more
the embodiment of enthusiasm and cheery optimism. He
had it now! At last the secret was within his grasp! Of his
ability to read the message, now that he was sure he had
the genuine one, he had no doubt. He had always liked
working out ciphers, and since he had succeeded in
extracting the hidden meaning from the stock and share
list which had been sent to the elusive Mrs. X in the
Gething murder case, his belief in his own powers had
become almost an obsession. He could hardly restrain his
eagerness to get to grips with this new problem until the
negatives should be dry and prints made.

The photographer was able to promise these for the
following day, and till then French had to possess his soul
in patience. But on his return from lunch he found on his
desk three excellent prints of the document.

They were only half-plate size, or about one-third that
of the tracing which had been given to Cheyne. He therefore instructed the photographer to prepare enlargements
which would bring the document up to more nearly the
size of the original. These were ready before it was time
for him to leave for home, and he sat down with ill-
controlled excitement to compare them with the document
at which he had already spent so much time.

And then he suddenly experienced one of the most bitter
disappointments of his life. To all intents and purposes the
two were the same! There were the same circles, the same
numbers, letters, and signs enclosed therein, the same
phrase, "England expects every man to do his duty,"
spaced round in the same way! The tracing had not been
very accurately done, as some of the circles seemed slightly
out of place, but the discrepancies were trifling, and
seemed obviously due to careless copying. He gave vent to
a single bitter oath, then sat motionless, wrapped in the
most profound gloom.

He took tracing and photographs home with him, and
spent the greater part of the evening making a minute

comparison between the two. The enlargement unfortunately was not exactly the same size as the tracing, and he therefore began his work by covering the surfaces of both with proportionate squares.

Taking the tracing first he drew parallel lines one inch apart both up and down it and across, thus covering its whole surface with inch squares. Then he divided the prints into the same number of equal parts both vertically and horizontally and ruled them up in squares also. These squares were slightly smaller than the others—about seven-eighths of an inch only—but relatively the lines fell on each in the same positions. A comparison according to the squares thus showed at a glance similarity or otherwise between the two documents.

As he examined them in detail certain interesting facts began to emerge. The general appearance, the words "England expects every man to do his duty," and the circles with their attendant letters and numbers were identical on both sheets. But there were striking variations. The position of certain of the circles was different. Those containing numbers and crooked lines were all slightly out of place, while those containing letters remained unmoved. Moreover, the little crooked lines, while preserving a rough resemblance to the originals, were altered in shape. The more he considered the matter the more evident it became to French that these divergences were intentional. The tracing which had been given to Cheyne was intended to resemble the other superficially—and did so resemble it, but it had clearly been faked to make it valueless.

If French were right so far, and he had but little doubt of it, it followed that the essential feature of the circles and crooked lines was position. This, he felt, should be a useful hint, but as yet he could not see where it led.

He pondered fruitlessly over the problem till the small hours, and next morning he took the documents back to the Yard to continue his studies. But he did not have an opportunity to do so. Other work was waiting for him. To his delight he found that Arnold Price had reached home, and that he and Cheyne were waiting to see him.

Price proved to be a lanky and rather despondent-looking individual with a skin burned to the color of copper and a pair of exceedingly shrewd blue eyes. He dropped into the chair French indicated, and instantly pulled out and lit a well-blackened cutty pipe.

"Got in yesterday morning," he announced laconically, "and wired Torquay I was going down. By the merest luck I got a reply before I started that Cheyne was in town. I looked him up and here I am."

French smiled pleasantly. Though interested in the man, he could not help noting with some amusement at once the restraint and the completeness of his statement. How refreshing, he thought, and how rare, to meet some one who will give you the pith of a story without frills!

"I'm glad to meet you, Mr. Price," he said cordially. "I suppose Mr. Cheyne has told you the effect that your letter has had on us all?"

The other nodded.

"Not altogether surprising," he declared. "There's money in the thing—or so I always believed, and this other crowd must believe it too; though how they got on to the affair licks me."

"We shall be very much interested to hear what you can tell us about it," French prompted. "Will you smoke, Mr. Cheyne?" He held out his cigar case.

"I can't tell you much," Price returned, "and nothing that will clear up this blessed mystery that seems to have started up. But this is my story for what it's worth. Before the war I was on one of the Hudson and Spence boats and I had the luck to get into the R.N.R. when hostilities broke out. I stayed on in my old ship till she was torpedoed a couple of years later, then I was appointed third officer on the *Maurania*. We were on a trip from South Africa to Brest with army stores, when one day, just as we came into the English Channel, we were attacked by a U-boat. We had an 18-pounder forward, and by a stroke of luck we

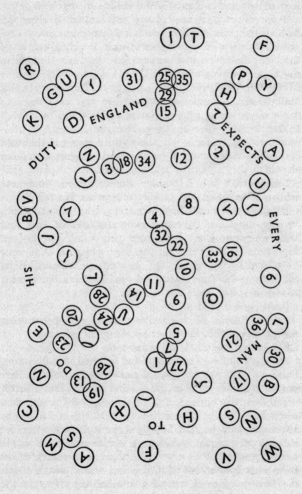

gave old Fritz one on the knob that did him in. The boat
went down and a dozen of the crew were left swimming.
We put out a boat and picked one or two of them up.
The skipper was clinging on to a lifebelt, but just as we
came up he let go and began to sink. I was in charge of
the boat, and some fool notion came over me—I think in
the hurry I forgot he was a U-boat skipper—but anyhow
like a fool I got overboard and got hold of him. It was
nothing like a dramatic rescue—there was no danger to
me—and we were back on board inside fifteen minutes."

French and Cheyne were listening intently to this
familiar story. So far it was almost word for word that told
by Dangle. Apparently, then, there was at least one point
on which the latter had told the truth.

"We weren't out of trouble," Price resumed, "and next
day we came up against another submarine. We exchanged
a few shots and then a British destroyer came up and drove
him off. But I had the luck to stop a splinter of shell, and
when we got to Brest I was sent to hospital. The U-boat
skipper had got a crack on the head when his boat went
down, and he was sent in too. By a chance we got side by
side beds in the same ward, and used to talk a bit, though
he was a rotter, even for a Boche."

Price paused to draw on his cutty pipe, expelling great
clouds of smoke of a peculiarly acrid and penetrating
quality. Then, the others not speaking, he went on:

"It turned out that the wound on Schulz's head—his
name was Schulz—was serious, and he grew steadily worse.
Then one night when the ward was quiet, he woke me and
said he knew his number was up and that he had a secret
to tell me. We listened, but all the other fellows seemed
asleep, and then he told me he could put me in the way of
a fortune—that he had hoped to get it himself after the
war, but now that it would be a job for someone else. He
said he would tell me the whole thing, and that I might
make what I could out of it, if only I would pledge myself
to give one-eighth of what I got to his wife. He gave me

the address—somewhere in Breslau. He asked me to swear this and I did, and then he took a packet from under his pillow and handed it to me. 'There,' he said, 'the whole thing's there. I put it in cipher for safety, but I'll tell you how to read it.' Well, he began to do so, but just then a sister came in, and he shut up till she would leave. But the excitement of talking about the thing must have been too much for him. He got a weak turn and never spoke again."

"But," Cheyne interposed, "what about the hard copper? Dangle told us about Schulz's discovery."

Price gazed at him vacantly for some moments and then suddenly smote the table.

"I've got it!" he cried with an oath. "Dangle! I remember that chap now! He was in the next bed on the other side of Schulz. That's right! I couldn't call him to mind when you mentioned him before. Of course! He heard the whole tale, and that's what started him on this do."

"I know," Cheyne returned. "He admitted that all right. But he told us about the hard copper. You haven't mentioned that."

Price shook his head.

"Don't know what you're talking about," he declared. "What do you mean by hard copper?"

"Dangle mentioned it. He was listening to the conversation. He told us all that about Schulz's story of the fortune, and about his wife and all that, just as you have, but he said Schulz went on to explain what the fortune was: that he had hit on a way of treating copper that made it as hard as steel. The cipher contained the formula."

Again Price shook his head.

"All spoof," he observed. "Not a word of truth in it. Schulz never mentioned copper or said anything more than I've told you."

French spoke for the first time.

"We found this Dangle a man of imagination, all through, and it is easy to see why he invented that particular yarn. By that time he had undoubtedly read the cipher, and he wanted something to mislead Mr. Cheyne as to its contents. The story of the hard copper would start a bias in Mr. Cheyne's mind which would tend to keep him off the real scent." He paused, but his companions not speaking, continued: "Now we have that bias cleared away, at least one interesting fact emerges. The whole business starts with the sea—the U-boat commander, Schulz, and it looks as if it was going to end up with the sea, the tramp, the *L'Escaut*."

As French said these words an idea flashed into his mind, and he went on deliberately, but with growing excitement:

"And when we connect the idea of a U-boat commander giving a message which ends with a sea expedition, with the fact, which I have just discovered, that the essence of his cipher is the *position* of the markings on it, we seem to be getting somewhere."

Price smote his thigh.

"By Jemima!" he cried. "I've got you. That blessed tracing is a map!"

"A map, yes. That's what I think," French answered eagerly, and then as suddenly he saw the possible significance of Nelson's exhortation, he went on dramatically: "A map of England!"

Cheyne swore softly.

"My word, if we aren't a set of blithering idiots!" he exclaimed. "Of course! 'England' is the title. That's as clear as day! The other words are added as a blind. Let's have the thing out, Inspector, and see if we can't make something of it now."

As French produced his enlarged photographs not one of the three men doubted that they were at last well on the way towards wresting the secret from the document which had so long baffled them.

CHAPTER XIX

The Message of the Tracing

INSPECTOR FRENCH spread the photograph on his desk, and Cheyne and Price having drawn up chairs, all three gazed at it as if expecting that in the light of their great idea its message would have become obvious.

But in this they were disappointed. The suggestion did not seem in any way to help either French or Cheyne, and Price, who of course had not seen the document before, was satisfactorily mystified. Granted that the thing was a map, granted even that it was a map of England, its meaning remained just as provokingly hidden as ever.

Presently Price gave vent to an exclamation. "Hang it all!" he cried irritably, and then: "I suppose those numbers couldn't be soundings? Could they give depths at the circles?"

"That's an idea," Cheyne cried, but French shook his head.

"I think there's more in it than that," he observed. "If you examine those numbers you'll find that they're consecutive, they run from one to thirty-six. Soundings wouldn't lend themselves to such an arrangement. You may be right, Mr. Price, and we must keep your idea in view, but I don't see it working out for the moment."

Silence reigned for a few moments, then Price sat back from the table and spoke again.

"Look here, Inspector," he said, knocking the ashes out of his pipe and beginning to fill it with his strong, black mixture, "you said something just now I didn't quite follow. Let's get your notion clear. You talked of this thing beginning with the sea—at Schulz, and ending with the sea—at *L'Escaut,* and Schulz's message being a map. Just what was in your mind?"

"Only the obvious suggestion that if you leave a message which provokes an expedition, you must also convey in your message the destination of that expedition, and a map seems the simplest way of doing it. But on second thoughts I question my first conclusion. There must be an explanation of the secret as well as a direction of how to profit by it, and it would seem to me doubtful that such an explanation could be covered by a map."

"Sounds all right, that," Price admitted. "Have you any idea what the secret might be? Sounds like treasure or salvage or something of that kind."

"I scarcely think salvage," French answered. "The *L'Escaut* is not a salvage boat, and a boat not specially fitted for the purpose would be of little use. But I thought of treasure all right. This Schulz might have robbed his ships—there would always be money aboard, and even during the war many women traveled with jewelry. The man might easily have made a cache of valuables somewhere round the coast."

"Easily," Cheyne intervened, "or he might have learned of some valuable deposit in some out of the way cove round the coast, like those chaps in that clinking tale of Maurice Drake's, *WO₂*."

"As at Terneuzen?" said French. "I read that book— one of the best I ever came across. It's a possibility, of course."

The talk here became somewhat rambling, Price not having read *WO₂* and wanting to know what it was about, but French soon reverted to his photograph. He reminded his hearers that they were all interested in its elucidation. Miss Merrill's safety, his own professional credit, Cheyne's peace of mind, and Price's fortune, all were at stake.

"We have," he went on, "evolved the idea that perhaps this tracing may be a map of England. On further thought that suggestion does not seem promising, but as we have no other let us work on it. Assume it is a map of England, and let us see if it leads us anywhere." There were mur-

murs of assent from his hearers, and he continued: "Now it seems to me the first thing to do is to try if we can fit these circles and lines into the map of England. Is there anything corresponding to them in English geography?"

No one being able to answer this query, French went on:

"I think we must distinguish between the letter circles on the one hand and those of the numbers and lines on the other. The position of the former was not altered in the faked copy; that of the latter was. From this may we not assume that the message lies in the numbers and lines only? Possibly the letters were added as a blind, as we have already assumed the words 'expects every man to do his duty' were added as a blind to 'England.' Suppose at all events that we eliminate the letter circles and concentrate on the others for our first effort?"

"That sounds all right."

"Good. Then let us go a step further. Have you noticed the distribution of the numbers, letters and lines? The numbers are bunched, roughly speaking, towards the center, the letters round the edge, and the irregular lines between the two. Does this central mass give us anything?"

"I get you," Price replied. He had risen and begun to pace the room, but now he returned to the table and stood looking down at the photograph. "You know, as a matter of fact," he went on slowly, "if, as you say, you take that central part which contains numbers only, the shape of the thing is not so very unlike England after all. Suppose the numbers represent land and the letters sea. Then this patch of letters in the top left-hand corner might be the Irish Sea, and this larger patch to the right the North Sea. And look, the letter circles form a band across the bottom. What price that for the English Channel?"

French crossed the room, and taking a small atlas from a shelf, opened it at the map of England and laid it down beside the photograph. With a rising excitement all three compared them. Then Cheyne burst out irritably:

"Confound the thing! It's like it and it's not like it.

Let's draw a line round those number circles and see if it makes anything like the shape." He seized the photograph and took out a pencil.

But just as in the scientific and industrial worlds discoveries and inventions seldom come singly, so among these three men the begetting of ideas begot more ideas. Scarcely had Cheyne spoken when French made a little gesture of comprehension.

"I believe I have it at last," he said quietly but with ill-concealed eagerness in his tones. "Those irregular lines in certain of the circles are broken bits of the coast line. See here, those two between 8 and U are surely the Wash, and that below H is Flamborough Head. Let's see if we can locate correspondingly shaped outlines on the atlas, and fill in between those on the photograph with pencil."

A few seconds' examination only were needed. Opposite, but slightly above the projection which French suggested as Flamborough Head was an angled line between GU and 31 which all three simultaneously pronounced St. Bee's Head. Short double lines on each side of 24 showed two parts of the estuary of the Severn, and projections along the bottom near X and 27 were evidently St. Alban's Head and Selsey Bill.

That they were on the right track there could now no longer be any doubt, and they set themselves with renewed energy to the problem still remaining—the meaning of the circles and the numbers they contained.

"We can't locate the blessed things this way," French pointed out. "We'll have to rule squares on the atlas to correspond. Then we can pencil in the coast line accurately, and see just where the circles lie."

For a time measuring and the drawing of lines were the order of the day. And then at last the positions of the circles were located. They were all drawn round towns.

"Towns!" Price exclaimed. "Guess we're getting on."

"Towns!" Cheyne echoed in his turn. "Then you must have been right, Inspector, about those letters being merely a blind."

"I think so," French admitted. "Look at it in this way. If only the towns and coast were marked, the shape of England would show too clearly. But adding those letter circles disguises the thing—prevents the shape becoming apparent. Now, I may be wrong, but I am beginning to question very much if this map has anything to do with indicating a position—I mean directly. I am beginning to think it is merely a cipher. Let us test this at all events. Let us write down the names of the towns in the order of the numbers and see if that gives us anything."

He took a sheet of paper, while Price found No. 1 on the photograph and Cheyne identified its position with that of a town on the atlas map.

"No. 1," said Cheyne, "is Salisbury."

French wrote down: "1, Salisbury."

"No. 2," went on Cheyne, "is Immingham."

"2, Immingham," wrote French, as he remarked, "Salisbury—Immingham: S—I. That goes all right so far."

The next three towns were Liverpool, Uttoxeter, and Reading, and though none of the men could see where SILUR was leading, it was at least pronounceable.

But when the next three letters were added French gave a mighty shout of victory. No. 6 was Ipswich, No. 7 Andover, and No. 8 Nottingham. IAN added to SILUR made Silurian.

"*Silurian!*" French cried, striking the table a mighty blow with his clenched fist. "*Silurian!* That begins to show a light!"

The others stared.

"Don't you recognize the name?" went on French. "The *Silurian* was a big Anchor liner, and she was torpedoed on her way to the States with two and a half millions in gold bars aboard!"

The others held their breath and their eyes grew round.

"Any of it recovered?"

"None: it was in mid-Atlantic."

"But," stammered Cheyne at last, "I don't follow—"

"I don't follow myself," French returned briskly, "but

when the cipher which leads to a maritime expedition begins with a wreck with two and a half millions aboard, well then, I say it is suggestive. Come along, let's read the rest of the thing. We'll know more then."

With breathless eagerness the other towns were looked up, and at last French's list read as follows:

1. Salisbury
2. Immingham
3. Liverpool
4. Uttoxeter
5. Reading
6. Ipswich
7. Andover
8. Nottingham
9. Oxford
10. Northampton
11. Evesham
12. Doncaster
13. Exeter
14. Gloucester
15. Ripon
16. Ely
17. Eastbourne
18. Wigan
19. Exmouth
20. Swansea
21. Tonbridge
22. Nuneaton
23. Ilfracombe
24. Newport
25. Eaglescliff
26. Taunton
27. Eastleigh
28. Ebbw Vale
29. Northallerton
30. Folkestone

31. Appleby
32. Tamworth
33. Huntingdon
34. Oldham
35. Middlesborough
36. Southend

Taking the initials in order read: Silurianonedegreewest-nineteen fathoms, or dividing it into its obvious words—*"Silurian* one degree west nineteen fathoms."

The three men stared at one another.

"Nineteen fathoms!" Price gasped at last. "But if she's in nineteen fathoms that gold will be salvable!"

French nodded.

"And I guess Dangle and Company have gone to salve it. They wouldn't want a salvage boat for gold. They'd get it with a diver's outfit."

"But," Cheyne went on in a puzzled tone, "I've not got this straight yet. If she's in nineteen fathoms, why has she not been salved by the Admiralty? Look at the *Laurentic*. She was put down off the Swilly in Ireland, and they salved her gold. Five million pounds' worth. Salved practically every penny, and in twenty fathoms too."

Price was considering another problem.

"One degree west," he murmured. "What under heaven does that mean? One degree west of what? Surely not the meridian of Greenwich. If so, what is the latitude: there's no mention of it?"

French could not answer either of the questions, and he did not try. Instead he picked up his telephone receiver and made a call.

"Hallo! Is that Lloyd's? Put me through to the Record Department, please . . . Is Mr. Sam Pullar there? Tell him Inspector French of Scotland Yard wants to speak to him . . . Hallo, Sam! . . . Yes . . . Haven't seen you for ages . . . Look here, Sam, I want you to do me a favor. It's rather urgent, and I'd be grateful if you could look after it just now. . . . Yes, I'll hold on. I want to know anything you can tell me about the sinking of the *Silurian*. You remember, she had two and a half millions on her in gold, and the U-boats got her somewhere between this country and the States, I think in '17 . . . What's that? . . . Yes, all that and anything else you can tell me." He took the receiver from his ear. "Friend of mine in Lloyd's," he explained. "We ought to get some light from his reply."

Silence reigned for a couple of minutes, then French spoke again. "Let me repeat that," he said, seizing a pad and scribbling furiously. "Latitude 41 degrees 36 minutes north, longitude 28 degrees 53 minutes west. Right. How was that known? . . . But there was no direct information? . . . Was the gold insured? . . . Well, it's an involved business, I could hardly tell you over the phone. I'll explain it first time we meet . . . Thank you, Sam. Much obliged."

He rang off and then made a departmental call.

"Put me through to Inspector Barnes . . . That you, Barnes? I'm on to something a bit in your line. Could you come down here for half an hour?"

"Barnes is our authority on things nautical," he told the others. "Began life as a sailor and has studied all branches of sea lore. We always give him shipping cases. We'll wait till he comes and then I'll tell you what I learned from Lloyd's."

"Isn't it a strange thing," Cheyne remarked, "that Schulz should have chosen England for his map and English for his cipher. Wouldn't the natural thing have been for him to have chosen Germany and German? He could have headed it, for instance, 'Deutschland über Alles,' and used the initials of German towns for his phrase."

"I thought of that," French returned, "but we have to remember he prepared the cipher to mislead Germans, not English. In that case I think he was right to use English. It made the thing more difficult."

He had scarcely finished speaking when the door opened, and a tall, alert-looking young man entered the room. French introduced him as Inspector Barnes and pointed to a chair.

"Seat yourself, Barnes, and listen to my tale. These gentlemen are concerned with a curious story," and he gave a brief résumé of the strange events which had led up to the existing situation. "Now," he went on, "when we found it was connected with the *Silurian* I rang up Sam Pullar at Lloyd's, and this is what he told me. The *Silurian* sailed from this country on the 16th of February, 1917. She was bound for New York, and she had two and a half millions on her in bullion as well as a fair number of passengers. She was a big boat—an Anchor liner of some 15,000 tons. You remember about her?"

"Well, I should think so," Barnes returned, as he lit a cigarette. "Why, I was on that job—getting her away, I mean. All kinds of precautions were taken. A tale was started that she would load up the gold at Plymouth and would sail—I forget the exact date now, but it was three days after she did sail. It was my job to see that the German spies about Plymouth got hold of this tale, and we had evidence that they did get it, and moreover sent it through to Germany, and that the U-boats were instructed accordingly. As a matter of fact the *Silurian* came from Brest, where she had landed army stores from South America, and the bullion went out in a tender from Folkestone, and was transferred at night in the Channel in the middle of a ring of destroyers. While preparations were being made at Plymouth for her arrival she was away hundreds of miles towards the States."

"But they got her all the same."

"Oh yes, they got her, but not all the same. She escaped the boats that were looking out for her. It was a chance boat that found her, somewhere, if I remember rightly, near the Azores."

"That's right," French answered. "Instead of going directly west, so Sam Pullar told me, she went south to avoid those submarines you spoke of and which were supposed to be operating off the Land's End. Her course was followed by wireless, down to near the Spanish coast, and then across fairly due west. She was last seen by a Cape boat some thirty miles west of Finisterre. Then a message was received from her when she was some 250 miles north of the Azores, that a U-boat had come along, and had ordered her to stop. The message gave her position and went on to say that a boat was coming aboard from the submarine. Then it stopped, and that was the last thing that was heard of her. Not a body or a boat or a bit of wreckage was ever picked up, and it was clear that every one on board was lost. Then after a time confirmation was obtained. Our intelligence people in Germany intercepted a report from the commander of the submarine who sank her, giving details. She had been sunk in latitude 41° 36′ north, longitude 28° 53′ west, which confirmed the figures sent out in her last wireless message. Four boats had got away, but the commander had fired on them and had sunk them one after another, so that not a single member of the passengers or crew should survive."

"Dirty savages," Barnes commented. "But people in open boats wouldn't have had much chance there anyway, particularly in February. If they had been able to keep afloat at all, they would probably have missed the Azores, and it's very unlikely they would have made the Spanish or Portuguese coast—it would have been too far."

French pushed forward his atlas.

"Just whereabouts did she sink?" he inquired.

"About there." Barnes indicated a point north of the Azores. "But this atlas is too small to see it. Send someone to my room for my large atlas. You'll see better on that."

French having telephoned his instructions Barnes went on.

"She's evidently lying on what is called the Dolphin

238

Rise. The Dolphin Rise is part of a great ridge which passes down the middle of the Atlantic from near Iceland to well down towards the Antarctic Ocean. This ridge is covered by an average of some 1,700 fathoms of water, with vastly greater depths on either side. It is volcanic and is covered by great submarine mountain chains. Where the tops of these mountains protrude above the surface we get, of course, islands, and the Azores are such a group."

A constable at that moment entered with the large atlas, and Barnes continued:

"Now we'll see in a moment." He ran his finger down the index of maps, then turned the pages. "Here we are. Here is a map of the North Atlantic Ocean: here are the Azores and hereabouts is your point, and—By Jove!" the young man looked actually excited, "here is what your cipher means all right!"

The other three crowded round in almost breathless excitement. Barnes pointed with a pencil slightly to the east of a white spot about a quarter of an inch in diameter which bore the figure 18.

"Look here," he went on, "there's about the point she is supposed to have sunk. You see it is colored light blue, which the reference tells us means over 1,000 fathoms. But measure one degree to the west—it is about fifty miles at that latitude—and it brings us into the middle of that white patch marked 18. That white patch is another mountain chain, just not high enough to become an island, and the 18 means that the peaks come within 18 fathoms of the surface. So that your cipher message is probably quite all right, and your Antwerp party are more than likely working away at the gold at the present time."

French swore comprehensively.

"You must be right," he agreed. "One can see now what that blackguard of a U-boat commander did. He evidently put some men aboard the *Silurian* to dismantle their wireless, then made them sail on parallel to his own course until he had by the use of his lead maneuvered them over the highest peak, and then put them down. The whole thing must have been quite deliberate. He returned to his own government a false statement of her position, which he knew would correspond with the last message she sent out, intending it to be believed that she was lost in over 1,000 fathoms. But he sank her where he could himself afterwards recover her bullion, or sell his secret to the highest bidder. The people on the *Silurian* would know all about that two or three hours' steam west, so they must be got rid of. Hence his destroying the boats one after another. No one must be left alive to give the thing away. To his own crew he no doubt told some tale to account for it, but he would be safe enough there, as no one except himself would know the actual facts. Dirty savage indeed!"

With this speech of French's a light seemed to Cheyne suddenly to shine out over all that strange adventure in which for so many weeks he had been involved. With it each puzzling fact seemed to become comprehensible and to drop into its natural place in the story as the pieces of a jigsaw puzzle eventually make a coherent whole. He pictured the thing from the beginning, the submarine coming up with the ship in deep water, but comparatively close to a shallow place where its treasure could be salved: the desire of the U-boat commander, Schulz, to save the gold, quite possibly in the first instance for the benefit of his nation. Then the temptation to keep what he had done secret so as, if possible later, to get the stuff for himself. His fall before this temptation, with its contingent false return to his government as to the position of the wreck. Then, Cheyne saw, the problem of passing on the secret in the event of his own death would arise, with the evolution and construction of the cipher as an attempted solution. As a result of Schulz's fatal wound the cipher was handed to Price, and Schulz was doubtless about to explain how it should be read, when he was interrupted by the nurse. Before another chance offered he was dead.

Given the fact that Dangle overheard the dying man's

story, and that Dangle's character was what it was, Cheyne now saw that the remainder of his adventure could scarcely have happened otherwise than as it had. To obtain the cipher was Dangle's obvious course, and there was no reason to doubt his own statement of how he set about it. A search among Price's papers showed the latter had sent the document to Cheyne, and from Cheyne Dangle had evidently decided to obtain it. But nothing could be done till after the war, nor, presumably, without financial and other help. In this lay, doubtless, the reason for the application to Blessington and Sime, and these two being roped in, the unscrupulous trio set themselves to work. Susan Dangle assisted by obtaining a post as servant at Warren Lodge, and thus gained detailed information which enabled the others to lay their plans. And so in a quite orderly sequence event had followed event, until now it looked as if the climax had been reached.

Like a flash these thoughts passed through Cheyne's mind, and like a flash he saw what depended on them. Now they knew where Joan Merrill had been taken. If she was still alive—and he simply could not bring himself to admit any other possibility—she was on that boat of Merkel's some two hundred and fifty miles north of the Azores! From that something surely followed. He turned to French and spoke in a voice which was hoarse from anxiety.

"What about an expedition to the place?"

French nodded decisively.

"We must arrange one without delay," he said. "I think the Admiralty is our hope. That gold wasn't insured—it was a government business. I'll go and tell the chief about it now, and get him to see the proper authorities. Meanwhile," he looked, for French, quite sharply at the others, "not a word of this must be breathed."

Intense interest was excited in the higher circles of the Admiralty by the news which reached them from the Yard. Great personages bestirred themselves to issue orders, with the result that with enormously more promptitude than the man in the street can bring himself to associate with a Government Department, a fast boat, well equipped with divers and gear, was got ready for sea. French put in a word for both Cheyne and Price, and when, some eight hours after their reading of the cipher, the boat put out into the Thames from Chatham Dockyard, it carried in addition to its regular crew not only Inspector French himself, but also his two protégés.

CHAPTER XX

The Goal of the "L'Escaut"

INSPECTOR FRENCH had gone to bed in the tiny but comfortable stateroom which had been put at his disposal by the officers of the Admiralty boat while that redoubtable vessel was slipping easily and on an even keel through the calm waters of the Straits of Dover. He awoke next morning to find her plunging and rolling and staggering through what, in comparison with his previous experiences of the sea, appeared to be a frightful storm. To his surprise, however, he did not feel any bad effects from the motion, and presently he arose, and having with extreme care performed the ticklish operation of shaving, dressed and climbed with the aid of railings and handles to the companionway, and so to the deck.

The sight which met his eyes on emerging made him hold his breath, as he clung to the rail at the companion door. It was a wonderful morning, clear and bright and fresh and invigorating. The sun shone down from a cloudless sky on to a dark sapphire sea of incredible purity, flecked over with foaming patches of dazzling white. As far as the eye could reach in every direction out to the hard sharp line of the horizon, great waves rolled relentlessly onward, wavelets dancing and churning and foaming on their slow-moving flanks. The wind caught French and, as if it were a solid, held him pinned against the deckhouse. He stood watching the bluff bows of the boat rise in the air, then crash back into the sea, throwing out a smother of water and foam some of which would seep over the fo'c'sle, and after swirling through the forward deck hamper, disappear through the scuppers amidships.

For some moments he watched, then moving round the deckhouse, he glanced up and saw Cheyne and Price beckoning to him from the bridge, where they had joined the officer of the watch.

"Some morning this, Inspector," Price cried, as he joined them in the lee of the weather canvas. "This will blow the London cobwebs out of our minds."

He was evidently keenly enjoying himself, and even Cheyne's anxious face showed appreciation of his surroundings. And soon French himself, having realized that they were not necessarily going to the bottom in a hurricane, but merely running down Channel in a fresh southwesterly breeze, began to feel the thrill of the sea, and to believe that the end of his quest was going to develop into a novel and delightful holiday trip.

The same weather held all that day and the next, but on the third the wind fell, and the sea gradually calmed down to a slow, easy swell. The sun grew hotter, and basking in it in the lee of the deckhouse became a delight. Little was said about the object of the expedition. French and Price were content to enjoy the present, and Cheyne managed to keep his anxieties to himself. The ship's officers were a jolly crowd, immensely excited by their quest, and conducting themselves as the kindly hosts of welcome guests.

On the fourth day it grew still warmer, indeed out of the breeze made by the ship's motion it was unpleasantly hot. French liked to get away forward, where it was cooler, and leaned by the hour over the bows, watching the sharp stem cut through the water and roll back in its frothing wave on either side. Dolphins were now to be seen swimming in the clear water, and two hung at the bows, one on each side, apparently motionless for long periods, until suddenly they would dart ahead, spiral round one another and then return to their places.

That fourth evening the captain joined his passengers as the trio were smoking on deck.

"If we carry on like this," he remarked, "we should reach the position about four A.M. But those beggars may be taking a risk and not showing a light, so I propose to slow down from now on, in order not to arrive till daylight. Come on deck about six. If they're here we should raise them between then and seven."

French, waking early next morning, could not control his excitement and remain in his berth until the allotted time. He rose at five, and went on deck with the somewhat shamefaced feeling that he was acting as a small boy, who on Christmas morning must needs get up on waking to investigate the possibilities of stockings. But he need not have feared ridicule from his companions. Both Cheyne and Price were already on the bridge, and the skipper stood with his telescope glued to his eye as he searched the horizon ahead. All three were evidently thrilled by the approaching finale, and a slight incoherence was discernible in their somewhat scrappy conversation.

The morning was calm and very clear. Once again the sky was cloudless, and the soft southwesterly wind barely ruffled the surface of the long flat swells. It was a pleasure to be alive, and it seemed impossible to associate crime and violence with the expedition. But beneath their smiles all concerned felt it might easily develop into a grim enough business. And that side of it became more apparent when at the captain's order the covers of the six-pounders mounted fore and aft were removed, and the weapons were prepared for action by their crews.

The hands of French's watch had just reached the quarter hour after six, when Captain Amery, who had once again been sweeping the horizon with his telescope, said quietly: "There she is." He handed the glass to French. "See there, about three points on the starboard bow."

French, with some difficulty steadying the tube, saw very faint and far off what looked like the upper part of a steamer's deck, with a funnel, and two masts like threads of the finest gossamer. "She's still hull down," the captain explained. "You'll see her better in a few minutes. We should be up with her in three-quarters of an hour."

In order to leave them free later on, it was decided to have breakfast at once, and by the time the hasty meal had been disposed of the stranger was clearly visible to the naked eye. She lay heading westward, as though anchored in the swing of the tide, and her fires appeared to be either out or banked, as no smoke was visible at her funnel. The glass revealed a flag at her forepeak, but she was still too far off to make out its coloring.

Now that the dramatic climax was approaching, the minds of the actors in the play became charged with a very real anxiety. Captain Amery, under almost any circumstances, would have to deal with a very ticklish situation. He had to get the gold, if it was salvable, and the fact that they were not in British waters would be a complication if the Belgian had already recovered it. French had to ascertain if his quarry were on board, and if so, see that they did not escape him—also a difficult job outside the three-mile limit. For Price a fortune hung in the balance—not of course all the gold that might be found, but the proportion allowed him by law; while for Cheyne there remained something a thousand times more important than the capture of a criminal or the acquisition of a fortune—for Cheyne the question of Joan Merrill's life was at stake. Their several anxieties were reflected on the faces of the men, as they stood in silence, watching the rapidly growing vessel.

Presently an exclamation came from Captain Amery.

"By Jove!" he said, "this is a rum business. I can see that flag now, and it's our red ensign. What's a Belgian boat doing with a British flag? And what's more, it's jack down —a flag of distress. What do you think of that?" He looked at the others with a puzzled expression, then went on: "I suppose they're not armed? You don't know, Inspector, do you? If they were armed it would be a likely enough ruse to get us close by, so as to make sure of hitting us in a vital place."

French shook his head. He had heard nothing about arms, though for all he knew to the contrary the *L'Escaut* might carry a gun.

"I don't see one," the captain continued, "but then if they have one they'd keep it hidden. But I don't like there being no signs of life aboard her. There's no smoke anywhere, either from her boilers or her galley. There's no one on the bridge, and I've not seen a movement on deck. It doesn't look well: in fact it looks as if they were lying low and waiting for us."

They were now within a mile of the stranger, and her details were clear even to the naked eye.

"It's the *L'Escaut* anyway," Captain Amery went on. "I can see the name on her bows. But I confess I don't like that flag and that silence. I think I'll see if I can wake her up."

He put his hand on the foghorn halliard and blew a number of resounding blasts. For a few seconds nothing happened, then suddenly two figures appeared at the deckhouse door, and after a moment's pause, rushed up on the bridge and began waving furiously. As they passed up the bridge ladder they came from behind the shelter of a boat and their silhouettes became visible against the sky. They were both women!

A strangled cry burst from Cheyne as he snatched the

captain's telescope and gazed at them, then with a shout of "It's she! It's she!" he leaped to the end of the bridge and began waving his hat frantically.

At this moment two other figures appeared on the fo'c'sle and, apparently moving to the vessel's side, stood watching the newcomers. Amery rang his engines down to half speed and, slightly porting his helm, headed for some distance astern of the other. Then starboarding, he swung round, and bringing up parallel to her and some couple of hundred yards away, he dropped anchor.

Without loss of a moment a boat was lowered, and French, Cheyne, Price, the first officer, and a half dozen men, all armed with service revolvers, tumbled in. Giving way lustily, they pulled for the Belgian.

It was by this time possible to distinguish the features of the women, and French was not surprised to learn they were Joan Merrill and Susan Dangle. Evidently they recognized Cheyne, who kept waving furiously as if he found the movement necessary to relieve his overwrought feelings. The two figures forward were those of men, and these stood watching the boat, though without exhibiting any of the transports of delight of their fellow shipmates on the bridge.

As they drew closer Joan made signs to them to go round to the other side of the ship, and dropping round her stern they saw a ladder rigged. In a few seconds they were alongside, and Cheyne, leaping out before the others, rushed up the steps and reached the deck.

If there had been any doubts as to the real relations between himself and Joan, these were set at rest at that moment. Instinctively he opened his arms, and Joan, swept off her feet by her emotion, threw herself into them and clung to him, while tears of joy and relief ran down her cheeks. As far as Cheyne was concerned, Susan Dangle, the figures on the fo'c'sle, French, and the men behind him might as well not have existed. He crushed Joan violently to him, covering her face and hair with burning

247

kisses, as he murmured brokenly of his love and of his thankfulness for her safety.

French, anxious to learn the state of affairs and seeing nothing was to be got from Joan, turned expectantly to Susan Dangle. What could these unexpected developments mean? Was Susan, the enemy, now a friend? Where were the others? Were the ship's company friends or foes? Could he ask her questions which might incriminate her without giving her a formal warning?

But his curiosity would brook no delay.

"I am Inspector French of Scotland Yard," he announced, while Price and the first officer stood round expectantly. "You are Miss Susan Dangle. Where are the other members of this expedition?"

The girl wrung her hands, and he noticed how terribly pale and drawn was her face and what horror shone in her eyes.

"Oh!" she cried, with a gesture as if to shut out the sight of some hideous dream. "Oh, it's been awful! I can't speak of it. They're dead! My brother James, Charles Sime, Mr. Merkel, most of the crew, dead—all dead! Mr. Blessington wounded—probably dying! They got fighting over the gold!" She began suddenly to laugh, a terrible high cackling laugh, that made her hearers shiver, and attracted the attention even of Joan and Cheyne.

French stepped quickly forward and seized her arm.

"There now, Miss Dangle," he said kindly but firmly. "Stop that and pull yourself together. Your terrible experiences are over now and you're in the hands of friends. But you mustn't give way like this. Make an effort, and you'll be better directly." He led her to a hatchway and made her sit down, while he continued soothing her as one would a fractious child.

But so great was the agitation of both girls that it was quite a considerable time before the tragic tale of the *L'Escaut's* expedition became fully unfolded. And when at last it was told it proved still but one more illustration of the old truth that the qualities of greed and envy and self-ishness have that seed of decay within themselves which leads their unhappy victims to overreach themselves, and instead of gaining what they seek, to lose their all. Shorn of incoherent phrases and irrelevant details the story was this.

On the 24th of May the *L'Escaut* had left Antwerp with twenty-eight souls aboard. Aft there were Joan, Susan, Blessington, Sime, Dangle, and Merkel, with the captain, first officer, and engineer—nine persons, while forward were three divers, six assistants, a cook, a steward, four seamen, and four engine-room staff, or nineteen alto-gether. Once clear of the Scheldt Joan's treatment had changed. Her food was no longer drugged, and when in a few days she got over the effects of the doses she had received, she found her jailers polite and friendly and anxious to minimize the inconvenience and anxiety she was suffering. They told her they did not wish her evil, and were taking her with them simply to prevent informa-tion as to themselves or their affairs leaking out through her. This, of course, she did not believe, since she did not possess sufficient information about them to enable her to interfere with their plans. But later their real motive dawned on her. Gradually she realized that Blessington had fallen in love with her, and though he was circum-spect enough, her distrust of him was such that she felt sick with horror and dread when she thought of him. Noth-ing, however, had occurred to which she could take excep-tion, and had it not been for her fears as to her own fate and her anxieties as to Cheyne's, the voyage would have been pleasant enough.

The *L'Escaut* was a fast boat, and four days had brought them to the spot referred to in the cipher. After three days' search they found the wreck, and all three divers had at once gone down. A week was spent in mak-ing an examination of the vessel, at the end of which time they had located the gold. It was in her stern, low down and not far from her port side. The divers recommended blowing her plates off at this spot, and ten days more sufficed for this. Through the hole thus made the divers were able to draw in tackle lowered from the *L'Escaut,* and the ingots of gold were slung to cradles and drawn up with really wonderful ease and speed. They had, moreover, been favored with a peculiarly fine stretch of weather, work having to be suspended on only eight days of the thirty-seven they were there.

On reaching the wreck in the first instance the captain had mustered his crew aft and had informed them—what he could no longer keep secret—that they were out for gold, and that if they found it in the quantities they hoped, every man on board would receive at the end of the trip a gift of £1,000 in addition to his pay. The men at first seemed more than satisfied, but as ingot after ingot was recovered the generosity of the offer shrank in their estimation. Four days before the appearance of French's party the divers had reported that another day would complete the work, and then appeared the first hint that all was not well. On that last evening before the completion of the diving the men came forward in a body and asked to see the captain. They explained that they had been reckoning up the value of the gold, and they weren't having £1,000 apiece: they wanted an even divide all round. The captain argued with them civilly enough at first— told them that they couldn't get the metal ashore and turned into money in secret, that the port officers or coast-guards wherever it was unloaded would be bound to learn what they were doing and that then the government would claim an enormous percentage of the whole, so that the £1,000 per man was an extremely liberal gift. The men declared that they would look after the unloading, and that they were going to have what they wanted. Hot words passed, and then the captain drew a revolver and said that he was captain there, and that what he said would go. Susan was watching the scene from the quarter-deck behind, but she could not be quite sure of what followed. One of the crew pressed forward and the captain raised his revolver. She did not think he meant to fire, but another of the men either genuinely or purposely misunderstood his action. He raised his hand, a shot rang out, and the captain fell dead. The mutineers were evidently terribly upset by a murder which they had apparently never intended, and had Blessington and Sime acted intelligently, the trouble might have gone no further. But at that moment these two worthies, who must have been in the chart-house all the time, began firing through the windows at the men. A regular pitched battle ensued, in which Sime and five of the crew were hit, three of the latter being killed. It was then war to the knife between those who berthed forward and those who berthed aft. All that night sporadic shots rang out at intervals, but at daybreak on the following day matters came to a head. The crew with considerable generalship made a feint on the fo'c'sle with some of their number while the remainder swarmed aft below decks. The defenders, taken in the rear, were shot down, and the mutineers were masters of the ship.

All that next day Joan and Susan, terror-stricken, clung to each other in the latter's cabin. The men were reasonably civil: told them they might get themselves food, and let them alone. But that night a further terrible quarrel burst out between, as they learned afterwards, those who wished to murder the girls and go off with the treasure and those who feared murder more than the loss of the gold. Once again there were the reports of shots and the groans of wounded men. The fusillade went on at intervals all night, until next morning one of the divers—a superior man with whom the girls had often talked—had come in with his head covered with blood, and asked the girls to bandage it. Susan had some slight surgical knowledge, and did what she could for him. Then the man told them that of the entire ship's company only themselves and seven others were alive, and that of these seven four were so badly wounded that they would probably not recover. Among these was Blessington. Sime and James Dangle were dead.

The slightly injured men threw the dead overboard and cleaned up the traces of the fighting, while the girls ministered to the seriously wounded. Of course, in the three days up till the arrival of the avengers—who had by a strange trick of fate become the rescuers—one man had died. Of the eight-and-twenty who sailed from Antwerp there were therefore left only nine: the two girls and four slightly and three seriously wounded men. None of those able to move understood either engineering or seamanship, so that they had luckily decided to remain at anchor in the hope of some ship picking up their flag of distress.

"There is just one thing I should like to understand," said Cheyne to Joan, when later on that day a prize crew had been put aboard the *L'Escaut* and steam was being raised for the return to England, "and that is what happened to you on the night that we burgled Earlswood. You got back to your rooms, then left again with Sime and Blessington?"

"There's not much to tell about that," Joan answered, smiling happily up into her lover's eyes. "I was, as you know, standing like a watchman before the door of Earlswood, when I saw Susan and her brother coming up. I rang and knocked and kept them talking as long as possible. Then when they opened the door I slipped away, but I heard your footsteps and realized that you had got out by the back way. I heard you run off down the lane with Dangle after you, then remembering your arrangement about throwing away the tracing, I climbed over the wall, picked it up and went back to my rooms. The first thing I did was to photograph it, then I hid it in my color box. I had scarcely done so when Sime called. He said you had met with an accident—been caught between two motor-cars and knocked down by one of them—and that you were seriously injured. He said you were conscious and had given him my address and were calling for me. I went down to find Blessington driving a car, though I didn't know then it was Blessington. As soon as we started Sime held a chloroformed cloth over my mouth, and I don't remember much more till we were on the *L'Escaut*."

"But how did Sime find your rooms?"

"Through Susan. Susan told me all about it afterwards. She went out after James and saw me climbing over the wall with the tracing. She followed me to my rooms and immediately telephoned to Sime. When Sime called she was with him, and while I changed my coat Sime let her into the studio and she hid behind an easel until we were gone. She searched till she found the tracing and then simply walked out. The gang had intended to go to Antwerp the following week in any case, but this business upset their plans and they decided to start immediately. Dangle went on and arranged for the *L'Escaut* to leave some days earlier. The rest of us put up at Ghent till she was ready to sail." But little further remains to be told. The few bars of gold still left on the *Silurian* were soon raised and the two ships set sail, reaching Chatham some five days later. All the bullion theoretically belonged to the Crown, but under the special circumstances a generous division was made whereby twenty-five per cent was returned to the finders. As Price refused to accept the whole amount an amicable agreement was come to, whereby Cheyne, Joan, and Price each received almost one-third, or £200,000 apiece. Of the balance of over £20,000, £10,000 was given to Susan Dangle by Joan's imperative directions. She said that Susan was not a bad girl and had turned up trumps during the trouble on the *L'Escaut*. £1,000 went to Inspector French—also Joan's gift, and the remainder was divided among the officers and men of the Admiralty salvage boat.

A few days after landing Maxwell Cheyne and Joan Merrill had occasion to pay a short visit to the church of

St. Margaret's in the Fields, after which Cheyne whirled his wife away to Devonshire, so that she might make the acquaintance of his family and see the country where began that strange series of events which in the beginning of the story I alluded to as THE CHEYNE MYSTERY.

PENGUIN CRIME

Penguin offers a varied selection of high-quality mystery and crime titles by favorite authors of the past and present. Here is a sampling of the Penguin list:

Margery Allingham
MYSTERY MILE

G. K. Chesterton
THE INNOCENCE OF FATHER BROWN

Edmund Crispin
THE MOVING TOYSHOP

Freeman Wills Crofts
INSPECTOR FRENCH'S GREATEST CASE
THE PIT-PROP SYNDICATE

Sir Arthur Conan Doyle
THE MEMOIRS OF SHERLOCK HOLMES

Elizabeth Ferrars
HANGED MAN'S HOUSE

Nicolas Freeling
DRESSING OF DIAMOND

Hugh Greene (Editor)
THE RIVALS OF SHERLOCK HOLMES:
EARLY DETECTIVE STORIES

Geoffrey Household
RED ANGER

Peter Lovesey
A CASE OF SPIRITS

Patricia Moyes
BLACK WIDOWER

S. L. Stebel
THE VOROVICH AFFAIR

Julian Symons
THE MAN WHO KILLED HIMSELF